Golden & Grey

The Nightmares That Ghosts Have

Also by Louise Arnold

Golden & Grey
(An Unremarkable Boy and a Rather Remarkable Ghost)

Margaret K. McElderry Books

Golden & Grey

The Nightmares That Ghosts Have

LOUISE ARNOLD

Margaret K. McElderry Books
New York   London   Toronto   Sydney

Margaret K. McElderry Books
An imprint of Simon & Schuster
Children's Publishing Division
1230 Avenue of the Americas, New York, New York 10020

Copyright © 2006 by Louise Arnold
Book design by Ann Zeak
The text for this book is set in Bembo.
Manufactured in the United States of America
2 4 6 8 10 9 7 5 3 1
Library of Congress Cataloging-in-Publication Data
Arnold, Louise, 1979–
Golden & Grey: the nightmares that ghosts have /
Louise Arnold.—1st ed.
p. cm.
Summary: In addition to continuing their work to stop school
bullies, eleven-year-old Tom Golden and Grey Arthur—along
with several spectral friends—try to discover why ghosts across
England are vanishing.
ISBN-13: 978-0-689-87586-1
ISBN-10: 0-689-87586-X (hardcover)
[1. Ghosts—Fiction. 2. Friendship—Fiction. 3. Bullies—Fiction.
4. Schools—Fiction. 5. England—Fiction.] I. Title: Golden and
Grey, the nightmares that ghosts have. II. Title.
PZ7.A73595Got 2006
[Fic]—dc22
2005028426

Dedicated to Ruth (tea lady extraordinaire), Joe (my first fan), Dan and Becks for their attempts to teach me history, Alice for the entertainment, and Kate and Karolina for making this all possible.

Golden
& Grey

The Nightmares That Ghosts Have

A New Beginning

LITTLE FRANK LONGFIELD BURST THROUGH THE DOOR, heart pounding, and skidded to a halt. He loosened his school tie, gasping in heavy breaths, lungs aching from running. A quick glance behind assured him that Big Ben was nowhere to be seen, but still an uneasy feeling crawled inside him, and couldn't be shaken.

Something felt wrong.

He had no idea where he was. He'd been so desperate to get away, so scared, that he'd run and run without a thought for where he was going, his feet always ten steps ahead of his mind. Big Ben had been behind him, so close behind, and Frank had simply run and run until the shouts grew distant, until the sound of chasing footsteps became fainter, and still he'd run, on and on, through labyrinth-like school corridors, running until he physically couldn't run any farther. His legs shook beneath him, scarcely able to carry his own weight. He took his schoolbag off his shoulder, and let it slide to the floor. He'd managed to lose his pursuer, so he should be safe now, but still that feeling inside him remained: a gnawing worry, a sense of being watched, of not being alone, just the knowledge, indescribable but definitely there, that something was *wrong*.

Frank glanced up and down the corridor, but it was utterly deserted. Rummaging in his bag, he managed to find the Thorbleton school map they had been given on the first day of term. It was flimsy now through overuse, holes appearing along the creases. No matter how he turned it, or screwed up his eyes with concentration as he read it, he still couldn't work out where he was. He scanned the walls for clues, but all the posters had been torn down, scrawled on, or covered in so much chewing gum that it was impossible to read the original message. The only poster that remained intact warned that it was an offense to set off the fire alarm without there actually being a fire, and had been hastily amended that morning to include a warning against setting a fire purely so you can pull the fire alarm. The doors to the classrooms had all had their numbers pried away, so only blank spaces remained. Frank glanced at his watch, and realized that the bell to signal the end of lunch would ring soon, and when that happened the last place he wanted to be was lost. He scrunched the map up, and threw it into his rucksack, hauling the bag back onto his shoulders. Slowly, he began walking forward, scanning the corridor for clues, any slight hint that might give away where he was. Crisp packets were strewn across the floor, but whoever had left them there was long gone. It was unusual for any place in school to be this empty, this still.

As Frank Longfield walked on, the sense of something being wrong grew and grew. He felt, no, he was *sure,* that there was someone else in the corridor with him, but whenever he glanced behind there was nobody to be seen. The hairs on the back of his neck began to stand on end, and goosebumps traced their way across his arms. It felt colder now, darker now, as if light and heat were slowly draining away. The sound of his own heart thumped loudly in his ears, and he walked slower, taking quiet steps, ears straining to pick out any noise. Nothing. Nobody. He looked over his shoulder again, and the corridor stretched out behind him: anonymous doors, tatty posters, shadows reaching out across the ground, empty, and yet . . . He stopped, wrapping his hands tightly around the straps of his bag, knuckles turning white, and called out, his voice echoing in front of him.

"Hello?"

The sense of fear that nestled inside Frank was suddenly swept away, and wild terror took its place, making his thoughts scream, his heart hammer, but leaving his feet firmly frozen to the spot. He swallowed dryly.

The Screamer stalked up behind Frank, breathing in light, shadows slowly streaming from his mouth. His long, curling toenails clicked on the floor as he edged forward, old bones creaking, ever closer . . .

Frank took in a deep breath, and held it, every ounce of his being willing him to run, and yet every muscle knotted in place. If he'd have looked behind, he wouldn't have seen a thing, because normal humans can't see ghosts, but he knew there was something there, something getting closer. . . .

The Screamer behind Frank Longfield stretched out a long, curled talon, and swiped the KICK ME sign from off his back.

Feeling something tug against his sweater, Frank

threw his bag to the ground, threw his arms into the air, and ran off screaming hysterically.

The Screamer, note impaled on his discolored nail, threw the scrap of paper into his mouth, and chewed it. Sharp, shard-like teeth reduced it to confetti in seconds. He then spat it out, soggy clumps of mangled note, threaded with specks of shadow, and raised his sinewy arms in the air, hissing triumphantly. Swirling shadows pooled at his feet. Frank Longfield disappeared, still screaming, into the distance.

A slow clapping sound disrupted the scene.

"Well yes, I suppose that's one way you could do it," said Grey Arthur, in the most polite tone he could muster. "Does anyone else want to tell the Harrowing Screamer how he could have perhaps handled this differently?"

As the bell to mark the end of the lunch break sounded, the rest of the school for Invisible Friends looked on in shocked silence as the Harrowing Screamer stamped on the remnants of the chewed-up note with both feet, howling all the while.

"Anyone?"

Where to Begin?

IT HAD ALL BEGUN A FEW WEEKS BACK, WHEN TOM and Arthur's normal lazy Sunday routine had been rudely interrupted by the arrival of a new ghost, clutching a copy of the *Daily Tell-Tale*.

Well, that's not strictly true. . . .

It had all begun a couple months back, when a lonely boy was befriended by a well-meaning ghost, when the rules of Ghost World and Real World had been shattered, when a human boy discovered he could see ghosts, and when a ghost discovered what he was meant to be.

Actually, that's not really true either. . . .

The beginning had begun, as so many beginnings do, way back at the very start. Way back, before color seeped into photographs, before photographs even existed, when the world was chronicled in hues of paint, or even etchings on a cave wall. It began when humans began, and when ghosts began, a footnote now faded in a long-stretching history. Maybe it had begun even before that—ghosts haunting dinosaurs, Screamers chasing terrified Tyrannosaurus Rexes across the tundra, Poltergeists "borrowing" eggs from nesting Pterodactyls, and swapping them with those of broody Diplodocuses, endlessly confusing all parties involved. Perhaps that was when it really started, though nobody is really sure anymore. Some Thespers will tell you they were there, way, way back when dinosaurs and not politicians ran the world, but Thespers are renowned for telling wild stories, and not all of them are true.

So it started somewhere way back when, and has been going on ever since. New chapters of this story emerged: the time when humans stopped seeing ghosts, when ghosts faded from truth and fact into legend and myth, when the world consigned them to bedtime stories and overactive imaginations. Skip many pages, and you will find the chapter where a human boy, with an unseen, unknown ghost friend, is struck by a car, and can suddenly see the Ghost World that is all around him. Skip forward again, and you will find the story of how the ghost community united to help save this boy from a man who wanted to use this power to see ghosts for his own greed. A little further, further still, then add a day or so more, and that is where this story starts.

So . . .

It had all begun a few weeks back, when Tom and Arthur's normal lazy Sunday morning routine had been rudely interrupted by the arrival of a new ghost, clutching a copy of the *Daily Tell-Tale*.

Not Such a Standard Sunday

SUNDAYS WERE TRUSTY, FAMILIAR DAYS, THE COMFORT blanket of the week. No alarm to rudely drag Tom out of bizarre dreams or just contented snoring, no school uniform waiting to be put on, no heavy schoolbag weighed down with homework and textbooks and whatever "interesting" concoction his mum has hidden inside a sandwich. There was no hurrying out the door, no urgency, no glancing at his watch every five seconds to make sure he wasn't late, and no panicking when he realized he was.

Tom wandered downstairs in his pajamas, pillow-hair making him look a little eccentric, but it didn't matter, because it was a Sunday, and everyone knows that nothing happens on a Sunday. He'd left Grey Arthur upstairs, playing the card game solitaire. He'd introduced Arthur to it a couple days ago, and it had been driving Arthur to within an inch of insanity ever since. One time he claimed to have completed it, but the trouble with being a ghost is that when you are slightly see-through, hiding cards in your pockets doesn't work so well. Tom had gently explained that you can't really cheat when you are the only person playing, and Arthur had sighed deeply and started all over again. And again. And again.

So Tom left Grey Arthur staring indignantly at the game, willing the cards to behave, and he wandered downstairs, pajamafied and bed-haired.

"So you finally decided to wake up then?" Dad asked, as Tom stumbled into the kitchen. As was Sunday's tradition, Dad was sitting next to a pile of newspapers that would take the best part of the day to read, and drinking tea from a cup that looked like it was made for giants. Tom smiled blearily, heading straight for the fridge for his traditional pint of milk. Mum was out in the back garden, battling with the wind to hang out bed sheets and school shirts and assorted damp laundry on the line. A particularly large gust of wind caught her off guard, and a T-shirt escaped halfway across the garden before she managed to catch it. She looked up, and seeing Tom watching her through the window, waved the t-shirt triumphantly. Tom smiled. Another typical Sunday.

The doorbell rang.

Tom's Dad looked up from his paper, and raised an eyebrow at Tom.

"You're not expecting anyone, are you?" Tom shook his head, and carried on reading the comic strips. Dad made a quizzical noise, and begrudgingly got up from his stack of newspapers, his pint of tea, and his chair to open the door.

Moments later Dad walked back in, frowning.

"Who was it?" asked Tom.

"Nobody there," Dad replied, settling back into his chair. Just as he was about to take another sip of tea, the doorbell went again. Dad sighed, and placed his mammoth cup back down again. Off he trotted back to the door, only to return seconds later. He was scowling. Tom looked at him inquisitively.

"Must be just some bored kids, playing knock-down ginger. You'd think they'd find better things to do on a Sunday." Dad resumed his Sunday morning pose, tea in hand, papers in front of him. The doorbell rang again. "Just ignore it. They'll get bored and leave us alone eventually."

The doorbell rang again.

And again.

And again.

"I'll go," Tom said. Dad just grunted, not even looking up. He was reading about how miserably Thorbleton FC had played in the regional cup, and shaking his head. There's nothing like a good soccer result to lift a dad's spirits, and a bad result to permanently sunder a good mood (and losing seven to nil definitely fits in the latter category).

Tom gulped down the last of his pint of milk, and wandered out into the hallway. He tugged open the latch, and flung the door open, hoping to catch someone fleeing down the path, giggling.

Which wasn't what happened at all.

"I assume this means I still don't look normal enough for humans to see?" asked the ghost on the doorstep. "How disagreeable."

She was a small ghost, who looked no older than Tom (though appearances aren't much to go on with ghosts. The oldest looking ghost might have only appeared last week, and the youngest could have been haunting people since the Middle Ages). She was wearing what would have appeared to be a school uniform, if the uniform had been designed by the most miserable of goths: black skirt, black knee-high socks, grey shirt, black tie, black shoes . . . She was pale, the kind of pale that would make your mother rush you to the doctor, with jet black hair cut at distinct right angles. It fell to just above her shoulders, and her face

9

was framed with an abrupt fringe, so meticulously straight it looked as if it had been done with a set square and a spirit level. Just beneath her fringe, set in that deathly pale face, were two startling eyes. One was entirely black, no iris, all pupil. The other had a small pupil circled with shocking green. She looked deathly serious, more somber than any child could ever possibly manage to look, with tight lips set in a line as straight as her fringe. At her feet was a battered old suitcase.

"Mildred Rattledust," she said simply, as Tom stared at her, mouth open. "I'm here about the job." She thrust a copy of the *Daily Tell-Tale* at Tom, who dutifully took it, and then she marched *straight through him,* dragging her suitcase behind.

There are several unpleasant sensations that everyone will experience at some stage in life. Treading in a wet patch while wearing socks. Having to rummage down the back of a settee through crumbs, and random stickiness, to find whatever you have lost. Fishing hair out of the plughole in the shower. Having a ghost walk through you easily beats any of these, without even breaking a sweat.

Tom shivered, grimaced, and shuddered all at once. Goosebumps leaped out all over his skin. Having a ghost walk through you, or walking through a ghost, feels cold, and slightly damp, and makes the hairs on the back of your neck jump up in shock. Every day, humans and ghosts cross paths, (although more polite ghosts will sidestep to avoid such a thing), and quite often the human will say "It felt like someone just walked over my grave," but really, that's not what it felt like at all. It actually felt like a ghost just walked straight through you, floating past your front, traipsing through your internal organs, gliding between lungs and heart and all other things that humans keep tucked inside, before appearing on the other side of you.

"So was there anybody there, Tom?" called Dad from the kitchen.

Tom composed himself, shaking his head to clear away the remaining tingles of being marched through. He turned away from the door, and saw Mildred dragging her suitcase up the stairs.

"No, Dad, you were right. Just someone playing tricks," he called back. He hoped he sounded normal. It was hard to sound normal just after a ghost has walked through you. "I'll be back in a tic, I just have something I need to sort out." Tom ran up the stairs, sidestepping the small ghost, and darted into his bedroom, ghostly newspaper still in his hand.

Arthur looked up as Tom burst in, a victorious look on his face.

"I completed it!" he cried, gesturing toward the finished game of solitaire. He looked exceptionally pleased with himself. Noticing the stern look on Tom's face, and the newspaper in Tom's hand, the pleased expression began to droop. Mildred Rattledust appeared round the corner, suitcase in hand, and the pleased look faded into a guilty, nervous grin.

"You have got some explaining to do," said Tom,

waving the newspaper in the same way you do when you see a naughty puppy doing something indoors that should only be done outside.

"Oh," said Arthur. *"That."*

Come One, Come All

"WHAT ON *EARTH* MADE YOU THINK THAT THIS WAS A good idea?" wailed Tom, as he looked at the front cover of the *Daily Tell-Tale*.

INVISIBLE FRIEND RECRUITMENT DRIVE, it read.

Mildred was busy unpacking her suitcase and putting various objects around the room: a Rubik's cube on the window sill, a stuffed hamster wearing a bowling hat on the desk, a sinister-looking, threadbare toy monkey with one drooping eye nestling on Tom's pillow.

"You know what journalists are like, Tom!" protested Arthur. "I just made one offhand comment to a Bug, and they exaggerate it, and twist it all around to make it sound better, and . . ."

"And what was this comment?" Tom demanded.

"Oh, it was nothing really," Arthur replied, packing away the solitaire.

"What kind of nothing? What did you say? *Exactly?*"

"Mrmph . . . mrmhsyshs . . . ," Arthur muttered,

putting his hands over his mouth to obscure the words. Mildred was emptying Tom's underwear drawer, throwing the contents out on the carpet, and filling the empty space with a seemingly endless supply of marbles from her suitcase.

"I didn't quite catch that, Arthur." Tom had his hands on his hips now, exactly the same way his mum did when she's trying to get the truth out of someone. Arthur blushed slightly, a hint of red infusing his usually grey cheeks.

"I said if anyone wants to be an Invisible Friend then they should come and stay with us, and I'd be happy to teach them," admitted Arthur, looking more than mildly guilty. Tom spluttered, at a loss for how to respond.

"Which is exactly why I am here. I've decided to put my Faintly Real skills to a new use. I shall become a friend to juvenile humans," said Mildred, floating up on Tom's bed. She stretched out, making herself comfortable, her head floating above Tom's pillow, pale hands clutching her menacing-looking monkey. "So, where will you be sleeping, Tom?"

"Oh, no. No, no, no, no, *no, no, no.*" Tom was shaking his head. He felt slightly giddy. On the front cover of the *Daily Tell-Tale,* beneath the headline, was a photo of Grey Arthur outside number 11 Aubergine Road, outside *Tom's house,* gesturing toward the front door. Tom glanced at Mildred settling on his bed, and then at Grey Arthur trying to look like butter wouldn't melt in his mouth (as a point of interest, butter actually wouldn't melt in his mouth, but that's neither here nor there). This couldn't be happening. . . .

"You can't stay here," he said finally.

Mildred sighed. "We can share the bed if you like. Top to tails though. It's not like I will take up much space. I'm noncorporeal."

"You're non *what* now?"

"It means that ghosts and humans can't touch. So you'll still have plenty of room."

Tom's head pounded.

"But—but—that's not the point!" stammered Tom. This was all far too much for a Sunday morning. "You can't stay there because it's *my* bed. And you can't stay in my house because things have only just gotten back to normal, as weird as my normal is. My mum would have a fit if she knew there were ghosts moving in."

"I was under the impression you were the only human able to see ghosts," answered Mildred, fixing her strange eyes on Tom.

"Well, yes . . . but—"

"Then she won't know."

Tom didn't quite know how to respond to that, so he just decided to ignore it. Instead, he turned his attention back to Arthur.

"You shouldn't have done this without asking me," he said. "In fact, you shouldn't have done this, full stop."

"I'm sorry. I'm really, really sorry," muttered Arthur.

"Well, that's a start," Tom replied.

"But . . ."

"Oh no, don't add a but!" Tom took his head in his hands, trying to block out what Grey Arthur was about to say.

"*But . . . ,*" continued Arthur, "you have to admit, it's a very good idea."

"No, it's a dreadful idea! A dreadful, *dreadful* idea!" wailed Tom. "One ghost in a house is enough, more than enough."

Arthur stood up a little taller, a distant look in his eyes, and began to respond—it sounded more than a little rehearsed, as if Arthur had been waiting for the right time to deliver this speech (of course, the ideal time would probably have been a long while before the article appeared in the ghostly newspaper). . . .

"Think of all the humans we could help. Lonely humans, bullied humans, having a little invisible helper to stop the notes that get stuck to their backs, to keep them company when nobody else is around."

"Oh, please don't guilt trip me," said Tom, rubbing his face with his hands.

"Think of how much it helped you, think of how much it meant to you. Think of the good it will do!"

"Oh, Arthur!" whined Tom, but he already knew he was fighting a losing battle. Arthur broke out of his scripted sales pitch, and resorted to begging instead.

"Pretty please, Tom. Pretty, pretty please?"

Tom sighed deeply, taking a moment to weigh it all up. It was a terrible idea, he knew that, and at the same time, he had to admit, a very good one. Arthur was grinning at him, already knowing what the answer would be.

"She can't have my bed," Tom said, after an age.

"Deal!" replied a gleeful Arthur.

"And she's not staying in my room. She can stay in the attic."

"That's fine." Arthur clapped his hands with excitement. Mildred simply sat up, cross-legged on the bed, watching everything unfold. Her monkey, which she clutched to her chest, seemed to be staring directly at Tom with its one good eye. Mildred studied her new home, taking in the desk cluttered with books and homework, the wall of memories smothered with photos and letters, the laundry basket into which only 50 percent of the dirty clothes had managed to make their way (the rest gathered untidily on the floor around it), the wardrobe brimming with school uniforms and weekend clothes, the rubber-band ball Tom had started making before rapidly losing interest, the television in the corner, and the collection of CDs (none of which had the correct album inside the box). She nodded to herself.

"This is our new home," she whispered to the monkey. Tom was quite relieved when the monkey didn't respond.

"This is so not a good idea . . . ," he uttered under his breath.

And *that* was how it had all begun.

The Burgling of Bees

THAT MONDAY MORNING STARTED AS ALL MONDAYS tended to do. The alarm beeped into life, and Tom groggily reached out and turned it to snooze. Five minutes later, the alarm went off again, and Tom reached out and turned it off again.

"Come on lazy bones, out of bed." Tom's mum strode into the room and pulled open the curtains, letting light stream into the room. Tom winced, and rolled over, pretending to still be asleep. "No you don't. Come on, out of bed." Tom sighed and sat up, and Mum ruffled his hair.

"Breakfast is on the table," she said on her way out of the room, closing the door behind her. Grey Arthur crawled out from underneath the bed, and tried to rearrange his hair into some semblance of normality. He failed, miserably, as always. So far, so typical. It was then that Mildred Rattledust floated down through the ceiling, school satchel on her arm, her hair in pigtails. Pigtails did not suit her. They looked faintly ridiculous when paired with such a stern-looking ghost. She landed gracefully on the floor right in front of Tom, and stared at him intently. Tom self-consciously patted down his bed hair, and pulled up his duvet cover to hide his cartoon pajamas.

"How do we commence?" she asked, head cocked slightly to one side. For an ex-Faintly Real, she seemed a long stretch from being even *remotely* real. There was something defiantly ghostly about her. No wonder humans had been unable to see her.

"Erm, well, breakfast first. And then we're off to school," replied Tom, feeling a little awkward. Mildred produced a notepad from thin air, and began writing notes. She had a little (black, obviously) pencil with her name, MILDRED RATTLEDUST, written down the side.

"Interesting," she said. Tom was pretty sure it wasn't interesting at all, but then maybe to a ghost it was. Arthur was pulling funny faces in the mirror, trying to get his ears to match up on each side. He'd tug at them until they were level, but they'd always slide out of place the moment he let go. Mildred continued to stare at Tom, and in the end he had to shoo her away, while he stepped into the wardrobe to get changed out of her sight. It was cramped, and a long way from being easy to do, but he'd rather do that than get changed with those eyes fixed on him.

This was going to be a long day, Tom thought.

If Tom had believed breakfast with one ghost at the table was hard work, then two was just ridiculous. Mum was ironing her uniform while eating a piece of toast (and dropping crumbs all over the blouse she was ironing), Dad was drawing pictures of new and wildly ambitious socks on a piece of paper, Grey Arthur was reading the cartoons in the newspaper, and Mildred stood in the corner, taking notes. Occasionally she would ask questions, questions like the ones Arthur had asked when he first moved in, and Tom would try his best to ignore her and let Arthur answer. After all, it doesn't do to talk to invisible ghosts in front of your parents while sitting at the breakfast table. So Mildred asked questions, Tom persevered in ignoring her, and Grey Arthur tried his best to play Invisible Friend Teacher. Some of the answers Arthur gave were stunningly inaccurate though, and some were just plain odd (from a human's point of view).

"What happens to the food after Tom puts it in his mouth?" Mildred asked.

"It's horrible—you don't want to know," Arthur replied.

"I need to know, it's for research."

Arthur had leaned over, and whispered something in Mildred's ear. Her eyes grew wide.

"And his parents *let* him do that?" she asked, clearly shocked.

"Oh, they do it too."

Mildred looked at Tom, aghast, and then wrote feverishly in her notebook. Tom blushed. There was a moment of brief, wonderful silence, before the questions resumed again.

"Do the parents need the brown liquid in order to function?"

"The brown liquid is tea, and yes, adult humans do. Though they can substitute it with coffee."

"What is the goo that the humans put on those slabs of brown?"

"That's honey. Humans get it from burgling bee's

houses. And the slabs of brown are called toast."

"Where does milk come from?"

"Again, that's horrible, and you don't want to know."

And on, and on it went.

Each answer caused Mildred to scrawl furiously in her notebook. Tom ate his breakfast as fast as humanly possible, and hurried out the door much earlier than was strictly necessary, in such a rush to get away that he forgot to bring his lunchbox. Luckily though, with two Invisible Friends at hand, it didn't remain forgotten. Mildred, under Arthur's careful instruction, stowed it away in her satchel, and chased Tom out the door.

The School Run

THINGS HAD PRETTY MUCH GOTTEN BACK TO NORMAL for Tom at Thorbleton Secondary School. After the celebrity status that newspaper headlines bring (the much gossiped-about escape from Dr. Brown), Tom had now faded back into relative obscurity. Five minutes of fame is only a temporary cure to the problem of loneliness, and once all the questions had been answered, and once the story had vanished from being current newspaper news, Tom went back to isolated lunchtimes, and the dubious title of Freak Boy. Grey

Arthur kept Tom company, and made Tom smile, but there's no magic wand to wave at the problem of how hateful some kids can behave, and so many things still remained the same. Big Ben was still to be avoided like the plague, the Spitting Kids were still a rotating point of local interest, cropping up here and there to spit, swear, and threaten people, and some of the girls in his class were still catty bundles of malevolence. This, however, is to be expected at school, and in his own way, Tom had grown used to it. Sure, it still hurt to be called names, and yes, it was never nice to be barged into or spat at, but the barbs failed to cut as deeply now that he had a friend, no matter how ghostly, to share it all with.

Grey Arthur pretty much left Tom to his own devices at school that day, and focused all his attentions on teaching Mildred Rattledust the intricacies of her new Invisible Friend tasks. Tom didn't mind though. After everything he had been through, what with being kidnapped by a known criminal, and coming face to face with a Screamer, nothing else seemed quite so scary anymore. He laughed in the face of double maths, stood firm against the adversity of science tests, and grinned defiantly at impromptu class debates. Okay, maybe he didn't quite go that far, but he'd definitely come a long way from the shy new kid who felt he was invisible, and then sometimes desperately wished he was.

Ballpoint Bill seemed quite excited at having a new ghost to talk to in the school (although he positively turned his nose up at the idea of changing careers and becoming an Invisible Friend himself, claiming that it all sounded "Far too much like hard work"). He did however agree to a role as an advisor, seeing as he'd spent longer in school than Grey Arthur had, and excitedly planned a lecture entitled "Pens and Your Human" for a later date. In English, all three ghosts sat together in the back row, chattering all the way through the lesson (which Tom did find a little distracting). Mildred seemed to be settling in quite well. She studied the human pupils with keen interest, occasionally modifying her appearance in order to blend in better, adding a couple earrings here, a bracelet there, and several doodles on her hand in pen (one read "I love Tommy B," even though she had no idea who Tommy B was, and probably wouldn't understand the concept of a childhood crush if it danced in front of her with a rose between its teeth). She still didn't look anywhere near normal, but it was definitely a start. Her grand ambition, she had stated loudly from the back of the class when Tom was trying very hard to listen to what Mrs. Lemon was saying, was to become good enough at seeming human that she could actually pass as one. Faintly Reals, by all accounts, are the most humanlike of ghosts, and those that are particularly good at what they do can actually appear for brief moments in front of humans. You have to be *exceptionally* good though, as humans automatically refuse to see anything that doesn't look real. And Mildred, much as she tried, was still a long, *long* way away from achieving visibility. There was just something so very *other* about her.

The hours flew by, and soon the bell came to tell them it was time to head home. Mildred actually groaned, which is another reason she was a long way from passing for a human child, but when Arthur explained that children went to school five days a week she perked up considerably.

"See Tom, it was fine. Didn't I tell you it would be fine?" Arthur asked as they walked home together. Mildred looked at Tom, and he couldn't quite be sure, but he thought that maybe, just maybe, she was trying to smile. At least, he's pretty convinced her lip twitched. Or spasmed. Tom simply hmmmed, that "hmmm" that adults use that means "I'm reserving judgment."

It was only day one, after all.

Say It with Socks!

LATER THAT EVENING, AFTER DINNER, TOM LEFT ARTHUR and Mildred downstairs watching television with his mum and dad, and wandered upstairs for some much needed alone time. It wasn't that he didn't enjoy their company, but it's just that two ghosts are twice as tiring as one, and sometimes you just need some time to day-dream, and listen to music, and not have someone ask you why toilet paper comes in different colors. He slunk up the stairs, feeling pretty close to exhausted, opened the door to his bedroom, wandered inside, and tripped head over heels over a pile of socks that reached nearly as high as his waist. A muffled cry of pain escaped him as he crashed to the floor.

"Who left them there?" he growled, picking himself back up. It was meant to be a rhetorical question, as he was meant to be alone, but it turned out not to be the case.

"Well, if that's the way you feel," came a disappointed voice, "I'll just take 'em back with me. I don't know, you make a nice gesture and people just complain. . . ." Tom twisted around to see where the voice was coming from, and saw a short Poltergeist boy pushing the socks hastily back into his pockets. He was scruffy, even by Poltergeist standards, which is very scruffy indeed. His hair had a streak of white running from the side of his head all the way down to the back of his neck, and it was all spiked up using heavens knows what. Possibly glue. His clothes all seemed a size too big for him, and he looked as if he'd been sleeping in rubbish bins (though thankfully, he didn't smell like it). The huge pile began rapidly shrinking as sock after sock was thrust into a seemingly bottomless pocket in his baggy and filth-encrusted trousers.

Some socks in the pile were so small that they looked

baby size, some a little bigger, with pictures of trucks or puppies or monkeys on them. One bore the embroidered message "Mummy's Special Boy." Larger socks for older feet were scattered throughout the pile: grey school socks from primary school; soccer socks; Christmas socks that played a tune; birthday socks that had a name, *Tom's name,* printed on them; rugby socks; garish bright socks that had once been in fashion but were now a mortal sin . . . Tom's life story, told through the medium of foot attire, lay on the floor in a rapidly shrinking pile of mismatched colors and contrasting shapes.

"Those are my socks!" gasped Tom, as he picked himself up from the floor.

"No," corrected the Poltergeist. "These are *my* socks. They used to be your socks, but then I stole 'em. These are all the odd socks I Poltergeisted from you over the years, and I was giving 'em back."

"Why?" asked Tom, utterly confused.

"Because I'm nice like that?" the ghost volunteered. Tom laughed.

"No, really. Why?"

"Because I heard your new socks stank?"

Tom raised an eyebrow.

"Okay, okay." The small Poltergeist took a deep breath, put on his most winning smile, and peered up at Tom. "I want to be an Invisible Friend and I thought if I did this you could put a word in with Grey Arthur."

Tom groaned. "The socks won't even fit me anymore."

"You might shrink."

"I won't shrink."

"You might."

It struck Tom that arguing with a ghost about whether or not he might shrink was utterly pointless, so he changed the subject.

"Why can't you just stay a Poltergeist? You seem to be quite good at it."

The Poltergeist shrugged. "Dunno. Fancied a change. Sounds like a laugh, this Invisible Friend stuff, and you've got to admit, a reformed Poltergeist, handy friend to have, eh? Eh?" He gestured toward all the socks he was returning, and grinned cheekily.

"I don't know how Arthur talked me into this . . . ," Tom moaned.

"Is that a yes? It is, isn't it? You beauty! You won't regret this. You won't even notice me," shouted the Poltergeist, leaping up and down for joy on the pile of socks, throwing handfuls in the air like oversize confetti. Won't even notice him? Tom didn't believe that for a second. "Oh, by the way, the name's Tike. Figured I should introduce myself, since we're going to be roomies."

"We're *not* going to be roomies. You're staying in the attic."

"Whatever you say, Boss," replied Tike, with a huge grin. "So, do you want these socks, or not?"

Tom sighed. Life had just got that little bit more complicated.

Enter, Stage Right

AFTER AN EVEN MORE EXHAUSTING OUTING AT SCHOOL the next day with not one, not two, but three ghosts for company (and that wasn't even counting Ballpoint Bill!), Tom staggered into his home a little bleary-eyed and almost yearning for bedtime. Tike had a disconcerting knack for stealing everything he could lay his hands on, and it was going to take him a while to break himself of the habit. At one stage he had even stolen Mr. Applegate's (a substitute teacher for art) toupee from off his head, without the teacher even noticing. A stern look from Tom meant the toupee got replaced before any of the class noticed, but Tike threw it back on in such a haphazard fashion that Mr. Applegate looked like he'd driven to school on a motorbike without a wearing a helmet. After shepherding the ghosts upstairs and putting on a film to keep them distracted, it was all Tom could do to stay awake while eating dinner. Which was exactly when Mum dropped the bombshell on him.

"Oh dear, I nearly forgot to tell you. I bumped into Mr. and Mrs. Dolchester on the way to work this morning," she said casually, as she tidied away Tom's plate.

"Mr. and Mrs. who?" Tom asked.

"You know, the couple from a few doors down who brought us over some stew when we first moved in."

Tom remembered. It smelled like a warm Snorgle, and probably tasted like one too, and had been liberally scattered with little lumps, hard as cannon balls, masquerading as dumplings.

"Well," continued Mum, "they've just come back from a caravan holiday in Wales, and they promised to come over for a cup of tea, and to show us their holiday snaps."

Tom visibly slumped in his chair.

"And," Mum added, "pre-emptively, no, you can't avoid it, yes, you have to stay, and yes, you have to pretend to be interested."

"Why?" Tom asked.

"Because it's polite," Mum chided. "And if that's not a good enough reason, then because I told you so."

"That's not fair," grumbled Tom.

"Nope. It's not. Parental privilege. If I have to endure two hundred photos of a caravan site, then so do you."

Dad, for about the fifth time in as many days, was working late at the Svelte Sock factory, and so was spared the hatefulness of other people's holiday photos. Dads seem to have an inbuilt sixth sense that tells them well in advance to avoid home in case of impending neighbors/relatives/canvassing politicians. Tom was about to protest, when the doorbell rang.

"That will be them. Remember, look as if you're interested," Mum whispered, as she dashed to the front door. There was much air kissing, and the exchanging of a jelly, before Mr. and Mrs. Dolchester made their way into the kitchen, where a dejected-looking Tom was slumped in the chair.

An hour later, Tom's eyes had all but glazed over.

"Here is the photo of the path leading to the caravan park that we stayed in," said Mr. Dolchester.

"This is the well that people dropped coins in to make wishes," said Mrs. Dolchester.

"This is a close-up photo of the mechanism that lowers the bucket into the well," said Mr. Dolchester.

"This is a photo of a rabbit that we saw in some grass. Except he jumped out of the frame just as we took the photo, so all you can see is the grass," said Mrs. Dolchester.

"This is a really nice omelette we had at the café just down the road," said Mr. Dolchester.

"This is a picture of our favorite waiter, Cyril," said Mrs. Dolchester.

Tom was on the verge of feigning death in order to get away when something happened that woke him up completely.

"This is a photo of an interesting shaped rock that we found that looks a little like an egg," said Mr. Dolchester.

The door to the kitchen burst open in a flash of light and a puff of blue smoke to the sound of trumpets. Tom nearly leaped out of his chair. A figure stood in the doorway, at least six feet tall in his top hat, swirling a cloak dramatically. From beneath the top hat,

and above the swirling cloak, a mustache twitched theatrically.

"Enter stage right!" intoned the voice. "Montague
Equador Scullion the Third!"

Tom's jaw practically landed in the two-inch-high
pile of photos on the table.

"Tom, be a sweetheart and shut the door. A draft
must have blown it open," said Mum, rubbing her eyes
in an attempt to keep a look of utter boredom at bay.

"And this is a photo of an interesting looking window that we passed in the street," continued Mrs.
Dolchester, oblivious to the drama going on in the
doorway. Tom just gawked silently. It was a Thesper, it
had to be a Thesper—only Thespers could turn walking
into a room into a full-fledged drama. As if life wasn't
complicated enough. The smoke began to dissipate, and
the figure in the doorway swished his cloak to drive the
rest of it away. The sound of trumpets faded. The ghost
grinned maniacally at Tom.

"Erm, Mum, I've just remembered that I forgot to
tidy my room," Tom muttered as he got up from his
chair, trying desperately to avoid staring at the new
arrival. Mum scowled.

"Oh, no you don't," she replied, glaring at him.
"You *promised*."

Tom was about to protest that he had done no such
thing when Mrs. Dolchester interrupted.

"Oh, let him go," she said. "After all, when a young
man volunteers to tidy his room, you should really

grasp the opportunity with both hands. Besides, we made copies of all the photos for you, so you can go through them at your leisure."

Mum simply stared at Tom, and he smiled apologetically. "It was lovely to see all your photos," he said politely to Mr. and Mrs. Dolchester, and quickly dived out of the room before Mum had a chance to block his escape. The caped Thesper bowed to everyone in the room, not that they saw it, and followed Tom as he left.

"What on earth was that?" demanded Tom, as soon as he was out of the adults' earshot, frowning as he marched up the stairs.

"That, dear Thomas, is what we call in the trade 'Making an Entrance,'" replied Montague. Tom could only sigh. As he made his way up the stairs, he noticed that a pool of light seemed to follow Montague wherever he went. Trust a Thesper to have its own personal spotlight. Tom opened the door to his bedroom, and stormed inside.

"I've got another recruit for you here, Arthur," he growled. "Apparently, his name is——"

"Montague Equador Scullion the Third!" gasped Grey Arthur. Tike clapped excitedly. Mildred, well, she didn't really react, but that was nothing out of the ordinary for Mildred.

"Oh, marvelous . . . You know him?"

"What ghost doesn't?" responded Tike, staring in wonder at the new guest. Grey Arthur whipped a piece of paper and a pen off Tom's desk, and thrust it toward the new ghost, who autographed it with all the flair and practiced ease of a professional. Grey Arthur clutched the piece of paper to his chest, grinning broadly, before tucking it away in his pocket. Tike was just staring up at Montague with all the adoration of a small child whose favorite soccer player just turned up on his doorstep, looking for someone to have a kick around with. Tom ushered Montague inside, and shut the bedroom door.

"So does someone want to fill me in then?" Tom asked.

"Montague Equador Scullion the Third is the most famous Thesper in England," responded Mildred.

"Thank you, darling, I couldn't have put it better myself," agreed Montague, easing himself into Tom's rickety desk chair. He managed to sit in it as if he was sitting in the finest of thrones.

"Then why on earth would you want to become an Invisible Friend?" A puzzled Tom sat down on his bed, next to Grey Arthur and Tike, who were both giddy with excitement. They kept nudging each other, then looking at Monty, then whispering, and nudging, and then looking some more. It was all a little embarrassing, but Montague seemed quite at home with this type of response.

"A fine actor is always looking for a new challenge, a new role . . . ," Montague explained, crafting his mustache into fine points. He took off his top hat, throwing it into the air, where it vanished in a puff of blue smoke. Arthur and Tike clapped gleefully. "And what bigger role can there be? To play an unseen part in someone's life. That's *art*." He leaned heavily on the word "art," overenunciating it, stabbing the air with his finger. Tom just nodded blankly.

"And what a story to pass on," continued Montague, delivering each line as if he was on stage. "To say I was one of the first-ever Invisible Friends. Too good an opportunity to miss. So I am here to learn, to observe, and to play my part—that is, of course, if you'll let me."

Grey Arthur made enthusiastic squeaking noises, which Montague took to mean yes. Tom noticed that he didn't even get a say this time.

"And who knows, maybe one day there will be plays about me—Montague Equador Scullion the Third, famed Thesper turned Invisible Friend!" He stood with a flourish, and clicked his fingers. There was more smoke, a blast of dramatic music, and when the air cleared the cloak had vanished. In its place, Montague was wearing a heavy cardigan with reinforced elbows, and his black trousers had been replaced with tweed. A few too many pens protruded from his top pocket. The theatrically pointy mustache had changed into a fuzzy little number that wouldn't look out of place on a geography teacher. Tike and Arthur burst into cheers at this change, clapping wildly, and even Mildred gave a small clap of appreciation. Montague bowed to his gathered audience, reveling in the applause.

Tom just sat in stunned silence. Every time he thought he'd just about managed to wrap his head around being able to see ghosts, something new happened that made him feel just as confused as ever, and now he had a ghost celebrity in his bedroom, dressed as a teacher.

"You should have seen him play the vampire in Hamlet," whispered Arthur to Tom. "He was *amazing*. I must have seen it at least five times."

Tom had never read *Hamlet*, but even so, he was fairly convinced there wasn't a vampire in it. At least not in the human version.

He decided to steer the conversation to something that felt vaguely sane.

"Okay, okay, okay . . . ," Tom said, trying to force his thoughts into some semblance of order. "Ground rules. You have to obey the ground rules. No talking to me when there are other humans around if you can help it, and that also means no trumpet playing, no puffs of smoke, no mustache twiddling; all of that is strictly off bounds."

"I will try my best," Montague said, nodding. Tom suspected that leaving such theatrics behind might be very difficult indeed for Montague.

"You live in the attic with the rest of the ghosts—well, other than Arthur, who stays in my room."

"How quaint. Of course, that will be fine. It will make a change from haunting backstage at the Globe Theatre. A few swashes of velvet, several mirrors, and it will feel like home in no time."

Tom was a little concerned about how Mum would react to finding a backstage re-created in her attic, but decided to cross that bridge when he came to it.

"And finally, your first task as an Invisible Friend will be to help me tidy my room, since I had to make an excuse to get away from the torture of caravan photos. Are we agreed?"

"On my life, Thomas Golden, *it shall be done!*"

Tom found himself sighing again. Sharing his home with not one, not two, not three, but *four* ghosts, one of whom was addicted to theatrics, was going to be very hard work indeed. . . .

Things That Go Bump in the Night

TOM FELL INTO A HEAVY SLEEP THAT NIGHT, thoroughly exhausted. His mum had stormed up some hour before, when the Dolchesters had finally left, ready to growl at him for his abrupt exit, but when she saw Tom's spotless room she relented a little. Only a little, though. As a punishment he had to look through the rest of the photos he'd missed, and write a letter to the Dolchesters, thanking them for their gift. It is very hard to find nice things to say about two hundred and nineteen photos of a caravan site and its contents, and it took Tom an age to finish it. Montague, ever the one for dramatic phrasing, had helped with some of the more outlandish compliments. After the note was written, Montague recited the ghost version of *Romeo and Juliet,* playing every single role (including Bintle the Enchanted Mushroom, and all seven of the happy dwarves) while Mildred, Tike, and Grey Arthur sat in mesmerized silence. Finally, the note completed, and *Romeo and Juliet* performed, Tom had herded the ghosts up into their attic bedroom, and settled down into bed. He was asleep as soon as his head hit the pillow.

He slept so heavily that for a while, he forgot to dream. Only for a while . . .

Everyone knows the type of dream, or nightmare, or waking horror, that Tom went through later that night. The one where you snap out of sleep, every muscle knotted in place, heartbeat soaring, convinced that someone is in the room with you. The one where you want to dive beneath the covers, or keep your eyes clenched tightly shut. The one where you don't dare move, or even breathe harder, because you hope that just by staying still, small, invisible, that whatever is there with you will lose interest, and go away.

Except, unluckily for Tom, this wasn't a dream, or a nightmare.

Every hair-raising second of this was real.

Tom fell out of sleep with a jolt, suddenly wide awake. The room was pitch black around him, and his eyes struggled to adjust. It was then, in that exact moment, that Tom realized that there was someone else in the room. He wanted to call out for Arthur, but he was too scared to move, to call out, to do anything. Instead, he just lay there, frozen, trying very hard to pretend to be asleep, and failing miserably. His heart hammered in his chest, and his teeth clenched together. As his eyes, squeezed together tightly to give the illusion of being shut, became more used to the dark, he could begin to make out a figure standing by the side of his bed, and Tom's breath caught in his throat. The thin, sinewy body, the long arms ending in long fingernails that twisted away in strange shapes, the swirling mist eyes . . . Tom's fingers dug into his duvet, gripping it tightly.

There was a Screamer standing over Tom's bed.

Tom screamed, and sat up in bed, his body literally propelling itself from lying down to sitting bolt upright in one swift movement. He clung to his duvet, dragging it up so that all but his head was covered, and still he screamed. The Screamer stared back at him, head slightly tilted, teeth bared.

Everything else happened so quickly. Arthur rushed out from beneath the bed, and at exactly the same time Tom's dad burst into the room, turning on the light. He was clutching a pint-glass full of water as a makeshift weapon (which would have been great if he was battling the Wicked Witch in *The Wizard of Oz,* but not much use against anything else) and he was managing to look bleary, confused, and wide awake all at the same time.

"What is it?" he yelled at Tom. *"What is it!?"*

Tom was staring at the Screamer, who was wincing at all the light flooding the room, shielding his eyes with his scrawny hands.

"It's okay, Tom! It's okay!" Arthur was calling, as Tom made strange gasping noises. The last time Tom had seen a Screamer had been at Thorblefort Castle, and that had been far from a pleasant experience. Waking up to find a Screamer standing over your bed though made that seem like a nice picnic in the sun. Arthur had got hold of the Screamer, and was leading him away from Tom's bed, all the while making soothing noises to Tom, and acting like this was nothing out of the ordinary.

"Tom. Are you okay? What's going on?" Dad demanded, looking warily around the room. Grey Arthur smiled reassuringly at Tom, and pushed the Screamer into Tom's wardrobe, straight through the closed door, out of sight.

Tom's mouth felt as dry as sandpaper, and he struggled to talk.

"I . . . erm . . ." Words fell out in stilted clumps. Dad was staring at him, panic etched on his face. "Nightmare. Thought I saw . . . Was a dream," he muttered weakly.

"Oh, thank goodness!" Dad visibly slumped, putting his weapon of water down on the night table. "You scared the life out of me! I thought we were being burgled, or that Dr.—" He stopped himself there, not wanting to mention Dr. Brown, not wanting to worry Tom, or to let Tom know that he himself was worried. "I just thought . . . well, it doesn't matter. You're okay, though?"

Tom glanced toward the wardrobe, and Grey Arthur was leaning against the closed door, smiling at Tom as if this was a normal, everyday occurrence. A disgruntled hissing noise was coming from inside.

"I'll be fine," Tom said, nodding.

"Do you want me to leave the light on?"

"Yeah, if you would."

Dad nodded, and took his pint of water back from the night table. "Good night, Tom," he said.

"Good night, Dad."

Dad gently shut the door behind him, and trundled off back to bed.

"What's it doing here?" gasped Tom at Grey Arthur, as soon as Dad was gone. "Why is there a Screamer in my bedroom? Make it go away!"

"It's okay, Tom. I think he's here to be an Invisible Friend."

"You *think*?"

Arthur shrugged, and smiled winningly.

Tom felt a massive sighing fit coming on. He was beginning to lose count of the number of ghosts in the house. This was turning into a full-fledged ghost school.

Shadows began pouring up from beneath the closed wardrobe door, and a low howling could be heard.

"Well, it can't stay. Tell it to go away," Tom hissed.

"Why can't he?"

"Because. Because he's a Screamer," replied Tom, as if it was the most obvious reason in the world. Arthur frowned.

"That's not fair."

"I don't care! I can't have a Screamer living in my attic. It'll give me nightmares."

"Don't be silly. I'm sure he's very nice, when you get to know him."

As if in agreement, there was a growling noise from inside the wardrobe. Tom, who was still partially hidden beneath his duvet, shook his head.

"No. You always manage to talk me round. At first there was just one extra ghost, and now there are three, AND a Screamer hiding in my wardrobe. There's no way. I won't have it in the house. Absolutely, one hundred percent, definitely, final answer, no."

And that was that. Tom refused to budge an inch on the matter.

Which is why there is now a Screamer living in Tom's parents' garden shed.

Full House

THE NEXT DAY AT BREAKFAST TOM WAS SITTING DOWN and eating toast; Dad was reading his newspaper; Grey Arthur was hovering above Tom's Dad's chair reading the newspaper over his shoulder; Mum was ironing her uniform; Mildred was busy writing in her journal; Tike was adjusting the dial on the toaster when nobody was looking from "brown toast" to "call the fire brigade toast"; Montague was posing in the mirror, practicing his "Invisible Friend" face; and the Screamer, who was apparently called the Harrowing Screamer—although how he managed to tell Arthur this when all he ever did was growl or hiss was beyond Tom—well, he was outside the kitchen, peering in through the window, and occasionally twitching his fingers like a weird magician about to pull something horrible out of a hat.

It was *total* chaos.

Tom dashed out of the front door on his way to school as soon as possible, again leaving his lunchbox forgotten in the hallway. It was a strange sight indeed, not that any humans could see it, to see a human boy darting out of his front door, followed by Grey Arthur, then an ex-Faintly Real, an ex-Poltergiest, an ex-celebrity Thesper, and a (possibly) ex-Screamer, who had managed (under Grey Arthur's guidance) to grab hold of Tom's forgotten lunchbox and hang the handle of it perilously from a discolored talon.

Strange days indeed.

So onward they marched, a very motley crew, toward Thorbleton Secondary School.

By all accounts, it was a baptism by fire, no pun intended. As they walked through the towering school gates, the roar of children's emotions swept into all the ghosts, bellowed whispers and roaring sighs, and while Grey Arthur didn't so much as blink, the new ghosts found it a struggle to cope. In fact, the Harrowing Screamer actually turned tail and fled, a muffled howl escaping him, and Arthur had to chase after him and drag him back. Screamers are used to hearing fear, but so many other emotions, all churned up and thrown together—well, it was enough to scare the scariest of ghosts.

"QUICK, THE TEACHER IS COMING . . ." "SHE'S SUCH A COW, WHO DOES SHE THINK SHE IS TALKING TO ME LIKE THAT. . . ." "PLEASE, PLEASE, I COULD HAVE SWORN I PUT MY HOMEWORK IN HERE SOME-WHERE. . . ." "SO, MUM SAYS SHE DOESN'T WANT TO LIVE WITH DAD ANYMORE. . . ." "THE CAPITAL OF GERMANY IS . . . IS . . . OH, COME ON, I KNOW THIS. . . ." On and on, the bar-rage of emotion went. Mildred clung to her satchel, her different colored eyes wide, silently wondering how long it would take until she became used to it all, like Grey Arthur seemed to be. Tike jiggled on the spot, a bundle of nervous energy, grubby hands clamped over his ghostly ears. Montague had closed his eyes, and was concentrating, taking deep breaths. The Harrowing Screamer, who had given up on trying to flee, was now just making a desperate hissing noise as he tried to clean some bubble gum off his long, curling toenails. The torrent of emotion made no sign of abating though, relentlessly pounding into the poor ghosts: "WHY DOES FIRST LESSON HAVE TO BE GEOGRAPHY? I HATE GEOGRAPHY!" "I CAN'T BELIEVE MUM MANAGED TO DYE MY SCHOOL SHIRT PINK...." "YOU'RE DUMPING ME?". . . and also, a little more worrying, spoken in such urgency that no ghost could miss it, *"IF YOU ADD SOME MORE PAPER, IT SHOULD CATCH ON FIRE QUICKER. . . ."* The ghosts exchanged anxious looks, and Arthur tried his hardest to give off a casual air of "just another day at school." Tom just looked a little bored—after all, he was spared the ghostly talent of being able to hear emotions, and so all he heard was the general roar of the playground, and by now he was very used to that. Instead, he just surveyed the masses of children swarming ahead, and took a deep breath. He didn't know whether to be more worried about the effect five ghosts would have on the school, or the effect the school would have on the ghosts.

The school, however, carried on, oblivious to its newest guests. There was a group of older boys surrounding a smaller boy, jostling him, while one rummaged around in his bag, pulling out its contents for everyone to laugh at. A group of girls were screaming insults at another group of girls, and occasionally throwing rude gestures to each other, but they all stayed a safe distance away, content to hiss and spit, but not actually scrap. A teacher, who was running late, darted past the ghosts, stopping briefly, out of breath, to reunite the jostled boy with his emptied schoolbag and its contents, and shoo the older boys away, before glancing again at his watch, and running in through the main entrance. A soccer ball was kicked against a glass window, coming perilously close to breaking it, and all the kids who saw gasped, and then giggled in relief. Montague looked at Tom in horror.

"This is madness," he said, shaking his head. Tom laughed.

"Welcome to my world," he said with a grin.

As Tom led everyone into the school corridor, he noticed the way was blocked off, with a group of boys gathered around a bin, whispering conspiratorially. Standing head and shoulders above them, at the center of the crowd, was Big Ben, lost in concentration. The sensible thing to do would be to get as far away as possible, as whatever it was they were doing, the last thing you wanted was to get caught up in it. But Tom wasn't always heavily filled with sensible, and what little sensible he did have right then was far outweighed by curious. Try as he might, though, he couldn't make out what they were saying, but suddenly they all darted away, screeching with laughter, and the smell of burning filled the air. The bin they had been huddled around was smoldering, occasional licks of flame peeping out from the top, while black smoke streamed free. Big Ben stood a moment longer, savoring his handiwork, huge hands with clumpy fingers hovering over the heat. Finally, satisfied, he turned to run away, and it was then that he locked eyes with Tom. In less time than it takes to blink, Ben had spanned the gap between them, his huge fingers coiled around Tom's collar, hoisting Tom up onto tiptoe. Instantly, Arthur was at Tom's side, bristling defensively, frantically looking around for teachers or ways to help. The other ghosts watched in stunned silence, unsure of what was going on.

"You didn't see me," Big Ben said sternly. Tom nodded quietly, and then Ben was gone, running out the exit, his giggling friends already as far away from the fire as possible. The trainee Invisible Friends watched him dart past, and then looked back at Tom, who was straightening out his collar and breathing a little unsteadily. Arthur, however, was already on the case, having located the nearest fire alarm, and he was trying to work out the right amount of force needed to break the glass.

"Is he meant to start fires?" asked Mildred, in all sincerity. Tom shook his head, a little delirious laugh escaping him, which escalated when he saw Mildred writing a note to that effect—HUMANS ARE NOT MEANT TO BURN THINGS WHILE WAITING FOR SCHOOL TO START—in her notebook. Given a little more time to compose himself, Tom would have given a proper response, and explained to the very confused ghosts standing in front of him the school etiquette of not setting things ablaze for entertainment, but his heart was still racing, and his mouth was still dry, and it was also at that point that the fire alarm wailed into life. Grey Arthur flashed a thumbs up toward Tom.

"What's that racket?" yelled Tike, and Tom had to shout back to be heard over the alarm.

"FIRE ALARM. GOT TO HEAD BACK OUT-SIDE."

Everything happened so quickly then, which is probably just as well, as dawdling when fire alarms go off isn't really recommended. The second the alarm sounded, the volume of emotion resonating through the school hit fever pitch. Poor Mildred, Tike, Monty and the Harrowing Screamer hadn't thought that it was possible for the noise to get worse, but as the excitement and worry of the fire alarm hit home, they realized they'd been very, very wrong in that belief. The walls practically creaked with the vibrations of nervous/animated voices, and within moments the corridor, which had previously been deserted apart from Tom and his ghostly companions, flooded with children, as if some unseen dam had been breached. The pupils surged toward the exit, and all the ghosts rapidly side-stepped out of the way, to avoid being run through, and Tom dived to the side to avoid being trampled. A teacher followed behind, trying very hard to keep some semblance of order—"Please, don't run. . . . No, this isn't a drill. . . . Just leave your stuff in your lockers, you can come back and get it later. . . . You all know where to go, we've done the drill umpteen times now. . . ." She stopped, and glanced at the burning bin, and Tom standing nearby it; then she frowned, rummaged in her bag, and pulled out a bottle of water. Expertly, she put out the fire, and stared at Tom.

"I suppose you're going to tell me you had nothing to do with this, and you don't know who did."

Tom nodded guiltily. "No idea, Miss."

"What a surprise." Tom burned red, hating the lying, but he also hated the thought of Big Ben being even more angry with him than usual, so he stayed quiet. The worst teachers can do is detention, or suspension, or expulsion, and the worst Big Ben could do?. . . Tom thought back on the memory of the broken glass bottle being held up close to his face, and he shuddered. The teacher tutted disapprovingly, and shooed him toward the exit. "Come on, outside with you. I know the fire is out, but we have to stay away until the fire brigade gives us the all clear."

And so Tom joined the tide of children pouring out of Thorbleton Secondary School, and his accompanying ghosts chased after him.

The playground, busy as it usually was, heaved with people, with teachers still clutching their pre-class cups of tea, and pupils giggling and socializing and trying their hardest to ignore the areas they were meant to be standing in. The alarm sounded quieter outside, but it was still a constant drone against a backdrop of excited chatter. Tom wandered over to join the queue where his class was waiting, as their teacher paced up and down the line, calling out names, and crossing them off the register. The ghosts huddled close by Tom, each a little overwhelmed by what was going on. Even Arthur, who was by now a seasoned professional at hanging around in school, was a little on edge—after all, this was his first real fire and, to make things that little bit more tense, Tom had chosen to stand next to the most hateful girl in school.

I say chose, and that's not strictly true. You are meant to stand in alphabetical order, to make calling the register that much easier for your teacher, and Tom, being a very obedient type of boy, had done exactly that. The only trouble is that Golden, Tom goes right after Getty, Kate, and Kate was The Most Awful Girl in the World. Or, at the very least, in Thorbleton. Kate's friends, Marianne and Isabelle, willfully defiant of any attempts to put them in alphabetical order because that would mean, oh horror of horrors, they would have to stop talking to each other for a few minutes, stood next to Kate, preening themselves in little mirrors they carried in their bags. Perhaps sensing Tom standing behind her, or perhaps feeling the smoky eyes of a Screamer burrowing into her back, or perhaps just glancing around to see who was admiring her latest hairstyle, Kate noticed Tom close by, and visibly snarled.

"Don't stand next to us!" she hissed. Her friends giggled, snapping their mirrors shut and throwing them back in their bags. "You'll infect us with weirdness."

"Is there any reason she's so mean to Tom?" asked Monty, and Arthur shrugged.

"I think she was just made that way," he replied.

"I can stand here if I want. I'm *meant* to stand here. It's alphabetical order," muttered Tom. Kate rolled her eyes.

"Go and stand over there. In the middle of the field or something."

"I don't want to," protested Tom.

"I don't care," snapped Kate.

"You know, if you asked the Red Rascal nicely, I reckon he could lose this Kate somewhere really far away. While she slept," volunteered Tike. Arthur shook his head, even though the idea made him chuckle.

"That's not quite how we do it," he replied.

"Maybe he fancies you. Maybe that's why he wants to be near you," suggested Marianne, and she and Isabelle shrieked with laughter at the idea. Kate's face reddened.

"I'd rather *die* than have Freak Boy fancy me." She stooped down, and peered into Tom's face. "You better not fancy me. If you do, I'll get my brother to beat you up."

Tom may well have fancied Kate, if he was attracted to horrible girls who spat on the ground, who wore so much makeup that their faces turned orange, and who spent their entire lives shouting and being as mean as possible, but luckily for him, he didn't, and quite honestly couldn't imagine why anyone would. That didn't stop him from blushing at the accusation though, or feeling a bit scared by the threat.

"Don't worry Tom, we'd never let him hurt you.

He'd have a tough job getting past five ghosts!" whispered Arthur. Tom smiled quietly at the reassurance.

"I don't know what you think you're smiling about, Freak Boy. My brother would destroy you," Kate snarled.

"Pssst . . . Tom!" A voice from behind Tom caught his attention. It was Peter, aka Pick-Nose Peter, and he waved cheerfully at Tom. "You can come stand with me if you like." Tom practically leaped at the offer. Not only was this the first time that anyone had called him over to chat in the whole time he had been at Thorbleton Secondary School, but Peter also had the added bonus of a very complicated Czechoslovakian surname, which saddled him firmly at the back of the line, as far away from Kate as possible.

All in all, too good an offer to miss.

"Maybe Tom's your secret boyfriend . . . ," suggested Isabelle. Marianne laughed so hard at that she actually snorted, and it sounded like someone had viciously squeezed a pig. Kate snapped, grabbing hold of Isabelle's hair, and yanking it as hard as she could. "What'd you do that for?" demanded Isabelle.

"You say anything like that again, and I'll slap you so hard your teeth will fall out."

"You wouldn't dare!"

Tom took this as the ideal moment to take his leave and join Peter, and leave the girls to pull each other's hair, and scratch each other, and do whatever it is girls do when they have a falling out.

Tom and Peter had spoken a few times in the past, but it was mostly just snippets of conversation in passing, and mostly about what had happened with Dr. Brown. Peter was though (once you got past the occasional nasal exploration) quite a decent chap. They weren't what you'd call friends yet, as friends takes a little time to happen, and this was the first time Peter had ever called him over to hang out together, but it was most definitely a start. Tom grinned as he made his way to where Peter was waiting.

"I saw the three witches were giving you a hard time, so I thought I'd give you a way out," Peter said, before leaning in, and adding, in a loud stage whisper, "Kate's just angry because someone's stolen her eyebrows."

As if sensing she was being talked about, Kate stopped bickering with Isabelle just long enough to shoot a filthy look over toward Tom and Peter. Sure enough, she had absolutely no eyebrows at all, and had, in her infinite wisdom, decided to cover up this fact by drawing on her own with what appeared to be felt-tip pen. Tom wasn't sure if she'd fallen victim to fashion, or a Poltergeist's sense of humor. The shock of it, paired with Kate's stern, mean face, made him laugh so hard that tears formed in his eyes, and then Peter started laughing at how much Tom was laughing, which made Tom laugh even more. It was a whole cycle of chortling.

"I can't believe I didn't notice! Now I won't be able to

look at anything else when I see her!" Tom gasped, between fits of giggles. Kate kept looking over, her expression fierce, her fake eyebrows scrunched up in a frown, and it just made Tom and Peter laugh even harder.

The ghosts stood a little ways away, watching Tom and Peter giggle together. Arthur was wearing the broadest of smiles. After all they'd been through in the past, it was just lovely to see Tom laughing. . . .

"You don't really fancy her, do you?" asked Peter, wiping away tears, his face aching from all the grinning. Tom, trying not very successfully to shake off the giggles, shook his head.

"Really, really, not. I've seen more attractive Snorgles."

"TOM!" hissed Arthur, jolted out of his smiling, shaking his head frantically. It doesn't do to name drop different types of ghosts into conversation with a plain old normal human.

"You've seen what now?" Peter asked, looking a bit perplexed. Tom glanced over at Arthur, who was shaking his head, and then back at Peter. He coughed to buy some time while he thought.

"It's, erm . . . slang, from where I used to live. It means . . . well, it just means she's ugly."

Grey Arthur gave Tom the thumbs up, and went back to explaining to the other ghosts why Tom kept the Ghost World secret.

Peter nodded slowly, thinking, "Snorgle . . . Heh. That's pretty cool. I think I'll use that. *Snorgle* . . ."

All the while Peter and Tom were giggling and chatting, Big Ben was strutting from line to line, reveling in the chaos he had caused. The fire engine roared into the playground, and all the kids clapped enthusiastically. Big Ben didn't. He was *far* too cool to clap. Instead, he just wandered to behind where Tom and Peter were, and stood there, trying hard to look a picture of innocence, while at the same time trying to look guilty enough that everyone knew this was his doing. It's very complex, being a bully. No point doing things like this if you don't get credit for them, and at the same time there's no point getting caught either. So he stood, trying to look innocently guilty, or guiltily innocent, and just succeeded in looking faintly deranged.

Every now and then he'd cough loudly, as if the smoke had badly affected his lungs (it's the bully equivalent of showing off your war wounds) and when Tom looked round to see what Ben was doing, he'd glare a warning at Tom. Tom just sighed tiredly.

"If you like, we can get the Screamer to follow him home, Tom. Don't think he'd look so tough at 2 a.m. screaming for his mum . . . ," suggested Tike.

Tom snorted with laughter at the suggestion, but shook his head. Peter looked at Tom, a confused but amused smile on his face.

"What's tickled you? Still thinking about her eyebrows?"

Tom shook his head. "No, it's nothing. Just thinking."

"You *are* a weird one, Tom," chuckled Peter. Tom looked crestfallen, all his laughter suddenly gone.

"I know, I know, Freak Boy, right," he muttered, staring at his feet.

"Actually, I meant it in a good way. I think it's pretty neat. Everyone else is so deathly dull, or evil. Anyway, there are worse nicknames to have. Have you heard what they call me?" Tom feigned complete ignorance. "*Pick-Nose Peter.* Yeah, really! It's not like I spend my life doing it, but you get caught doing it once, okay, maybe twice, in class, and mix that up with the fact my name begins with a *P,* and well . . . there you go. Pick-Nose Peter. I'd swap that for Freak Boy any day."

Tom and Peter shared a grin, as Mr. Hammond wandered though the lines, checking for the final time that everybody was where they were meant to be. He stopped next to Big Ben, just behind Peter and Tom, and sighed wearily.

"So, you're going to tell me that you had absolutely nothing to do with this, aren't you Ben?" he asked.

"Can't accuse me of nothing without proof," said Ben, by way of response.

"You mean like the fact you stink of lighter fluid and smoke? Yes, I'm utterly sure that's a coincidence. You can go to the headmistress's office, and see if they believe that too." Mr. Hammond pointed toward the entrance to the school, and all eyes were on Big Ben as he slowly made his way, scowling all the while, toward the much feared headmistress's room. There was a ripple of "ooooh" noises as he passed. Mr. Hammond cleared his throat, and spoke loudly, addressing everyone still waiting. "As you might have guessed, that means that the fire brigade have given us the all clear, and it's safe to go back inside." A disappointed moan rose from all the children. "AND, if you hurry, *without* running, pushing, or shoving, then you won't have to work through the tea break to make up for all the time you've lost."

It was a bluff, of course, and most of the older kids knew that—it was hard enough to persuade kids to attend detention these days, let alone keep an entire school in during its tea break—but once a few people started moving, everyone else seemed to follow, no matter how begrudgingly.

"Well, that's the excitement over for today," sighed Peter. The fire engine roared away into the distance, having real fires to fight and real lives to save, instead of having to deal with the fallout of Big Ben's attention seeking.

"Yeah . . ." Tom agreed, a little disappointedly. He'd been enjoying just standing around and chatting with Peter.

"Do you want to sit next to me in class? The seat is free," offered Peter.

Now, that sounds like the smallest question in the world, and Tom tried so incredibly hard to be all laid back in his response, but inside he felt like tap dancing. He glanced over to where Grey Arthur was standing with the other ghosts, and Arthur nodded enthusiastically. He hadn't thought that Arthur would mind, but it's always polite to check. "That would be great," replied Tom.

"You're sure? I know you usually like to sit on your own. . . ."

Tom never sat on his own, he always had Grey Arthur sitting at his side, but since Peter couldn't see ghosts there's no way he'd know that.

"I'm sure."

And so that is how Tom Golden made friends with Peter, aka Pick-Nose Peter. Grey Arthur and his group of trainee Invisible Friends followed behind the two boys as they talked, laughed, and compared notes on who were the most evil people in school. Arthur would have been lying if he said it didn't make him feel a little odd, a little left out, watching Tom sit down with Peter, but sometimes being a good friend does make you a little sad, as you have to do what's right and not what feels best. Tom making good friends with a human was definitely right, and Arthur was incredibly happy for Tom, but there was still a faint smudge of sadness that they wouldn't be sitting together in class anymore.

Still, Arthur had plenty to distract him, as he tried to stop the Harrowing Screamer from running away for the second time, and tried to stop Tike going through a pupil's bag while his back was turned. It wasn't as if he was going to be bored.

Helium, and Radium, and Boredom . . .

THE FIRST LESSON OF THE DAY WAS SCIENCE, AND TOM AND the boy formerly known as Pick-Nose Peter sat down together at the back of the class, while all the ghosts huddled together near the teacher's desk. Ballpoint Bill had come to join them as well, delighted that his favorite Thesper was in the vicinity. He even had his lecture all penned and ready for later on (although the handwriting was so bad that there were doubts that even he would be able to read it).

The teacher burst into class a few moments after everyone had arrived, looking a little flustered and more than mildly nervous. Perhaps she had good reason to be— she was the sixth substitute teacher they'd had for that class this term. The proper teacher had been off for months now with what was officially described as "fatigue," but everyone knew that was just teacher slang for stress. With a class like this though, stress was hardly surprising. Big Ben and Kate between them managed to break the hardiest of teachers. Two of the substitute teachers had left in floods of tears, one had shouted until his eyes went bloodshot, one disappeared to get a pen and was last seen driving away at great speed, and one was blatantly a French teacher who had been coerced into teaching a subject she knew nothing about. That lesson had consisted of making them copy entire sections of the textbook, word for word, while the teacher had demanded, in the strongest of French accents, *"Silence maintenant!"*

Tom had learned very little in science so far, other than:

- If you make a teacher cry, they send in a PE teacher to shout at you, because PE teachers are very good at shouting.
- If you make two teachers in a row cry, the Head of Year is summoned.
- *Maintenant* is French for "now."
- Copying from books is very dull indeed.

Tom remembered when he had first entered the science room, full of posters of periodic tables and glass bottles with scary labels, being convinced that this was going to be the most exciting class of all. So far, the most exciting thing that had happened was the angry teacher screaming that they were a "bunch of hateful deviants" when Kate had poured sulfuric acid into his bag.

Still, the ghosts seemed to find it all very interesting indeed. Tike was sniffing the contents of all the different chemical bottles (it was just as well he wasn't human, as Tom was convinced that was the kind of thing that made humans die, or at the very least, bleed from the nose or faint). Mildred was copying down science formulas into her little book. Montague was studying the teacher, trying to impersonate the voice she used when begging the class to behave. Ballpoint Bill was still slightly in awe of Montague, and kept offering him ink cartridges to eat, and the Harrowing Screamer decided to hide in the supply cupboard, away from the bright fluorescent lights. Grey

Arthur was just doing his utmost to keep the chaos to a minimum so Tom would have at least half a chance to learn something.

That is, if he was being taught anything worth learning in the first place.

Which he wasn't.

Yet another pointless class of copying out of the book came and went, but at least this time, with Big Ben still in the headmistress's office, the substitute teacher survived the experience relatively unscathed.

The ghosts continued to follow Tom around for the rest of the morning, making it incredibly hard to get any work done at all, or to chat with Peter without being interrupted, and by lunchtime Tom had had enough, and ordered them to go away with Arthur and practice whatever it is that Invisible Friends need to practice.

Which was when little Frank Longfield sprinted past, a KICK ME note on his back, with the infamous school bully, Big Ben, freshly liberated from the headmistress's office, in hot pursuit. Which brings us neatly back to where we began. . . .

So Where Were We?

THE SCREAMER STALKED UP BEHIND FRANK, BREATHING in light, shadows slowly streaming from his mouth. His long, curling toenails clicked on the floor as he edged forward, old bones creaking, ever closer . . .

Frank took in a deep breath and held it, every ounce of his being willing him to run, and yet every muscle knotted in place. If he'd have looked behind, he wouldn't have seen a thing, because normal humans can't see ghosts, but he knew there was something there, something getting closer . . .

The Screamer behind Frank Longfield stretched out a long, curled talon, and swiped the KICK ME sign from off his back.

Feeling something tug against his sweater, Frank threw his bag to the ground, threw his arms into the air, and ran off screaming hysterically.

The Screamer, note impaled on his discolored nail, threw the scrap of paper into his mouth, and chewed it. Sharp, shardlike teeth reduced it to confetti in seconds. He then spat it out, soggy clumps of mangled note, threaded with specks of shadow, and raised his sinewy arms in the air, hissing triumphantly. Swirling shadows pooled at his feet. Frank Longfield disappeared, still screaming, into the distance.

A slow clapping sound disrupted the scene.

"Well yes, I suppose that's one way you could do it," said Grey Arthur, in the most polite voice he could muster. "Does anyone else want to tell the Harrowing Screamer how he could have perhaps handled this differently?"

As the bell to mark the end of the lunch break

sounded, the rest of the School for Invisible Friends looked on in shocked silence as the Harrowing Screamer stamped on the remnants of the chewed-up note with both feet, howling all the while.

"Anyone?"

"Not meaning to be rude or anything, but I think you really scared him," said Tike, barely hiding a grin. The Harrowing Screamer looked very pleased at that. "Which you're not really supposed to do. Are you? Arthur?"

"Erm, no, you're not," agreed Arthur. The Harrowing Screamer looked disappointed, or sad, or possibly bored. It's quite hard to tell what a Screamer is feeling when they are all sharp teeth, old bones, and shadows. He looked like he was feeling something, at any rate. "Okay, anyone else?"

"Would it not have been possible to hold the door shut, preventing the large angry child from chasing after him in the first place?" Mildred asked, pen poised.

"Well done, Mildred, that's another way to deal with this." Mildred scrawled notes in her book. "Another thing you could have done would be to try to find a teacher, and get his or her attention. Bullies hate being caught." More furious writing from Mildred. Montague stood in silence, taking in the scene, breathing in the ambience, the smallest details, smiling to himself.

"Okay class, gather round then. We're going to have a small lecture now from Ballpoint Bill, who is our school expert, having lived here for many years. Bill is going to explain the importance of pens and pencils within the school day, and how making sure your child is fully stocked with writing equipment can keep them out of trouble. So, I'll hand you over now to Bill."

Arthur led them all through the corridor to the empty classroom where Ballpoint Bill had holed himself away, readying himself for his lecture. Each table had even been carefully prepared with a selection of writing equipment for the trainee Invisible Friends to study, and written on the white board, in what could only be loosely described as handwriting, was the title PENS + UR HUMAN. A LECTCHURE BY BALLPOINT BILL.

There was only one problem, though.

Ballpoint Bill was nowhere to be seen.

"Where is he? He was here just a second ago," Arthur asked, scratching his head. Assorted murmurings from the other ghosts said that nobody else knew where he was either. "Where are you, Bill?" Arthur called. "He can't have just vanished."

"Well, yeah, he could have done," replied Tike.

"Okay, yes, he *could* have done. But Bill wouldn't have. He's far too . . ." Arthur searched for a kinder word, but couldn't find one. "Lazy."

He wandered over to where he had last seen Bill, calling out his name.

It was then that he noticed them, left, abandoned on the floor. Two pen cartridges, both chewed to rupturing, spilling ink on the floor. Bill would never abandon good ink like that. Arthur reached down, and touched the ink, rubbing it between his fingers. It was still wet. Freshly spilled. He looked up at the other ghosts, unable to hide the alarm on his face.

"Something is wrong," he said, his expression grave. "Something is very, very wrong."

Tom Golden, Designer of Top Quality Sewers!

TOM WAS DAYDREAMING. IT WASN'T LIKE HE'D MADE a conscious decision to do so—Mr. Hammond was in the middle of a rather involved speech about how the Romans were the first civilization to invent sewers, and without Grey Arthur at his side to nudge the table when his attention wandered Tom had gently drifted away, grinning dozily at his desk and staring off into the distance. Peter was sitting by him, but Peter was daydreaming too, so he wasn't much help at all.

Tom's wasn't even a particularly good daydream, as daydreams go. In fact, it was all a little random. Tom had designed a new type of sewer that used lasers, and solar power, and was run by Capuchin monkeys in little boiler suits.

"*Tom . . .*"

World leaders and eminent scientists had gathered

around for the official opening of the first ever Golden Design Sewer, and they were all cheering wildly, throwing their hats in the air, proclaiming it the "Greatest Leap in Sewer Technology Since the Romans."

"Tom . . ."

Tom was smiling, waving graciously at the gathered crowds, making sure his best side was turned to the assembled TV cameras, lapping up all the attention. "I'm just glad I could help!" he cried above the rapturous applause. "Just glad to help!"

"TOM!"

"Yes sir?" Tom replied on reflex, snapping back into reality from his daydream. Mr. Hammond looked at him, a bemused expression on his face. It was no wonder he looked a bit confused, since it had been Grey Arthur calling out Tom's name, and not Mr. Hammond at all. Peter had stopped daydreaming too now, and was staring at Tom, trying not to giggle.

"Pssst! Over here!" called Arthur, waving to get Tom's attention.

Tom blushed, and let his head sink into his hands. Through spread fingers he could see Grey Arthur in the doorway, and the rest of the trainee Invisible Friends gathered outside, peering in.

"Catch you daydreaming, Tom?" asked Mr. Hammond with a grin. The rest of the class were chuckling.

Tom was about to glare at Arthur to let him see

how annoyed he was when he noticed the worried look on Arthur's face, and the frown fell away to an unspoken question. Arthur pointed at Mr. Hammond to let Tom know he should answer his teacher.

"Sorry? What did you say?" Tom asked, flustered. The class laughed again.

"I was wondering if you were daydreaming, but I don't really think I need an answer." Mr. Hammond was stifling a grin.

"Erm, no. Well, yes. A little," admitted Tom. "But I didn't mean to. I just remembered . . . that I need the toilet."

"You remembered?"

"Yes."

"Meaning that, for a while, you forgot?" Mr. Hammond was trying so very hard to look serious, but not quite managing.

"Erm, I guess so, yeah . . . ," mumbled Tom, burning redder by the second. You'd think by now that Tom would be better at making on the spot excuses, but it wasn't something that came naturally to him, and he always seemed to embarrass himself further when he tried. Like now.

"Well, you'd better hurry up and go then. We wouldn't want you to forget again, would we?"

Tom nodded gratefully, and made his way out of the classroom, past giggling classmates, to where the group of ghosts was huddled in the corridor. Tom marched straight past them toward the boys' toilets, and they all scurried after him. Tom was still red cheeked, but it could have been worse. At least, this time, he hadn't called Mr. Hammond Dad. . . .

The Silence of an Empty Loo

DURING BREAK TIMES, THE TOILETS ARE ONE OF THE busiest places in the school. The boys' toilets not as much as the girls, since girls always seemed to need to go to the toilets in herds for some mysterious reason, but even so there was always a constant stream of people in there. Some of the older, naughtier kids would even hide in the toilets to smoke—as if toilets didn't smell bad enough as it was! Tom couldn't understand how anything could be considered cool when it meant you had to hang out in a place that smells of wee in order to do it, but then if that's what it took to be cool, he was quite happy to not understand, thank you very much.

During lesson times though, the toilets were always deserted, and eerily quiet. The sound of a dripping tap was magnified tenfold, splashing loudly into the sink (whose plughole had been filled with tissue paper). His footsteps echoed as he marched in. After checking to make sure all the stalls were empty, and that he was genuinely alone, Tom turned to face the ghosts.

"So what is it? What's going on?" he asked. The

ghosts exchanged glances, unsure who should answer.

"Ballpoint Bill has vanished," Arthur replied, looking deadly serious. Tom wasn't used to seeing Arthur serious. He was usually all goofy smiles and never far away from laughing, so seeing him all full of concern felt unsettling.

"But why is that unusual? I thought you ghosts can vanish."

"Some can," agreed Montague, peering at his surroundings with thinly veiled horror. It seemed the famed Thesper hadn't been in a school toilet before. It wasn't as if the toilet was as bad as it had been in the past—there had been occasions when Tom had marched in, and the place had made your eyes water. Maybe Thespers are just more delicate ghosts than most. Montague covered his mouth with a handkerchief from his tweed trousers, and continued, "But this is distinctly out of character for Ballpoint Bill."

"And Arthur's all worried 'cause he found some ink on the floor, didn't you?" added Tike.

"Meaning?" asked Tom. He was finding it hard to see what all the fuss was about. A ghost doing something out of the ordinary? Isn't that what ghosts ordinarily do?

"Meaning he left in a hurry. Bill would never leave any ink behind. Something must have happened. Something terrible." Arthur was wringing his hands, and pacing.

"You don't know that. Maybe he just, I don't know,

got bored. Or hungry. Or remembered he had to be somewhere." Tom shrugged. Arthur didn't look convinced. The other ghosts didn't seem too alarmed by all this, but then they didn't know Ballpoint Bill. Not like Arthur did. "I'm sure it's nothing. He'll show up."

"And if he doesn't?" Mildred asked. Tom wasn't sure why they were all asking him the questions. It wasn't like he was an expert. It was only a few months ago that he was plodding along through life, quite unaware that ghosts even existed, and now here he was, hiding in the boys' toilets, being asked advice on a vanished ghost. It wasn't even as if he was the oldest one there— Grey Arthur was at least three hundred years old, and if you believed Montague, then he was so old that he used to haunt the early Viking invaders, and Tom was sure that Tike, Mildred, and the Harrowing Screamer would be old enough to at least get a free bus pass, if they gave free bus passes to ghosts.

"Well, there's nothing we can do about it right now. I've got to get back to my lesson before Mr. Hammond thinks I've fallen down the toilet. You guys look around for Bill, and we'll talk about it later. Okay?" Tom tried to look upbeat, and while the rest of the ghosts managed to look fairly unfazed, Grey Arthur remained a puddle of misery. "I really have to go. I'm sorry. You'll figure it out."

Tom nodded briskly, and waved a brief good-bye to the Invisible Friends before disappearing out into the corridor and wandering back to his lesson.

If Tom had been more on the ball, he might have realized something else when he was in the toilets. He might have thought, when he searched the toilets to make sure they were alone, that it was unusual that they were. He might have figured it out when he noticed the air didn't smell quite so offensive as usual in there. But he didn't. And none of the other ghosts did either, so distracted by Arthur's worry. But, *if* he had paid better attention, and *if* the other ghosts had thought about it, they would have realized that Ballpoint Bill wasn't the only ghost missing.

There had been no Snorgle in the toilets. For the last few months, a Snorgle had been living in the third stall from the entrance, emanating foul odors, and occasionally burping and swearing in turn. Tom and Grey Arthur had even bribed him a while back, getting him to chase Big Ben around all day, leaving the bully surrounded by the worst aromas.

Funny the things you can miss when your mind is elsewhere.

To Absent Friends

THE REST OF THE DAY PASSED IN A BLUR. EVERY NOW and then in lessons, Tom would hear the ghosts roaming the corridors, calling out Ballpoint Bill's name, but they never managed to find him. Every inch of the school had been searched, and then searched again, and a third time for good measure, but to no avail. Arthur had even created a pile of pens that Tike had "borrowed" from Mrs. Lemon's stationary drawer, and he left them out to try and lure Bill from hiding, but that didn't work either. Wherever Bill was, it was nowhere nearby, or else he would have a mouth crammed full of ink before you could say "pencil case." As the day wore on, Arthur had become more and more upset. The other ghosts had tried to comfort him, Montague even telling a story about his great-uncle Benjamin the Lost, who had vanished mid-conversation one day, and only reappeared a whole century later, in exactly the same spot, picking up the discussion where he left it. Ghosts are inherently unpredictable creatures, and Arthur was probably worrying about nothing, they'd said. Arthur had simply nodded quietly, trying very hard to believe them, but inside he couldn't shake the feeling that this wasn't right at all. . . .

Tom had waved good-bye to Peter at the gates, and set off home with his ghostly entourage in tow. As they walked together, everyone tried desperately to cheer Arthur up, but even Agatha Tibbles, perched on the wall outside Mrs. Scruffles' home, couldn't raise a smile from him. She'd pulled every trick out of the book, ranging from her trademark *MOW* for attention, to rolling around on her back purring, all the way through to tangling herself around Arthur's feet, and none of it managed to drive away Arthur's gloom. In the end, dejected, she settled for a quick fuss from Montague. Tike even tried telling his collection of "Screamers are so stupid" jokes, but when the Harrowing Screamer started hissing, and Arthur still hadn't even so much as raised a chuckle, he decided it was probably best to stop.

Back in Tom's room, they talked, and Arthur paced, and then they talked more and Arthur paced more, before they all decided that they were just going round in circles. Ballpoint Bill had vanished, yes, but there could be a hundred and one reasons for a ghost to vanish, and worrying about all the "could haves" and "might ofs" was utterly pointless, and only served to make Arthur even more agitated. He was working himself into such a pickle, even getting to the stage of drawing little posters in Tom's A4 notepad with pictures of Ballpoint Bill on them, and written above in Grey Arthur's best handwriting, the message HAVE YOU SEEN THIS GHOST? The picture wasn't a bad likeness, but Tom couldn't help but feel that postering the neighborhood was a little premature.

"After all," he'd explained to Arthur, who was holding up the poster for the other ghosts to approve, "he's only been missing a couple hours. When humans go missing they make you wait twenty-four hours until you are *officially* missing. They said so on the news."

"That's stupid. A person is missing as soon as you

71

can't find them," Arthur had sniffed, blue-tacking the poster to Tom's window. Tom couldn't really argue with that.

"Well, it's not doing us any good to sit here worrying. We'll take a couple hours rest, to clear our heads, since my dad says that sometimes you need to step back from something so you can see it better. After dinner we'll meet back up, sit down and decide what to do, okay? It's been a long day, Arthur. We could all do with a break."

Arthur nodded quietly. "Sure. Of course. Class dismissed. Go and have a bit of a rest, and I'll just stay here, and, you know . . ." Panic. Flap. Worry. Draw posters and then draw some more. Panic again. ". . . Think."

As the other ghosts floated out of the room to wherever it was they decided to go, Tom and Arthur were left alone. Grey Arthur looked smaller, greyer, and sadder than Tom had ever seen him before.

"It will be fine, Arthur," he said, sitting down on the bed next to where his ghostly friend was slumped. Arthur nodded, simply looking at the floor. "It will be. We'll find him. And you'll see, it will all have been a big fuss over nothing. You know Bill, they probably just opened a new stationary shop somewhere in town, and he's in there, happy as Larry, stuffing his face full of pens and completely unaware that we're here worrying away." He grinned, and Arthur managed a halfhearted smile. "I'm going to go downstairs and just chill out for a bit. You'll be okay?" Arthur nodded again, but as soon as Tom left the room, he was back at the notepad, drawing another "Missing" poster, and frowning all the while. As much as everyone tried to reassure him that everything was going to be fine, deep down, Arthur had a terrible feeling that it wasn't going to be fine at all. . . .

And On Tonight's News . . .

When Tom wandered downstairs, Mum was busy cleaning the kitchen, with the TV playing the news, and so Tom left her to it. If you get too close to a tidying parent, they have a terrible habit of trying to get you to tidy too, and before you know it you're wearing marigolds and firmly trapped at the sink. Dad was, yet again, working late at the factory. Tom slipped into the lounge, hoping for some peace and quiet, only to find Tike already there. He was sprawled in Dad's huge armchair, which only served to accentuate just how small he was. Tom was worried that he'd leave stains and smudges all over it, since he was looking particularly grimy today, but thought better of asking him to move. Poltergeists, or even ex-Poltergeists, have an annoying habit of doing the exact opposite of what you want anyway. Instead, Tom just settled down on the settee, and flicked on the television just in time to catch the tail end of the news.

"... spate of thefts all over the country that has police puzzled. In no less than six different locations, some hundred miles apart, towns have reported entire wishing wells to have been emptied of coins. Some of these coins had been there for hundreds of years, which leads police to speculate that this may well be the work of antique coin collectors, although they are not ruling out the possibility of coordinated theft by gangs simply picking a soft target. Police are asking that anyone with information regarding these thefts contact them on the helpline listed at the bottom of the screen. At this stage, they are *wishing* for a lead."

The presenter chuckled weakly at that joke, shuffled the papers on his desk, and continued.

"And in business news this week, Svelte Socks—the socks that say style with a smile—"

(Tom sat up at hearing the name of Dad's business mentioned.)

"looked to be frowning today, as word of an unexpected slump in sales caused chaos in the boardroom and a plummet in stock prices, amidst talks of many factories being forced to close. Company representatives seem unable to explain this radical drop in sales, simply claiming that an unprecedented decline in demand seems to be—"

Mum dashed into the room, and switched off the TV, halting the presenter mid sentence.

"Don't you have homework to be doing?" she asked, ushering Tom off the settee. Tom was still gawking at the now blank television screen.

"Did you see that on the news, Mum?"

"I know, how low can you get, stealing from wishing wells? I swear, I don't know *what* the world is coming to."

"Mum, I meant—"

Mum busied herself, tidying the coffee table, straightening the magazines that gather there, relocating the fruit bowl, little touches that didn't need doing, and she continued to talk over Tom, not giving him any time to respond.

"Mrs. Stanton at the Fish and Chip shop had her charity box stolen the other day. *A charity box!* It's a sad state of affairs when people have to stoop to such things."

"Mum . . ."

"Mind you, it will catch up with them in the end. These things always do. Karma, that's what they call it. *Stealing from wishing wells!*"

"MUM!" cried Tom, raising his voice to get her

attention. She stopped what she was doing, and looked at him, a little anxiously, biting her lip. "Is Dad's job okay?"

"What? Why? Oh, because of what the TV said? Nothing for you to worry about." She began tidying again, wiping away imaginary dust from a shelf. "You know how these journalists can be, always making things sound so much more exciting than they are."

"Honestly? It's nothing more than that?" he asked.

"Would you look at the time? I'd best put dinner on—your dad will be home any second. And you, you have homework to be getting on with." With that, she made a hurried exit to the kitchen.

"Wow," said Tike, stretching lazily in Dad's armchair. "That doesn't sound good."

"What do you mean? What doesn't sound good?"

"You know, the way your mum tried to avoid the subject, then left all quickly. I bet it's *really* bad." Tom glared at Tike, who looked confused. "What? Why are you looking at me like that?"

"You really need to work on your friendly chatter," he replied glumly. With that, Tom left the room, turning around briefly to catch a glimpse of Tike undoing the little touches Mum had done in tidying—making sure the magazines were stacked at an odd angle, pushing the fruit bowl to one side . . . Noticing Tom watching him, Tike quickly sat back in the chair, whistling innocently. Or at least, as innocently as a Poltergeist can, which really wasn't very. Tom grabbed his school bag from the hallway, and went back up to his bedroom to join Grey Arthur. So much for taking a break to unwind . . .

It didn't take long for the rest of the ghosts to slowly drift back into the room, and so Tom made Arthur teach an impromptu class on Invisible Friending to distract him from his frantic poster factory (nineteen posters and counting by the time Tom had returned), while Tom wrote up his homework on Roman sewers. It would have been a lot easier to do if he hadn't daydreamed the class away, and if he hadn't been called out of class by an anxious Arthur, if there wasn't a very distracting room full of ghosts chattering away behind him, and if he wasn't secretly worrying about what the TV presenter had said.

Socks and Shares

MUM WAS CHECKING (FOR THE THIRD TIME IN AS MANY minutes, not being a very patient cook) the contents of the oven when Dad walked in. He sighed deeply, laying his briefcase down on the table, and sinking into his chair. He looked through the letters stacked on the table, all with formally printed addresses, all still sealed, and he couldn't summon the courage to open them and read the outstanding bills inside. No doubt more than a fair share of them boasted the words "Final Demand" in red letters at the top. Instead he pushed them to one side, as if distancing them from him by a few inches could make them disappear, and he loosened his tie. Mum wandered over, and kissed him hello. Dad smiled wearily back at her.

"How was work?" she asked.

"Where's Tom?" he replied.

"Upstairs. Doing his homework. He can't hear us. How was work?"

"As good as it can be when you find your manager crying in the toilets, clutching a copy of the *Financial Times*," Dad muttered, deciding to take his tie off completely and then shoving it in his pocket. He looked tired.

"Not that good then," Mum responded, in a case of monumental understatement. She filled the kettle up, and began making tea. Tea was a necessity in such situations.

"I just don't understand it." Dad rubbed at his forehead, trying to chase away a growing headache. "Nothing's changed! The socks are as good as ever, if not better, the prices haven't gone up; our competitors are suffering just as much as we are, so nobody is taking over the market. . . . It just doesn't make any sense. It seems that people just don't need to buy as many new pairs of socks, which is ridiculous. Isn't that ridiculous?" Mum simply nodded, throwing teabags into the pot. "People *always* need socks. They're the staple gift of Christmases and birthdays. If you wear shoes, then you need socks. Unless they're sandals." He sat up straighter, as if a thought had suddenly occurred to him. "Is everyone wearing sandals these days? Is it some new trend that research has somehow missed?"

"I haven't noticed an increase in sandals," said Mum gently.

Dad slumped back down into his chair again, tracing his fingers on the table in a figure eight. "Then I just don't get it. Fifteen years I've been working in the sock industry, and I've never seen anything like it. Our shares have hit rock bottom. If it doesn't pick up in the next week or so, they're going to have to lose a few factories. The Thorbleton one included."

Mum stood for a while, letting that information sink in. "So when are you going to let Tom know what's going on?" she said finally, her voice quiet. She poured the tea into mugs, adding a splash of milk, a few too many sugars, and passed the cup to Dad.

"I wasn't going to."

"You'll have to tell him *something*, sweetheart. He already heard a bit about it on the news earlier on, and he was asking me questions. We can't keep this secret from him for long, and I don't like lying to him if he asks me."

"It's not lying, really, is it? We're just protecting him from the truth. It's entirely different."

"Is it?" They held eye contact for a while then, before Dad broke away, and went back to tracing his fingers across the table.

"Of course it is. He's been through an awful lot

recently, and the last thing he needs is to worry about something that he can do absolutely nothing about. It's not like he can go out there and suddenly make the world need more socks, is it? So what's the point of telling him unless we absolutely have to?"

"I suppose."

"I was thinking that, maybe, you could, possibly, get some more shifts at the castle until this all gets sorted? Just to cover us until we know what's going on?" There was a brief change of expression on Mum's face, just a flicker, and Dad saw it. "What? What is it?"

"It's nothing," she said, putting the teabags back in the cupboard.

"It's something. I saw your face. What is it?"

"I didn't want to say, what with you being worried about work . . ."

"But?"

"But . . . things aren't going so well at Ye Olde Tea Shoppe. Things aren't going so well at the castle, full stop."

Dad shook his head in disbelief. "It's a castle. What is there to not go well? It's old, and drafty, and full of pigeons. That's what castles *do*."

"Exactly! I don't know. I don't understand it. Nobody does. The tourists just aren't coming anymore, and those that do, don't tend to stay. Certainly they don't stick around for cream tea and scones. It just feels . . . different there, somehow. Less special. People say it feels like wandering around a lounge instead of an ancient castle. There's none of that"—she gestured wildly to symbolize a feeling you can't quite put into words—"about the place anymore. The tourists say it just feels ordinary. *Ordinary!*" She shook her head, too, unable to comprehend it all. "We scarcely have enough work to occupy ourselves. Look in the fridge. I brought home nine sandwiches today that weren't sold, and Janet took home twelve. Usually, we're lucky if the sandwiches last the day. There's certainly no extra work going. I'm sorry, honey, if I could, I would, but I'm working five days a week already, and I'm not even sure if they'll continue to need me at all if this keeps up."

"Marvelous," sighed Dad, sinking deeper in his chair. "That's just what we needed. More bad news."

"That's why I didn't want to tell you, sweetheart," Mum said sadly. Dad tried his best to smile at her.

"No, no, it's good you did. It's best we know exactly where we stand. I don't want you to have to keep secrets from me."

Mum sat down next to Dad at the table, her cup of tea next to his, and they looked at each other, their faces a mirror of each other's worry. "And so what about us keeping secrets from Tom?" she asked softly. "We'll have to tell him soon enough, if your wages don't come through, if we can't even pay the mortgage. I think he'll notice if the bank repossesses the house."

"Well, hopefully it won't come to that. We've got some new marketing ideas to work through, and my Anti-Static-Shock-Socks should be ready for the factories soon. We'll pull something out of the bag in time, I'm sure. I just don't get how things have gotten so bad, so quickly. It seems like only yesterday I had a nice new promotion, a nice pay raise, moving into a nice new home in a nice new area that has a nice garden and a nice-sized kitchen, and you got yourself a nice new job too, and so quickly, it's all . . ." He caught himself getting morose, and consciously pushed it aside. He took hold of Mum's hand, and gave it a reassuring squeeze. "It'll be okay. Things will pick up. They always do. Tom doesn't need to worry about it."

"Worry about what?"

Tom was standing in the doorway, empty glass in his hand from when he'd come down to get some juice. Mum and Dad shared a wide-eyed look of shock at being overheard, before quickly trying to look as normal as possible.

"Worry about what?" Tom repeated.

"Oh, nothing honey. We were just talking about whether . . . I . . . had . . . cooked enough dinner for us, and I think I have, so there's nothing for you to worry about," stumbled Mum, her face burning red.

Tom looked at Dad for confirmation, but he couldn't look Tom in the eye. Tom knew then, knew it was something bad, knew Tike had been right. Butterflies fluttered in his stomach, and his pulse quickened.

"I'm not stupid. I know something's going on," Tom said. "So are you going to tell me? Dad? Mum?"

"Tell you what, honey?" asked Mum, trying hard to look a picture of innocence. Her blushing cheeks betrayed the lie. It was obvious from whom Tom inherited his inability to fib.

"Fine," replied Tom. "Fine! Don't tell me." He left his empty glass on the counter, and turned his back, walking away into the hallway.

"Tom . . . ," Dad called after him. Tom broke into a trot, dashing up the stairs toward his room. *"TOM!"*

The Truth Is Out There

TOM DARTED THROUGH THE DOOR TO HIS BEDROOM, AND pulled it shut behind him, cutting off the sound of his dad calling his name. Grey Arthur was hovering above the bed, giving a talk on "Why Human Children Drink Juice," to the trainee Invisible Friends, which slammed to an abrupt halt when Tom burst in. The room looked very crowded with everyone in there. Tike was sitting on the laundry basket, Mildred on the floor, Montague leaning nonchalantly against the wardrobe and the Harrowing Screamer standing, as ever, in the darkest corner of the room, picking something indescribable from out of his teeth with a curling fingernail.

"What's wrong?" Arthur asked, seeing the frown Tom was wearing. The sound of heavy footsteps— Dad's footsteps—could be heard coming up the stairs.

"I just need a bit of privacy, if you don't mind," whispered Tom. There was a knock—Dad's knock—and when Tom glanced at the door and then back at the room, all the ghosts had vanished. Nothing like being able to float through walls and ceilings to help make a fast exit.

"Tom, can I come in?" Dad asked through the door. "We need to talk."

We need to talk. One of the most unsettling things a parent can ever say to a child.

"I guess," replied Tom, letting Dad in and then wandering over to the bed, where he took a seat. "As long as you aren't still pretending this is to do with there not being enough dinner."

Tom's Dad closed the door behind him as he entered, and sat down next to Tom on the bed.

"Mum's not a very convincing liar, is she?" Dad said, with a soft smile. Tom couldn't help but laugh a little at that.

"No," he agreed. "She's really not."

"So I suppose you want to know what's really going on?" asked Dad.

"Would be nice," said Tom, nodding. "Has this got anything to do with what was on the news earlier?"

"Yeah, Mum said you saw that. No getting past you, is there?"

"It was on *the news,* Dad. It was a bit hard to miss." Tom rolled his eyes, and Dad smiled affectionately. "So what's going on then?"

And so Tom listened intently as Dad explained how sales were down, how the factory might close, how moving house was a very expensive business and how he'd left the bills for a bit, waiting for more paychecks, and how the bills were all stacking up, and how the mortgage needed paying too, and just how little fun it is being an adult, especially when you had no money, and that if things got any worse it looked like they might lose the house. Tom sat, taking it all in, nodding in silence until Dad was finished.

"So why were you keeping this a secret from me?" asked Tom, eyebrows knotted quizzically.

"It wasn't keeping it a secret, as such."

"Yes, it was," interrupted Tom.

"Okay, maybe it was a little bit keeping it a secret, but mostly it isn't something for eleven-year-old boys to have to worry about."

"But I want to help."

"I know you do, Tom, which is why I wanted to keep this from you. Unless you can work out why sock sales have plummeted by eighty-two percent, then there's nothing you can do. And if our entire team of market researchers can't figure it out, then no one is expecting you to. It's just one of those things, Tom. Business, enterprise, sales, it's a fickle game. And you've got homework, and lessons, and tests, and goodness knows what else to concern yourself with."

"But you shouldn't have tried to keep it secret from me," muttered Tom.

"Well, people keep secrets from other people all the time, Tom. You know that as well as I do. And sometimes they think they have good reason to." It was obvious what Dad was referring to.

Grey Arthur.

Tom looked at his Dad, surprised. Ever since the incident with Dr. Brown, the whole thing with Tom and ghosts had just vanished from conversation, never to be mentioned again. Until now.

"But that really *is* nothing for you to worry about, Dad," dismissed Tom, feeling a bit awkward about where the conversation was headed.

"Because it's not happening anymore, or just because there's nothing to worry about?"

"Erm, the last part." Tom suddenly stumbled, realizing what his Dad had just implied. "So, hang on, you believe that I can . . . you know?" Tom stopped short of saying "see ghosts." It felt too strange, after all this time of being secretive, to talk about it now.

"Let's just say that maybe I am open to the possibility." Unseen, in Dad's wallet, folded so many times it was no larger than a stamp, was Grey Arthur's note, the note that had let Dad know where Dr. Brown had taken Tom, nestled among receipts and a photo of Tom as a baby. "So . . . do you want to talk about it?"

"Erm, no, not really. Feels a bit weird."

"Well, maybe one day, if you ever feel like it . . . well, you can."

"Does Mum . . . ?"

"Oh, no. No. Thinks it was just one of those things. A phase, perhaps. But no, she doesn't."

"But you . . . ?"

"Ish. I guess, yeah. I mean, why not?"

They sat in silence for a while, each taking in the conversation about ghosts that had somehow managed to take place without ever once mentioning what they were talking about.

"So, are we done talking now?" asked Tom.

Dad laughed. "Yes, we're done." As if to herald the end of the conversation, the fire alarm went off, and from downstairs Mum could be heard crying out "Oh, no, no, no!"

"Sounds like dinner is ready, anyway." Dad chuckled. "You coming down?"

"Yep, just give me a tic," answered Tom.

"Right you are. I'll see you down there. Oh, and Tom?"

"Yes?"

"Please, promise me you aren't going to worry about this. There's honestly nothing you can do. It *will* sort itself out."

Tom nodded, and Dad ruffled his hair before leaving the room, shutting the door behind him. When Dad was a safe distance down the stairs, Tom spoke up.

"It's okay, you guys can come out now."

On cue, Tike climbed out of the laundry box, the Harrowing Screamer materialized from the shadows beneath Tom's desk, Arthur crawled out from beneath the bed, Mildred floated serenely through the ceiling and Montague strode out through the wardrobe door.

"So I take it you all heard what was said?" asked Tom. An assorted murmuring indicated they had. "Good," responded Tom. "So now we have *two* problems. Ballpoint Bill vanishing and my dad's work. So here's what I want you to do. Tike, I want you to visit some of your old haunting friends. If anyone is an expert on the comings and goings of socks, it's the Poltergeist community."

"Easy peasy," replied Tike, cracking his knuckles.

"Montague, I want you to ask around the Thespers, see if they've heard any gossip about either Ballpoint Bill or socks."

Montague smiled. "If there's a story out there, the Thespers will know it already."

"Mildred, you pop over to see Mrs. Scruffles, see if she knows anything that could help us. Arthur, since you've already made the posters, you might as well pop out and put them up around the neighborhood." The Harrowing Screamer hissed in the corner, awaiting instruction. "You, erm, can guard my desk." The Screamer seemed satisfied at that, and perched on top of the desk, gnashing his teeth.

"And what is your task, Thomas?" asked Mildred.

"I," replied Tom, with dramatic flair, "am going to eat some burnt lasagna for dinner and pretend that everything is normal. It's what we humans do best."

Piecing It All Together

DINNER TOOK FOREVER—HEAVY SILENCES AND HEAVIER lasagna made the experience very awkward indeed. Nobody quite knew what to say, so they chewed, and smiled, and chewed some more. In the end, Tom resorted to the tried and tested method of spreading the food as thinly as possible on his plate to make it look like he was finished. Liberated at last, Tom rushed up the stairs.

Tike and Arthur were already back and talking animatedly when Tom burst in. The Harrowing Screamer was still perched on the desk, guarding it with all his might, but he relaxed a little when he saw that Tom had returned.

"So?" Tom demanded, as he shut the door. "Anything?"

"Tell him," Arthur said, wringing his hands.

"Okay, right, well I went to speak to Mike and Miranda, the Mischief Twins, see if they knew what was going on," Tike began. Tom nodded, encouraging him on. "Only, thing is—there is no Mike and Miranda anymore. Miranda's gone. Vanished. Just like Bill."

"What?" Tom asked, jaw dropping open.

"Exactly. Not good. Mike's really shook up. Seems they had an argument, over a Poltergeisting job from the *Daily Tell-Tale*. Mike wanted to do it, Miranda didn't, so he went off on his own. When he got back, she was gone. Vanished. He feels terrible, like it's his fault. I tried to tell him it wasn't, but . . . you know how it is. Can't help feeling guilty, can you? So then I ask him about the socks. It's been a couple days now, maybe longer, since Miranda vanished, so he hasn't been out on the Laundry Run since it happened. Says he can't face it alone. Says it don't feel right."

"So he doesn't know anything about the socks, but he *does* know another ghost who vanished?" Tom said out loud, trying to work it all out.

"Yeah, I know, a bit too weird, huh? So I figured I'd go and ask some of my other Poltergeisty friends, see if they've heard anything. Except—get this. I can't find any. Not a single one. They've gone. Just like Bill. Just like Miranda."

"So how are we going to find out what's happening to all the socks if we can't find any Poltergeists to ask?" Tom sighed.

"He's a bit slow off the mark, isn't he?" Tike asked Arthur, ignoring Tom. Arthur nodded glumly. Tike turned to Tom, spelling it out very slowly so he was sure that Tom would understand. "If all these Poltergeists are disappearing, then there's no ghosts stealing socks. Follow? No ghosts stealing socks, no people realizing none of their socks match, no people going out to buy new socks. Get it?"

"So you're telling me my very human dad might be going out of business because of a *Poltergeist* shortage?" It all seemed too bizarre to be true. Tom shook his head, trying to wrap his mind around it.

"It's not just a Poltergeist shortage." Montague Equador Scullion the Third floated through the bedroom window, throwing himself straight into the conversation, just as if he'd been sitting in the wings, waiting for his cue. "It's everywhere, all over the country, all different types of ghosts. It's all the Thespers are talking about. And here, look . . ." Montague threw a copy of the *Daily Tell-Tale* down on the bed, and it fell open to the private advertisements, next to the section of "Mischief Tasks for Freelance Poltergeists." "See anything odd there?"

Tom peered at the paper. Section after section began with the words "Missing," "Lost," or "Have You Seen?" A Thesper here, a Sadness Summoner there, a Screamer vanished, a Poltergeist searching for his Laundry Run companion, whole castles missing their ghostly occupants. As Tom stared at the page, advertisements for mischief dissolved from sight as they were completed, and new ones formed in their place: "Number 2, Belton Drive, Miss E. Bell has lied about losing her keys as a reason for being late for work. Poltergeist needed to hide keys in obscure location"; "Flat 14, Sunset House, Francesco and Anna-Marie have lied to parent, claiming not to know where his favorite record has gone. Record is lying in several pieces beneath Anna-Marie's bed after unfortunate Frisbee accident. Poltergeist needed to cause broken record to be found . . ." Adverts would appear and vanish in the blink of the eye, but the section where people were looking for lost friends, that simply grew and grew as Tom watched. "Does anyone know the whereabouts of Englebert the Ectoplasmic? Last seen on Monday at Arundel Castle." "Missing—Betty the Bridesmaid. Last spotted trying on wedding dresses in Wolverhampton. Much missed. Come home." "Where are you, Wailing Screamer? Barnard Castle isn't the same without you." Advertisement after advertisement surged onto the page, and not a single one disappeared. For a while, everyone just watched the page in stony silence, until Montague, deciding that they had seen enough, gently closed the paper. The front page boasted a story about the Red Rascal, and his recent attempt at stealing an entire mountain.

"So why isn't this on the front cover? Why is it tucked away in the private section? It's not even a story! They should be warning ghosts, or at least doing *something*!" Tom cried, voice rising in alarm.

"Because, Tom, panic can be a terrible thing," Montague explained. "Until they know what's going on, they don't want to print a story that will cause alarm. At the moment, all they do know is that more ghosts than normal are disappearing. That's all anyone knows."

"I told you, Tom!" Arthur wailed, looking at the closed paper. "I told you! I knew something was wrong."

"I have to agree, Arthur. Something is *terribly* wrong. Something that could have grave implications for both ghosts and humans." It was an incredibly dramatic way of phrasing it (what else do you expect from Montague) but everyone in the room knew, dramatic or not, that Monty was telling the truth. Arthur slumped down on the bed, head in his hands. Tike was pacing nervously, and the Harrowing Screamer began howling, a low, sad noise.

Ghosts sometimes vanish, and sometimes they reappear. Sometimes day by day they fade so much that one day they simply no longer *are*. Sometimes ghosts just exist for one hour, one night, one dance in the moonlight, one maniacal laugh, and they cease to be as quickly as they came to be. None of this was unusual, not for ghosts. But to have ghost after ghost vanish, so many, so fast, that was unusual. It was worryingly so. Tom only needed to look at the fear on everyone's faces to see that.

Mildred stormed into the room, marching straight through the shut bedroom door, hands on her hips.

"Lots of ghosts have vanished," she said, looking stern. Tom sighed.

"You're about five minutes too late," he responded. "We already know."

Mildred didn't even blink in response. Nothing seemed to shock her. "Mrs. Scruffles wants you to come over after school tomorrow to discuss the matter with her. She said she had some research to do, but by then she should have a better idea of what is going on. She also made me bring over some cupcakes she made, to keep your spirits up."

The Harrowing Screamer darted forward, snatched a fairy cake from Mildred's outstretched hand, and threw it into his mouth, razor-sharp teeth making short work of it. He hissed gratefully, and retreated back into the shadows, trailing crumbs behind him. It was a bit of a surprise, to see the Harrowing Screamer eat something so very human and sweet. Perhaps he was trying to fit in, after all. The rest of the cakes were left untouched though—nobody else felt much like eating.

"So what do we do in the meantime?" asked Montague. Just like in the boys' toilets at school, all eyes were fixed on Tom, waiting for a response. It made Tom feel a little awkward. He thought for a while before responding.

"In the meantime, you all stick together. We will all go to school tomorrow, we will still do everything the same, but nobody is ever to be left on their own. Until we know what's going on, it might not be safe."

Everyone seemed to agree with that. That night, instead of sleeping in the attic with the boxes and the cobwebs or, for the Screamer, in the shed with the spades and the watering cans, all the ghosts piled into Tom's room to sleep, and Tom didn't complain, not even when he opened one sleepy eye to see the Harrowing Screamer practicing his scary face in the mirror.

Tom didn't complain because he knew they were scared. Because he knew they were afraid that something terrible was happening.

Tom didn't complain because you really know something is wrong when it is the ghosts staying in your room who ask you to leave the light on at night.

Going Through the Paces

SCHOOL WAS THE LAST THING ON EVERYONE'S MIND THE next day, but these things had to be done, and Montague was particularly keen that they carry on just as they would normally.

"The show must go on," he'd said that morning, while Tom was packing his schoolbag. He hadn't so much said it as *intoned* it, his voice rich with drama. "Because what we are learning to do, namely what Arthur does every day, is important. We shouldn't let anything get in the way of that."

Tom smiled at that, touched. Adults seem to have this horrible knack of looking back on being a kid, and remembering all the good, and the fun, and the summers running through fields, and spectacularly forget just how difficult it is to be young. They forget that feeling, like soggy lead inside you, when people call you names. They forget the bleeding noses, the shoves in the back, the twisting of collars, the Chinese burns. They forget the notes, the whispers, the shouts, the horror of finding graffiti with your name in it, the terror of a group of Spitting Kids blocking your path, and somehow they look back on it all, wash away everything bad, and just remember sand castles, and daisy chains, and summer holidays. And maybe, just perhaps, that's what it was like when all the adults he knew were younger, but Tom found that hard to believe. It was a strange but wonderful thing, to see that ghosts understood something that many adults fail to do.

Battle Stations

BIG BEN WAS IN A PARTICULARLY FOUL MOOD THAT day. Tom was waiting for the first lesson to start when Ben marched up, toe to toe with Tom, towering head and shoulders above him. He stank of stale cigarettes, and just general "boy who doesn't wash enough" aromas. Everyone else waiting in queue for the teacher to arrive suddenly took two or three paces away from Tom. Peter, who was rather good at conversation and making you laugh, was a bit out of his depth when it came to fending off bullies, especially ones who seemed nearly adult size and had a fearsome reputation for violence. To his credit though, he didn't distance himself from Tom like the rest of the class had, standing firmly at Tom's side, licking his lips nervously. Tom looked in desperation toward Arthur, who was already way ahead of him. Tom swallowed dryly.

"Okay guys, battle stations. We have an angry bully squaring up to Tom. Anyone have any idea of what we should do?"

Tom was desperate for Arthur to hurry this along. Big Ben wasn't even saying anything, just glaring, enjoying watching the fear on Tom's face. There was an awkward silence from the Invisible Friends, as they mulled over their choices. *Quick . . . Quick . . . Quick . . .* thought Tom anxiously. Montague began to say something, and then trailed off into silence. Mildred was frantically flipping through her notebook, trying to find some notes that might help her work out what to do. The Harrowing Screamer was just hissing, jumping up and down on the spot excitedly.

"Come on, guys, you can do this!" Precious seconds passed, and Ben was poised to do something deeply unpleasant to Tom when one of the ghosts finally had an idea.

In the end, it was Tike who leaped to Tom's defense. He dashed forward, and with hands as fast as, well, very fast ghost hands, he stole the belt from around Big Ben's trousers. Without it to hold up his ludicrously baggy school uniform, Ben's trousers slid down into a pool around his ankles, and at just that exact same moment, Mrs. Lemon walked around the corner.

"What on EARTH are you doing, Ben?" she screeched, breaking into a trot toward him, her hands flying to her face in shock. Ben stared down in horror at his exposed underwear, his cheeks flushing hot red. The boxer shorts had cartoon pictures of a bear, holding a heart, on them. The whole class was in hysterics. He gathered his trousers up quickly, yanking them back around his waist. Mrs. Lemon was glaring at him.

"I have no idea what that was all about, and quite frankly, I don't think I want to know. Go to the head-mistress's office, and you can explain there why you thought it was a good idea to show everyone your underwear."

Ben, face still red, muttered darkly under his breath, one hand holding up his trousers, the other clenched into a fist, and marched off into the distance, the sound of everyone's laughter ringing in his ears.

There was an added swagger in Tike's step, a new-found confidence. And he wore the belt wrapped twice around his waist, as a trophy of his brave deed.

When the final bell went, the ghosts actually sighed, disappointed that the day was over, disappointed that they hadn't had more problems to solve.

"Don't worry," Arthur had said, ushering the ghosts out of the school toward home. "Things like that hap-pen in school all the time. You'll all get a chance."

For those brief few hours, they'd almost managed

to forget what was going on in the Ghost World around them. As soon as they stepped foot outside the school gates though, as soon as they remembered the reason why Tom and Arthur had to stop off at Mrs. Scruffles' house, all those concerns came crashing back, and the mood dipped.

After all, there's only so long you can postpone worry before it comes bowling back into you, twice as loud as before to make up for lost time.

Can't Be Too Safe

TOM AND GREY ARTHUR PUSHED OPEN THE RUSTY, creaking gate, and slowly made their way through the tangled mass of foliage that masqueraded as Mrs. Scruffles' garden. The path had all but disappeared since Tom had last visited, and a lump of green and leaves was all that was left to show of the shopping trolley that had been dumped in the garden some months ago. Bramble thorns tugged at Tom's clothes, and strange things crunched under his feet, out of sight, hidden by unruly grass and weeds. Tom had a worrying feeling that they might be snails. Feeling a little guilty, he tried to take longer steps, tiptoeing delicately as he waded toward the door. Grey Arthur wasn't affected at all, gliding through the garden as if it wasn't even there.

New graffiti had been added to the rash-red door, although Mrs. Scruffles had taken care to cover some of the less appealing words with Wite-Out. The front window was still boarded up, although it seemed as if someone had recently attempted to pry the boarding away. A broken piece of wood, littered with splinters and crooked nails, lay abandoned on the ground where it had fallen. Ivy was already crawling over it. Tom knocked on the door, and waited.

Nothing.

"Maybe she's not in?" Tom asked. Arthur shook his head.

"Try again."

Tom knocked louder this time. Flecks of old paint fell away where he hit the door, revealing bare wood beneath.

There was the sound of many bolts being slid out of place, and the door opened a crack, a chain preventing it from opening fully. This was new. Tom glanced at Arthur, who shrugged, as confused as Tom.

"Hello?" Tom called through the gap in the door. No response. "Mrs. Scruffles, it's Tom and Grey Arthur. You asked us to call over after school?"

The door chain fell away, and the door swung open. Tom and Arthur stepped hesitantly through into the hallway, and as soon as their feet were firmly planted on the welcome mat, the door slammed shut behind them of its own accord. The chains magically leaped back into place, bolts locking shut into the door frame. Tom and Grey Arthur frowned at each other.

"I know, I know, it's all very severe, but you really can't afford to take any chances these days." Mrs. Scruffles floated out into the hallway, and the familiar smell of freshly baked cookies, vanilla, and caramel followed her. She looked as cuddly, and as warm, and as friendly as ever, but the smile didn't quite reach her pastel eyes, eyes that looked worried. It made Tom feel sad. "Come in, come in, don't forget to wipe your feet. I've put a nice fresh pot of tea on for us. In times like this, we all need a good cup of tea."

Times like this? Tom and Grey Arthur both dutifully wiped their feet, though Tom was sure Arthur just did it for effect, and they followed Mrs. Scruffles through the corridor into the kitchen and dining room.

Everything was pretty much as it was the last time Tom and Grey Arthur had visited, and yet at the same time, subtle differences stood stark against the back drop of homeliness. The same watercolors hung on the wall, soothing countryside scenes that seemed to subtly alter each time you looked at them. The old grandfather clock stood proudly against the flowery wallpaper, ticking enthusiastically. Cats lined the room, monopolizing every spare inch of space, sprawled on the floor, cluttering work surfaces, clinging tenaciously to shelves, meowing and purring and sleeping and eating, as cats tend to do. Mrs. Scruffles was a terrible softy for stray cats, and it seemed that every feline within a twenty-mile radius knew it. There were even more cats than last time, which Tom had previously thought would have been impossible. There were cats in the drawers, cats perched on top of the door, cats above the cupboards, even a cat asleep in the breadbin, filling it completely. Agatha Tibbles, the large fierce-looking Persian, and Carrot Cake, the distinctly past-his-prime ginger tom, were milling around Mrs. Scruffles' feet, trying very hard to distract her as she set down the large tea pot in the center of the table, after having to force several more cats to relocate to make space. So far, so familiar. However, the floral curtains at the back of the room were shut tight, preventing light from spilling in, and it made the room gloomy. Several old books were piled up on the table, all dusty colors and leather bound. A fat old cat was sitting on top, guarding them, but when Tom tilted his head he could read the names written down the spines: *Foul Portents and You—A Guide to Ghostly Woe, Something Wicked This Way Comes, Ghost Disasters from Time Beginning*, and finally, ominously, *The Nightmares That Ghosts Have*.

Mrs. Scruffles gestured for Tom and Arthur to take a seat, and she joined them at the table. She pushed a strand of grey wispy hair out of her eyes, and poured three cups of steaming hot tea, before adding so much sugar that each cup nearly overflowed. She gulped back her cup of tea in one go, as if to settle her nerves, and poured another.

"Where to start?" she said to herself. Agatha

Tibbles leaped up onto her lap, and Mrs. Scruffles began to trace her fingers through Agatha's long fur. Unlike humans, cats can be touched by ghosts, if they so decide, and Agatha looked to be taking full advantage of this, purring merrily to herself as Mrs. Scruffles stroked her. Tom and Grey Arthur sipped their tea, waiting to hear what had to be said. Tom already knew that it wouldn't be good. Mrs. Scruffles was warm smiles, and caramel smells, and everything friendly and safe feeling, and so when Mrs. Scruffles looked worried, you couldn't help but feel worried too.

"Well, let's start with yesterday then. It's as good a place as any." She pushed a plate loaded with custard cream biscuits toward Tom and Arthur. "When Mildred called round last night, and mentioned Ballpoint Bill disappearing, and about the socks, I made a couple phone calls—"

"You use a phone?" interrupted Tom, forgetting his manners completely.

"Of course, you can't just shout at each other across the country, can you?" she replied, smiling at the question as if this was the most obvious thing in the world.

"Well, I suppose not . . . ," mumbled Tom. Sure enough, as Tom looked about the room, he spotted a bright red, old-fashioned phone. It was large, and plastic, and instead of buttons to dial with, it had a little circle on the front, with holes in which to put your fingers to spin the wheel to dial. He was sure it hadn't been there last time he called round, but then maybe it was only there when Mrs. Scruffles wanted it to be. The Ghost World was strange like that.

"So, erm, where was I?" She paused, gulped down another cup of tea, and poured some more into the bone-china cup. "Oh yes, phone calls. It took me a while to get through to anyone, which was very odd, but eventually I managed to reach an old ghost friend, Nigel—"

"You know a ghost called *Nigel*?" Tom couldn't help himself. These questions kept popping out of his mouth before he could stop them. Arthur was scowling at him across the table to stop interrupting, and Tom mouthed "Sorry" back at him.

"I know a Faintly Real called Nigel, yes. Terribly nice fellow. Volunteers at a Red Cross Charity Shop up in Glasgow. Still has a slight problem getting his hair quite right, so he always wears a hat, even in summer, but other than that he's really rather good at appearing human. Which is just as well really, or the humans wouldn't be able to see anyone at the register, and—oh, look what you've made me do now. I've gone off on a tangent. Where was I?"

"You phoned Nigel," Arthur said helpfully.

"Right, yes, of course I did. So, I spoke to Nigel, and well, long story short so I can't get distracted again, he'd heard stories of other ghosts disappearing, too. So we phoned around." She paused, stirring her tea, ruffling Agatha Tibbles behind the ears. Tears suddenly gathered in her pastel-colored eyes, and she dabbed them away with a doily before they could fall. Tom and

Grey Arthur exchanged worried looks. She took a deep breath, composing herself, and continued, her voice quiet. "So many old friends gone. You know how it is, ten, twenty years, a century slides past, you fall out of touch, you don't even realize it's happened, and then, by the time you do . . ." She dabbed at her eyes again. "Ethereal Erik, gone. John of the Green Trousers, gone. Stretch-Smiled Susan, gone. Monsieur Grindle, Abigail of the Broken Flowers, Jimmy the Salesman . . . they've all gone. Every single one."

She threw two more sugar lumps into her tea, but didn't take a sip. Agatha Tibbles nudged Mrs. Scruffles' hand gently with her nose, as if willing her to continue.

"It shouldn't have been able to happen like this. We should have known sooner. I should have realized sooner. But when the world changed, we had to change with it. Towns, cities, everything is so much bigger, busier, than it used to be, and the old haunts get knocked down so you have to move on, find new places to live, new locations to call home. Everyone is so scattered these days. So far apart. Old networks crumble, old friends disappear, and it takes a human boy and some Invisible Friends to point out what we should have all noticed so much sooner. Ghosts are vanishing. All over the country. And we didn't even see it."

She sighed, stirring her tea, unable to continue. Grey Arthur sat in stunned silence, unsure of what to say. Tom had already had an inkling that whatever was happening was bad, but it was only now, seeing the tears in Mrs. Scruffles' eyes, hearing the list of lost ghost friends, that he realized just how truly bad it was.

"We've all been so distracted recently," Mrs. Scruffles sighed, "with the big news story of you, Tom. Not that it's your fault, not at all, it's just we never saw this one creeping up on us."

"So what could have done this?" Tom asked, his voice not much more than a whisper.

"That's the thing." Mrs. Scruffles looked up at Tom and Arthur, her face serious. "There's nothing that can do this. But . . ." She hesitated, unsure whether to continue. "But maybe once there was."

"Maybe?" Tom was leaning forward in his chair now, urging Mrs. Scruffles on.

"Maybe," agreed Mrs. Scruffles. She looked at Arthur, and some unspoken understanding passed between them, and as it did Arthur paled, dusty grey cheeks fading to white. Just seeing that made Tom's stomach lurch.

"The Collector," Grey Arthur said.

"The Collector," repeated Mrs. Scruffles in agreement.

"The *who* now?" Tom asked.

"I could be wrong," continued Mrs. Scruffles, "I dearly hope I am."

"What are you talking about?" demanded Tom.

"You better do all your haunting chores,
You better give humans a fright,
Or the Collector will come to do his rounds,
And steal you away in the night."

Arthur recited slowly, as if remembering each line as he went from some murky long-buried memory. Mrs. Scruffles nodded, her expression dark.

"You've completely lost me." Tom leaned back in his chair, feeling a little frustrated. Sometimes it felt like these ghosts were talking a completely different language.

"I'm sorry, Tom. It's sometimes hard to remember that you're only human." Mrs. Scruffles smiled apologetically, and topped up Tom's tea. "The Collector is a story that you tell to young ghosts; it's a ghost-tale, a myth. One of those silly legends you tell around the portcullis at castles, or when everyone is gathered for a full moon. Just something to encourage the youngsters to make ectoplasm, to warn them against staying up all day, that kind of thing. It's not meant to be real."

"But you think it might be?"

"Maybe," she agreed.

"Maybe? You've got to stop saying maybe! Maybe isn't much help. Who would know for sure?"

Mrs. Scruffles nodded to herself, head slightly tilted, as if running through ideas in her mind.

"Well, there is one ghost I know of that would be old enough to say for sure. Old enough to know when the stories started. Old enough to know if they came from truth, or if they were just from the imagination of a bored Thesper."

"Okay, brilliant." Tom clapped his hands, raring to go. "So, enough chat. Let's go visit them."

"You won't like it."

Tom slumped back in his chair.

"Now why doesn't that surprise me?"

"Because you're getting used to how this whole ghost thing works, I suppose." She dunked a biscuit in her tea, and then quickly ate it before it could crumble. "You've met her before."

"Oh no . . ." Tom had a sneaking suspicion he knew what was coming. Really, he'd known from the moment Mrs. Scruffles had mentioned the existence of such a ghost, but he'd pushed the thought aside, hoping, wishing, that he was wrong.

"At Thorblefort Castle . . ."

"Oh, no, no . . ." Tom was shaking his head, making little whining noises.

"Her name is . . ."

"I'm way ahead of you. It's Sorrow Jane. Isn't it? Tell me I'm right. I'm right, aren't I? It's Sorrow Jane. Marvelous. That's just . . . marvelous."

"She's the oldest ghost I know. Maybe she's even the oldest ghost there is."

Tom slumped as far back in his chair as humanly possible, staring at his tea. He kept sighing, then taking in a deep breath to speak before thinking the better of it and just sighing again. Sorrow Jane. The world's most powerful Sadness Summoner. The ghost who had reduced Tom to a quivering wreck of snot and tears and sobbing on the school trip to the castle. The ghost that sang such painfully sad songs that you felt you were drowning in them, and that nothing else existed. Tom would have done anything to avoid going through that again, and now he was being asked to voluntarily march up to her and ask *questions*?

"Well, why do I have to talk to her? Can't you just, I don't know, phone her? Or send someone else? Why can't Arthur go? Why don't you go, Arthur? Or Monty, we could send Monty. Or anyone. Anyone else can go. Why does it have to be me?" In his head, these questions had sounded a lot less whiny, but it all came out as one long torrent of whinging. Mrs. Scruffles just smiled patiently.

"Sorrow Jane hasn't spoken to any other ghost for more centuries than I care to count. She's just sat, and sung, lost in her own little world, oblivious to everything else around her. Until she met you. You're something new, Tom. A human who can see ghosts. Something different enough to attract even Sorrow Jane's attention. You were the first person she's interacted with in known history. You should feel honored."

Honored? Tom would have laughed, if he'd been able to, if his mouth wasn't dry and if his heart wasn't sinking.

"I didn't feel honored! I felt miserable. And teary. And Mum had to take me home while I cried. It was horrible." Tom was sulky now, staring at his tea as he stirred it for no good reason other than the fact that he didn't know what else to do.

"Oh, I know, sweetheart. I know it's not fair. Life rarely is. But this is important. For your friends. For your dad. For ghosts and humans. We need to know what's going on. The human world leans heavily on the Ghost World, and although humans don't see it, or know it, the two are firmly tied together. Take your dad's socks, for example. A lack of Poltergeists means a lack of socks going missing, which means factories closing and people out of jobs. A lack of Sadness Summoners could mean that chocolate sales fall, since sad people love to eat chocolate, or it could mean that cinemas showing sad films would be empty, since the sad films just wouldn't feel so miserable anymore. A lack of ghosts at castles would mean that they lose that feeling of history, of times gone by, of being special. A lack of Invisible Friends . . ." She trailed into silence, but then she didn't need to continue. Tom knew what that would mean. It would mean no Mildred, no Tike, no Montague, no Harrowing Screamer . . . It would mean no Grey Arthur. Tom looked at Arthur, who was staring at the table, lost in thought. Mrs. Scruffles continued. "It's important, Tom. We need to know."

"Of course I'll do it," Tom replied glumly. "You know I will. But it doesn't mean that I can't grumble about it. I don't have to be grown-up about it, because I'm not a grown-up."

"Well then, grumble away." Mrs. Scruffles smiled warmly at Tom, and Tom tried to smile back, but couldn't. His mouth felt like sawdust, and his lips clung to his teeth, holding a stern pout in place. He swilled back some tea to make the sticky tongue sensation go away. Mrs. Scruffles topped up the cup as soon as it hit the table. "I'll bake you a nice big cake to cheer you up afterward. With glacier cherries. And marzipan."

"You don't have to do that," muttered Tom. "Just don't . . . disappear, or anything."

"I'll try my very hardest."

Tom sighed, growled, whined, and then made a "GAH" noise, just to get it all out of his system. Arthur and Mrs. Scruffles looked at him, a little bemused, but sympathetic. It was hard enough for ghosts to be around Sorrow Jane, so they could only guess how upsetting it must be for a human boy. They just let him carry on making strange noises until he was done. It didn't take too long. Tom straightened up in his chair, and smiled unconvincingly.

"Well, I guess I'd best head home and let Mum know I'll be popping up to see her at the castle tomorrow." He tried exceedingly hard to sound upbeat, and almost pulled it off. He gathered up his schoolbag, and gulped down the last of his tea, and stood up on slightly shaky legs. Arthur and Mrs. Scruffles stood up too, and as they walked toward the door, Tom hesitated. Out of curiosity, he leaned over and picked up the receiver of the big red phone, and put it to his ear. It was silent. As he placed it back down again, he saw that the phone wires ended in an abrupt mess, and weren't plugged in anywhere. Tom noticed Mrs. Scruffles watching him, and he smiled at her sheepishly.

"Just checking," he said.

"What else did you expect from a ghost phone?" she asked, with a grin.

Out of the blue, Arthur ran up to Mrs. Scruffles, and he gave her a big hug. She hugged him back, arms wrapped around his see-through body, and just for that brief moment Tom was acutely aware of how unfair it was that humans and ghosts couldn't touch. Arthur finally let go, and stepped back, his expression concerned.

"Why don't you come back with us?" he asked. "There are quite a few ghosts at Tom's. You'll be safe there. Or at least, safer. Just until we know what's going on. Tom wouldn't mind. Would you, Tom?"

Tom shook his head. "Not at all. You'd be more than welcome. I've even got a spare sleeping bag—that is, if you sleep. And I make an okay cup of tea."

Mrs. Scruffles ruffled Arthur's hair affectionately and smiled kindly at Tom. "That's very sweet of you both to be concerned. But I can't. Who'd look after the cats while I was gone?"

Agatha Tibbles mowed, and Mrs. Scruffles picked the cat up off her lap, and tucked her under her arm. "Let me see you to the door." Carrot Cake followed behind, and as they waited for each and every lock and bolt on the door to open, they all shared a fond farewell. "Now, you take care of yourself, Arthur. And you too, Tom. Let me know how it goes tomorrow."

The door swung open, and Tom and Arthur stepped out into the fading evening light. Mrs. Scruffles stood in the doorway, waving them good-bye, and although everyone wore wide smiles, they all felt heavy inside, and uneasy. Though nobody mentioned it, they all knew there was a chance, with ghosts vanishing all over the country, that they might not see each other again. But they smiled, and they waved, and they said nothing. What was there to say? The door shut as Tom and Arthur were halfway to the gate, and the sound of locking bolts followed them as they wandered out of the overgrown garden.

Tom and Arthur were nearly home before they realized they were being followed. Carrot Cake, out of boredom, or curiosity, had decided to escort them back, his four legs racing to keep up with Tom and Arthur. Tom picked up the cat, who felt uncomfortably bony in his old age, and carried him on his shoulder. It felt like picking up a xylophone, wrapped in fluff. Tom and Arthur walked in reflective silence for a while, the only noise being the rattling sound of Carrot Cake's purr.

"Well, tomorrow should be interesting . . . ," Tom finally said, reaching whole new depths of understatement. He felt he had to say something to break the silence, and that was as good a thing as any.

"I really appreciate you doing this, Tom. I know you don't want to." Arthur was floating alongside him, feet a good inch off the floor, and he petted the ginger mess of cat that Tom was carrying. "It means a lot to me. To all of us."

"Pffft," Tom replied, trying to sound a lot more relaxed than he felt. "What are friends for?"

Stiff Upper Lip

"Thomas Golden, you put down that stray cat this instant!"

Mum had walked into the kitchen, loaded down with shopping bags, to find Tom holding a ginger knot of paws and fur, rummaging in the fridge to find him something to eat. Tom turned round guiltily, and shut the fridge door. Grey Arthur was perched on the counter, sniffing the contents of Mum's spice rack.

"Honestly, Tom, put him outside. You'll get fleas. Or lice. Or rabies." Mum was looking at Carrot Cake in horror while pointing sternly at the back door. Carrot Cake meowed happily at her.

"Don't be silly, Mum. We don't have rabies in England."

"Well, okay, maybe we don't, but we definitely have

fleas in England, and that cat looks like he's riddled with them."

Tom covered Carrot Cake's ears, and looked at Mum in mock horror.

"Aww, don't be mean. He doesn't have fleas."

Mum frowned at the cat. "Are you feeding him? You shouldn't feed strays. They just keep on coming back, and then more cats come, and the next thing you know all the cats in the neighborhood will know that they can get fed here, and then you're inundated with cats, and then I'll be known as the crazy cat lady, and I'm far too young to be the crazy cat lady, and—"

"Fine! Fine. I'll put him outside." There was no point trying to reason with Mum once she had descended into full-blown rant. Tom had learned that a long time ago. He opened the back door, and gently dropped Carrot Cake outside. The cat meowed a feeble good-bye, and sprinted off into the garden, surprisingly agile when he wanted to be, leaping over the back fence out of sight. "See, he's gone now."

"Good." Mum began rummaging through the shopping bags, and putting everything where it belonged. Grey Arthur coughed, a polite nudge to remind Tom what he had to do, and Tom seized the moment while she was distracted.

"So, Mum, are you working late at the castle tomorrow?" Tom tried ever so hard to make that sound very casual, but mums have a built-in radar for questions that sound casual but really aren't. She paused

115

what she was doing, and looked suspiciously at Tom.

"Why?"

"Are you?" Tom asked, avoiding eye contact under the guise of helping Mum unpack. Mums also have an uncanny ability to sense the truth if you let them look you in the eye mid lie, so it was always best to avoid it. Tom studied the bananas he pulled out of the bag as if he'd never seen yellow fruit before.

Mum wasn't fooled.

"That depends on why you're asking," she said.

"I was just thinking of coming down to meet you after school if you were."

Mum turned to face Tom full on, so he couldn't look away. She managed to look deathly serious while holding a can of baked beans in her hand, which was a mean feat.

"Now, why would you want to do that after what happened last time?"

It was a good question.

"Because, castles are important. They're full of, you know, culture . . . and history . . . and stuff."

Grey Arthur cringed.

"Culture, and history, and *stuff*?" repeated a blatantly cynical Mum. "What kind of *stuff*?"

"Pigeons?" Tom volunteered. Grey Arthur held his head in his hands, unable to watch.

"Pigeons . . ." Mum said, raising an eyebrow. "You don't have to lie to me, Tom. I know what this is about."

"You do?" asked Tom.

"I'm pretty sure she doesn't . . . ," muttered Arthur.

"Yes Tom, I do. I wasn't born yesterday. I'm your mum, and mums know these things. You want to go back so you can prove to me that you're all right now, that everything is better."

Tom nearly laughed with relief, but he managed to rein it in just in time.

"That's it. That's exactly it. Because they say, if you fall off a horse, you should get straight back on, so that's what I want to do. Except, of course, it's a castle, and not a horse, and I didn't fall off the castle, I just kind of fell down and cried, but it's the same difference I suppose, in a way, if by the same you mean different. . . ."

"You're babbling," Mum interrupted.

"She's right. You really are," agreed Grey Arthur.

"Sorry. Sorry . . ." Tom took a second to focus. "So, can I? Come down and meet you? I'll get a bus straight there, and that way I should have enough time to look around before you finish. That's if you are working late, and that's if I'm allowed. So are you? And am I?"

The expression on Mum's face softened, and she put down the can of beans.

"Sweetheart, you don't have to prove anything to me. If you say you're all right now, then I believe you. You don't have to come all the way down to where I work just to show me."

"I want to, Mum. For me. I want to do this for me."

Mum nodded, and leaned forward to give Tom a peck on the cheek. Tom grimaced, and wiped the lipstick smudges away. "What was that for?" he asked.

"For being you. I'm very proud of you, you know. Of course you can come down and meet me. I'd love you to." And with that, Mum carried on unpacking the shopping, smiling to herself.

Grey Arthur clapped, and Tom grinned happily. Well, that was the easy part out of the way. He had a sneaking suspicion that striking up a conversation with Sorrow Jane was going to be the hard part.

The More, the Miserabler

AFTER GETTING ALL THE OTHER GHOSTS UP TO SPEED ON today's events, Grey Arthur excused himself for a private mission. He was very vague about what he was up to, but insisted Tom couldn't come because he had to travel quite a long way, and Tom only had "short, stumpy, human legs." Tom was sure he hadn't meant it as an insult, but it really didn't come across as very flattering either. On Tom's insistence though he had taken the Harrowing Screamer along with him, as a guard ghost. After visiting Mrs. Scruffles, and seeing the way she'd turned her house from a domestic haven into Fort Knox, Tom knew that now wasn't the time to be taking any chances.

Some hours later, the two of them returned, diving

through the bedroom window. Tike, Mildred, and Montague had already retreated to the attic where, under Montague's supervision, they were role playing Human and Invisible Friend. It basically involved Tike saying things like "I'm so human, I can't even walk through walls," then giggling, and Montague telling him off, and demanding he "got into character." Mildred, as ever, looked on sternly, taking notes. Tom was quite glad he didn't have to watch that.

"Okay, so what's going on?" Tom asked. Grey Arthur smiled knowingly.

"Are you ready?"

"Ready for what? It might help me decide if I'm ready or not if you tell me what's going on."

"It's a bit like a vaccination. A small dose of sadness to prepare you for tomorrow. You know, build up an immunity."

"Why doesn't this sound like fun?"

Grey Arthur ignored the question. "Are you ready?"

"What are you going to do? Make me watch *Watership Down* or something?"

"Make you watch what now?" Arthur was looking at Tom, more than a little confused.

"Oh, never mind. It's a cartoon with lots of rabbits in it."

"And that's sad?"

"You've obviously never seen it."

Arthur shrugged. Humans can be ever so strange.

"No, it's nothing to do with rabbits. I've brought a guest over, partly because of what Mrs. Scruffles said about losing touch with friends, partly because I didn't want him to be alone when all this was going on, and partly because he'll be able to help you with meeting Sorrow Jane tomorrow. You've met him before, just fleetingly, in Duskridge Woods, but you were a bit distracted at the time." Arthur gestured toward the closed window. "This is my oldest, bestest friend—Woeful William."

An old, foppish-looking ghost, draped in velvet clothing with frilly sleeves, glided in through the closed curtains. He was pale blue, like Sorrow Jane had been, but where Sorrow Jane had been the blue of drowning seas and biting cold, Woeful William's blue was the color of an overcast day when all your friends are ignoring you. His gaunt face hung in a permanent mope, and lank hair flopped over his eyes. He sighed melodramatically, flapped a handkerchief in welcome, and settled down into Tom's desk chair in a miserable-looking heap. As soon as he entered the room, Tom felt his mood dive. It was like a cloud of depression just swallowed Tom up, wrapping him from head to toe in sighs, and bleakness, and just pure, unadulterated, *miserable*. It was all he could do to stop his bottom lip from wobbling.

"It's delightful to meet you," Woeful William sighed. Tom was sure that William looked a million miles away from being delighted. "Terrible business with all these vanishing ghosts. Utterly terrible. Depressing, really. Makes one feel quite down. More so than usual." He sighed again, and Tom found himself sighing, too.

"Is it working?" Arthur asked excitedly. Tom could only pout in response, which Arthur took as a yes. "Excellent. Oh, don't look at me like that, Tom, it's for your own good. Okay, now William, I was thinking you could read Tom some of your poetry. How's that one go again, oh, you know, the one about the girl, and the disease, and the lame puppy . . ."

And so the night dragged on. Poem after morbid poem, recital after recital, sigh after sigh, until even the Harrowing Screamer began to take on just the faintest hint of blue around the edges. Tom sniffed, and listened, and finally fell asleep, steeped in misery, as Woeful William told his very own bedtime story of "The Ugly Duckling," except in this version, there was no swan in sight.

The Show Must Go On

"BEHOLD—A HAPPY HUMAN."

At school the next day, William had decided that he should pull his weight, and help out with teaching the Invisible Friends. There was no point sitting around moping, he'd said, which Tom had found a very funny thing for a Sadness Summoner to say, but there you go. Tom was quite happy to let the class go off on their own, and leave him to study, not least because every time he so much as looked at William he remembered that awful poem about the poor lame puppy, and it made him want to cry. So William, Arthur, Tike, Mildred, Montague, and the Harrowing Screamer had wandered off, exploring the school, in search of a place to hold their latest lesson.

Which is how they ended up in the school library.

The school library was quite possibly the best place to practice being an Invisible Friend. It was the refuge of the lonely, who would immerse themselves in books and stories, and a sanctuary for the bullied, as it tended to be riddled with adults, and also because the worst bullies wouldn't be seen dead in there—heaven forbid anyone might think they were trying to learn something.

As libraries go, it was a fairly pitiful affair—while there were a good number of books to be borrowed, it was a lottery as to what condition they were in. Sometimes people had scrawled in the margins—if you were lucky, it would just be something daft, like who they fancy or who they hate. If you were unlucky, an arrow would point to a section of text with monstrous spoilers, like "He doesn't really die," or "She's the murderer." Frequently, readers would stumble across missing pages—usually, you'd have a good idea about whether or not you were taking a gamble on a book, depending on the amount of yellowing tape bound to its spine, but occasionally it came as a horrible shock to discover someone had maliciously torn out the last page. But even with all its many faults, kids still came to the library, still came to throw themselves into stories, or simply hide themselves away out of sight, and out of harm.

Frank Longfield was one such kid.

He was holed up in a corner, sitting on his own, smiling away happily as he read a book. He was obviously enjoying it, as every now and then he would chuckle, or smile to himself. Woeful William pointed to Frank, attracting the attention of the class of Invisible Friends. The ghosts stood a distance away, and observed as Woeful William continued.

"In order to assist a human's well-being, you must first learn to recognize their moods, which is frightfully hard in humans as they don't change color greatly. It's easy to hear the emotion when they talk, but in a silent human, such as the type you find in a library, you must search for other clues, you must look for subtle changes. As a Sadness Summoner, I am finely tuned in to emotion to such a degree that I can actually see the emotion surrounding humans. I can perceive an aura of sadness around people. I can—"

"How does it look?" interrupted Tike. Woeful William faltered, his flow broken.

"Sorry?"

"Emotions. How do they look? I mean, like sadness. What's sadness look like?" Tike was scratching his head, and everyone else now had their eyes fixed on William, waiting for an answer. Mildred had her pen poised.

William paused thoughtfully. "It looks . . . like rain feels," he said finally.

"It looks *wet*?" Tike looked at William quizzically.

"I don't think he meant it quite so literally, Tike," whispered Montague. Tike went to ask another question, but Grey Arthur nudged him to be quiet, and so William continued.

"So . . . where was I? Ahh, yes. Recognizing emotion." He pointed at Frank Longfield again, encouraging the class to pay attention. "Note the way the mouth twitches upward into a smile. This denotes happiness. Now . . ." Woeful William took a step closer to Frank, and instantly his smile faded away. "This is what we call in the trade 'marginally miserable.' See the straight mouth?" The class nodded, and Woeful William took yet another step closer. Frank's mouth began to drag down at the corners, and his bottom lip jutted out slightly. His eyebrows slumped down. "This stage here is what I like to call 'the melancholies.' It's at this point that the smallest nudge either way can make a human cry or smile again. And if I take one more step forward . . ." William did so with a flourish, waving his handkerchief, and poor little Frank Longfield's face crumbled. His bottom lip wobbled, and his eyes filled with tears. William quickly leaped back a few paces, and the moment passed. Frank shook his head, did a small confused laugh, checking to make sure nobody had seen his brief lapse into sadness, and then carried on reading as before. The Invisible Friend class burst into rapturous applause. Montague was particularly impressed, clapping wildly.

"So, now class," Arthur said, stepping in, "I want you to put what you've learned to use. Have a look around, and see if you can spot a miserable child, and we'll see if we can cheer them up. After all, that's what friends are for."

The ghosts began roaming the room excitedly, peering into the faces of unsuspecting pupils, studying their mouths, sniffing them to see if they smelled sad, or if they were radiating any misery. Mildred shot her hand up in the air, having discovered a rather down in the dumps Holly Mayer, hiding in a corner of the room. In her bag was a letter from some girls, who she thought had been her friends, telling her exactly why she was "rubbish" and why they never wanted to hang out with her again (it was something really quite silly, to do with buying a top the same color as another girl's, and for fancying the wrong boy). Mildred pointed at Holly.

"This child is sad," she said, quite accurately.

"Oh yes, she absolutely reeks of misery. It's lovely," agreed William, before hastily correcting himself, having caught Arthur's eye. "Lovely if you are a Sadness

Summoner. Which you aren't. So in which case, I suppose it's bad." Arthur nodded, finding it hard not to laugh.

"Okay, Mildred, so you've found a sad child." Arthur looked at her encouragingly. "How are you going to cheer her up?"

Mildred paused, thinking. "Buy her a puppy?" she volunteered. Arthur smiled.

"I was thinking of something a little less fluffy."

"A lizard?"

Arthur shook his head, grinning. "I was thinking that you could talk to her."

Mildred looked at Arthur, slowly shaking her head. "I've never been able to appear normal enough for a human to see me."

"Well, then that's a good reason to keep on trying. Go on, what harm can it do? The worst that will happen is that she just won't know you're there. Everyone here is going to be a different kind of Invisible Friend, and maybe you can get to be an occasionally *visible* Invisible Friend."

"It won't work," Mildred said flatly.

"It might. You don't know unless you try. Just give it a go." Arthur looked at the odd-eyed, seriously pale, childlike ghost in front of him, dressed from head to toe in a black uniform, and he smiled reassuringly. "You can do this."

Montague put an arm around Mildred, and whispered in her ear. "Just concentrate. Picture yourself as a real child. Focus. Take a deep breath, hold it, let go. You *can* do this. I have every faith in you."

Mildred took a deep breath, and after a gentle push in the right direction from Monty, wandered over to where the child was sitting. She sank into the chair next to her, and turned to look at Grey Arthur, who nodded encouragingly. Holly sniffed loudly, rubbing her nose. She was penning the beginning of an angry retort in her notebook, which began with the very obvious lie "I don't care what you think."

"Greetings, lonesome human child," Mildred said. Holly sniffed again, staring into space. Mildred glanced over at the class of Invisible Friends, and shrugged. Montague gave her the thumbs up, and gestured for her to continue. Mildred took another deep breath, concentrating as hard as possible to appear as real as possible. Her slightly translucent skin became less misty, although it was still as white as a very serious polar bear. Another deep breath, another burst of concentration, and a couple hairbands appeared on her wrist.

Montague clapped. "That's my girl!" he said, urging her on. "You can do this!"

Mildred strained, effort written all over her face, eyes nearly crossed with the exertion of it all, and three little freckles appeared on her nose. They were black, instead of brown, but it was only a small fault. She coughed, for no other reason than the fact that she'd heard children cough before, and tried again.

"I could not help but notice the miserable expression

on your face, and I wish to offer you companionship."
No response. Holly crossed out the beginning of her
note, pen pressed so heavily that the paper tore, and
turned over a new page, starting again. Mildred looked
over anxiously at Montague, ready to give up, but Monty
shook his head at her, and Mildred sighed. She smoothed
down her incredibly straight, incredibly black hair, and
attempted something heart wrenchingly difficult.

Mildred was trying to smile.

Every ghostly muscle in her face strained, creaked,
and twitched under the unnatural demand. A hushed
silence swept over the class of Invisible Friends as they
realized what Mildred was doing. Arthur crossed his
fingers. Montague held his breath. Mildred's lips curled
at the edges, creeping upwards, dimples burrowing into
her pale white cheeks. Tike was jumping on the spot,
urging her on. The Harrowing Screamer hissed quietly.
Mildred struggled on. Through slightly parted lips you
could see dusty white teeth.

She'd done it.

She'd actually done it!

Mildred Rattledust was smiling!

Okay, so the Mona Lisa was hardly going to feel
threatened by this, worried about losing her place in
the world's most beautiful smile competition, and if
you smiled like this for your annual school photo then
your Mum would open the envelope, take out the picture, pale slightly, laugh a little nervously, and then slip
the photo straight back into the envelope and refuse to

buy it, let alone put it up on her shelf, but it was undeniably a smile, which was a start.

Mildred turned this slightly sickly, heavily unnatural-looking smile on Holly Mayer, tilting her head slightly (though her hair stayed firmly in place at the side of her head). "Hello," Mildred said. "Do you wish to have a conversation?"

Holly nearly leaped out of her skin as she became aware of a very strange-looking girl sitting uncomfortably close to her, smiling like she'd just chewed a particularly bitter wasp. The weird girl clapped excitedly, and looked over to an empty part of the library. "She can see me!" she called, although there was nobody there to hear her. Holly stared at this bundle of oddness in wide-eyed shock, pushing back her chair to try to reclaim her personal body space. The weird girl's smile broadened, and Holly was convinced she actually heard the girl's lips creak as she did so.

"I'm Mildred Rattledust, and I am—"

"A freak!" Holly gasped, hurriedly throwing her notebook back into her schoolbag. "I can't sit next to you. I'm getting picked on badly enough as it is, without having some freak sitting next to me talking to thin air!" Holly leaped up from the chair, and scampered across to the far corner of the library. Once she was a safe distance away, safe as in "nobody will think she's with me" away, she turned round to scowl at the bizarre girl who'd been sitting by her, but the chair was, once again, empty. Holly shook her head, confused, but the moment soon passed. It's a very human skill to explain away the irrational, and Holly was no different. She assumed the girl had fled under her withering gaze, so fast that Holly hadn't even seen her go.

Unseen once again, Mildred sat in the chair, her black freckles fading from her nose, her skin returning to see-through, and watched Holly flee across the library. She turned to face the other ghosts, who were all wearing suitably sympathetic expressions. They expected misery, maybe even tears, but Mildred had let the smile fall away and was wearing the same stern expression as ever.

"That was . . . ," she said, hesitating as she sought out the right word. The ghosts waited with bated breath. ". . . *Fantastic!*"

The Invisible Friends and Woeful William clapped loudly, and Mildred even stood up on the table, curtsying, enjoying her moment. For the first time ever in Mildred's entire ghostly life, there was a hint of a genuine smile on her lips. It was faint, and unless you knew what you were looking for there is no way you'd see it, but it was definitely, undeniably, there.

Grey Arthur grinned widely. It was moments like this, pockets of pride in worrying times, that made everything worthwhile.

Mildred wrote pages upon pages of notes in her little book about her appearance to Holly, and made Arthur draw little black stars next to what she had written, and give it a big tic, just so she could prove it was all true.

After school, the ghosts walked Tom to the bus stop, and on the way Mildred told him, in great detail, about just how spectacular she'd been. Tom couldn't help but grin. It was just the little dose of happiness he needed to carry him through all the way to the castle. He was dreading it, dreading meeting Sorrow Jane again, but he looked at the ghost faces all around him, and he knew that he had to do it.

Woeful William bowed deeply before Tom, waving his handkerchief. "You're exceedingly lucky, to meet such a delightfully tragic ghost as Sorrow Jane. She's always been my idol. Just remember, as with any great emotion, it will pass. You simply have to endure it, and realize that it won't last forever."

Tom nodded. After last night's epic misery-a-thon, he realized that he didn't feel quite so low when standing near William. Sure, he didn't feel like tap dancing, and he kept getting horrible flashes of the sad puppy poem, but compared to the all-encompassing woe that he first felt, this was a definite improvement. Maybe it would help when meeting Sorrow Jane after all.

Tom and Grey Arthur stepped onto the bus together, and they waved good-bye to the ghosts left standing on the pavement. If the bus driver thought Tom was a little strange waving good-bye to an empty bus shelter, he didn't say so. Bus drivers see a lot stranger things on their daily travels.

Empty Courtyards and Forgotten Songs

THE BUS GROANED TO A HALT JUST OUTSIDE THE entrance to Thorblefort Castle, and Tom and Grey Arthur stepped outside. Dark clouds were gathering in the sky, and the sun had long ago given up on its battle to shine through. Tom wrapped his coat tighter around him, and shuddered.

"Deep breaths, Tom, deep breaths . . . ," he muttered to himself.

"You'll do fine," Grey Arthur said. Tom didn't reply. He just nodded, staring at the imposing castle that loomed ahead.

Thorblefort Castle stood, ancient and proud, tired and hollow, before them. The bleak sky seemed to frame it perfectly, a somber backdrop, making the crumbling stonework and broken towers seem even more forlorn. There was a grandeur here, a defiant sense of history nestled against the stretching sea horizon. Moss-sprawled stones held on to silent memories of kings and armies, of dwindling centuries, of a time before electricity made the dark night paler, before cars and trains made the country seem smaller. Time had spun on, the world had changed, and yet Thorblefort Castle had stood defiantly. Although invading armies, heavy storms, and the gradual creeping erosion of years had worn it bare in places, there was still something giant, majestic, noble about it.

"Let's get this over and done with," said Tom. He marched toward the entrance, head held high, his small frame dwarfed by the large portcullis entrance. Grey Arthur hurried behind him.

The last time Tom had been to the castle, on the school trip, it was literally heaving with ghosts, all there waiting to meet the miraculous Tom Golden, He-Who-Can-See-Ghosts. This time was different. There were no crowds, no fanfare, no ghosts waiting at the entrance. Tom walked into the cobbled courtyard, and it was deserted. The castle felt lonely. Empty. It was as if the history, the spirit, the heart of the place had just drained away, leaving a hollow shell of crumbling brickwork. No wonder the tourists were staying away. The castle felt cold and dead. Grey Arthur looked around, an expression of horror clear on his face.

"This isn't right," he whispered, as if afraid to break the silence that clung to the courtyard. "They can't all be gone."

"Maybe they're just staying indoors?" Tom replied. Grey Arthur shrugged, but deep down, he didn't believe it.

"Come on, let's find her. Let's work out what's going on and get out of here." Arthur walked forward, Tom at his side, toward the old graveyard, toward where they last had seen Sorrow Jane. He just hoped that she was still there. If she wasn't . . . He shook his head, trying to shake that thought loose. She had to be there.

They wandered through the castle grounds,

shocked into silence at the lack of life within. Even the pigeons who lived in the nooks and crannies in the stonework seemed subdued, snug in puffed up feathers, scorning the skies for the sanctuary of their nests. Pillars of stone, which had once belonged to something majestic, jutted out from the ground like broken teeth. Moss stretched over the walls, creeping green.

Tom's footsteps echoed as he walked. Arthur's made no sound.

And suddenly, there she was. Standing, alone, in the middle of the graveyard, looking toward them, simply waiting, as if she'd known they were coming. Arthur glanced anxiously at Tom, but Tom was staring straight ahead at Sorrow Jane, and it was as if nothing else existed.

"You'll be fine," Arthur said again, but Tom didn't hear him. He was walking toward her, lost to everything else.

Sorrow Jane's dark blue dress pooled in rags at her feet—delicate blue, cold feet that hovered a clear inch above the leaf strewn ground. Deep within the material of her dress lights shimmered and flickered before disappearing, like stars dying in a far off sky. Her long hair hung in tangled strands to below her waist, and jewels woven into her hair glinted with a magical glow. Her light blue, drowning-blue skin was dusty and pale, and her face was as beautiful and as sad as any heroine's in any tragedy. Tom was transfixed, unaware of his feet carrying him onward, unaware of anything but the magnificent, mesmerizing, ancient ghost before him. As he approached, she began to glide forward, bare blue feet never touching the ground, the ragged ends of her dress trailing through the leaves on the ground.

Tom was aware of the world fading around him, aware of everything else paling and muting until it seemed that there was nothing else other than him and Sorrow Jane, no other time than now. He struggled to keep control, to fight against the tide of tears and sadness that threatened to drown him, he fought to keep hold of the question he had to ask, the answers he had to know, but everything felt liquid, and no matter how hard he tried to grasp it, it all simply flowed away. His knees buckled beneath him, sending him kneeling to the ground, and all the while he looked up, his eyes locked with hers, with those eyes swimming with centuries of tears. She was standing right in front of him now, so close he could feel her breath, cold like the wind from the sea, and he reached inside himself, desperately searching, desperately trying to remember what had bought him here, trying to remember . . . something. . . . Tears streamed down his cheeks, and he didn't even notice. She reached out a delicate hand, her blue sleeves falling away to reveal thin, blue, porcelain arms, and she touched Tom's face, her cold misty fingers passing through him as if he wasn't even there.

The rest of the world fell away.

It was as if he was watching life through water, everything faintly warped and out of scale. Colors shifted gently, the world swimming, and it took Tom a while to realize that he was no longer in the castle grounds. He was on an old cobbled street, crooked buildings jutting up on either side. A horse and cart charged toward him, and Tom raised his hands, but the cart hurtled straight through him as if he wasn't there. He glanced behind, and the cart continued along its path, its driver oblivious to Tom's presence. The scene shifted again, pitching Tom forward, and he was led down the street. A Snorgle was sifting through the contents of a bucket that had been tipped out into the street below, filling his pockets and looking around furtively. Something shifted nearby in an alleyway, and the Snorgle looked up, alarmed. He began running away, his little stumpy legs propelling him forward, and Tom was drawn after him, through the narrow streets.

The Snorgle darted into an open doorway, and rested against the wall, his broad chest heaving. Tom was standing in the middle of the room. It was dark inside, candles struggling to drive away the gloom. It was someone's home, but unlike any home Tom had ever seen. No electricity, no television, no comfy settee. Wooden chairs, a wooden table, bare dirt floor. The ceiling was low, and rested on thick, wooden beams. The Snorgle glanced out the door, and gasped in horror at whatever he saw, dashing back inside. He looked around frantically for somewhere to hide, but the stark surroundings offered little refuge. A dark figure appeared in the doorway, draped in a heavy hooded cloak, and at his side hung a large, velvet drawstring bag. Tom tried to call out a warning, but no sound came.

The dark figure walked in the door, slowly advancing, and the Snorgle actually squealed in fear. The cloaked ghost rummaged in the bag, and took out something, holding it tight in his hand. The cape completely obscured his face. The Snorgle was backing away, and he became trapped against the wall, the figure between him and the door. Tom could scarcely bear to watch, but he couldn't turn away. The Snorgle grabbed something off the table, and held it in front of him, a sad makeshift shield. Tom couldn't quite work out what it was, and he strained to see, but the watery vision made everything vague. The hooded entity advanced, and the Snorgle held the item out, cowering behind it.

Suddenly, the shrouded ghost faltered. He screamed, throwing his arms in front of his face. It was as if he was collapsing in on himself, diminishing, and a low howl filled the room. His hand withered, retreating into the cloak, and what he had been clutching fell benignly to the floor. It was a coin, old, well worn, and it spun on the dirt before settling, face up. There was a final scream, and then the crumpled cloak on the floor vanished, dragged back to some distant lair, the ghost inside no longer strong enough to fill it. Tom knew though, knew with a certainty he couldn't explain, that the ghost was still alive, if alive was the right word to use. He could feel a distant noise, tugging at him, a screech like twisted nails down a blackboard, and he knew, he just knew, that it wasn't over.

Tom found himself back on the ground at the castle, hands digging into the mulch and leaves on the ground. Sorrow Jane was looking at him, and Tom understood. He understood what she had shown him, he understood what she knew.

The Collector was coming.

Tom staggered to his feet, brushing the broken leaves from his trousers and wiping tears from his face with muddy hands. Sorrow Jane floated up onto the wall, her back to them. Her song still drifted on the air—beautiful, heartbreaking, silvery notes in a language so old that she was the only one who remembered it.

"The Collector is real, Arthur."

Arthur nodded. "It's okay, Tom. At least now we know."

Sorrow Jane sat up on the wall, and Tom knew what she was doing. She was waiting. Waiting for the Collector to come for her too. Waiting for it all to be over.

"We have to do something."

"And we will," agreed Arthur.

"But we can't just leave her there!" Tom looked at Arthur, his eyes red. Arthur smiled sadly.

"What would you do, Tom? Take her home with us? Look at her, Tom. She's ancient, and magical, and wild. Putting her in a home with radiators, and television, and talk of what's for dinner . . . it would never work. It would destroy her. She has to stay here. It's where she belongs."

Tom looked at the dusky blue ghost, singing to herself, and he knew Arthur was right.

It didn't make it any easier, though.

Life Is Full of Surprises

IT WASN'T HARD TO FIND THE TEA SHOP. IT WAS PERCHED right by the exit, a tourist trap designed to lure people in with the promise of cream tea, scones, and more Earl Grey than you could shake a stick at. Inside, it was decorated in true castle style, with little flags adorning the walls, and red velvet cushions on the chairs. A suit of armor stood in the corner, with a maid's apron tied round its waist. Even the menu was written in Olde English style, with everything described as "Regal Tea Cakes" or "Medieval Pork Pie." Mum was waiting inside, in her little uniform, a broad grin ready for her son. Tom had taken a slight detour via the toilets to wash away the last of the tears, and the mud from his hands, and he hoped that he looked suitably upbeat. If he didn't, well, Mum didn't notice.

"There you are! I was wondering when you'd turn up. I've been keeping a sandwich here, ready for you." Mum thrust the doorstep sandwich toward Tom, and it was overflowing with bacon. "We've had another slow day. Heaven knows where all the tourists have gone. So we had lots of fillings left over. I thought you might be hungry."

Tom was. Ravenous. Nothing like being taken back into a vision of the past by an ancient Sadness Summoner for building up an appetite. Mum was calling out to someone in the kitchen, and holding

Tom in front of her by the shoulders, the same way you'd hold a huge trophy that you were very proud of winning.

"Janet, Janet, come over here and meet my son. Tom's come up to the castle to have a proper look around. Tom, this is Janet, my workmate, and Janet, this is Tom, my son." A strange, tall woman appeared from the kitchen, and wandered over to where Tom and Arthur were standing. She had bright green eyes, and the reddest hair Tom had ever seen. Tom imagined that if you were to touch that hair, it would feel warm, like a hot water bottle. He went to shake her hand, but she was holding a stack of plates, so instead he bobbed his head in greeting.

"So you're the famous Tom Golden. I've heard a lot about you." She smiled widely at Tom, and Tom's mum grinned with pride. Tom shifted awkwardly, a little embarrassed. Janet noticed Tom cringing and laughed, before saying to Tom's mum in a stage whisper that Tom was meant to hear, "You've got yourself a very special boy there." Tom couldn't see his mum behind him, but he knew that she would be glowing at that. Tom was glowing too, but for a different reason, his cheeks flushed hot with blushing.

"Well, let me get my bag, and we'll be heading off home then, Tom," Mum said, wandering behind the counter. As soon as Mum turned her back, Janet smiled at Tom, knowingly. She leaned in toward him, and whispered in his ear.

"I just hope Sorrow Jane didn't give you *too* hard a time."

Tom looked at Janet in confused silence, but she simply smiled again, and walked away. As she passed the window, Tom gasped in shock. The light coming in shone, just ever so subtly, *through* Janet.

Janet was a Faintly Real!

"Don't stare, Tom, it's rude," Mum said, pushing her handbag up onto her shoulder, as she noticed the way he was looking at Janet. Tom quickly concentrated on his sandwich instead, trying to hide his surprise. "So, was it okay this time?" Mum asked, studying Tom's face. Tom nodded, mouthful of bread and bacon, and he chewed hastily to respond.

"It was fine, Mum. I'm glad I came."

"I am too." And with that, Mum swept him up in a huge hug. Tom groaned, but not too much, because after meeting Sorrow Jane, and knowing who, or what, was coming, deep down a hug was what he really needed.

Calling an Emergency Meeting

AFTER THE LONG DRIVE HOME, DURING WHICH TOM slept fitfully, and Arthur stuck his head out of the window all the way (without even having to unwind it),

Mum finally pulled up outside the house. Dad's car still wasn't there—ever since things had started going wrong at work, he'd been working such long hours, returning home with dark shadows under his eyes, and a briefcase bulging with plans.

Arthur rushed upstairs to gather the rest of the ghosts, while Tom made some excuses to Mum about wanting to go for a walk to help him wake up. Mum, still all brimming with happiness after having Tom visit her at work, agreed, but on the condition that he was only gone for an hour at most. Ever since the Dr. Brown incident, Mum worried. A lot. She'd creep in to check on him while he was sleeping, she'd watch him out of the window on the way to school, and she'd sometimes—not that Tom knew, as the school secretary was very discreet—but she'd sometimes even phone the school from work, just to make sure he was there, that her son was still okay. So she said he could go, on the strict condition that he was an hour at most, and Tom agreed. Hopefully, it wouldn't take that long. They'd tell Mrs. Scruffles what had happened, and she'd know exactly how to make everything right, and that would be it. Job done. Everything back to normal, everyone happy, everyone back exactly where they should be. At least, that was the theory.

All the ghosts crowded on the doorstep outside Mrs. Scruffles' house, and waited as Tom knocked on the door. The same as last time, there was no response. Tike twitched impatiently.

"Why can't we just float through the door? Why do we have to flap about with all this knocking business?" he asked, peering through the letter box.

"Because it's polite," said Tom. Tike made a *pffft* noise, as Poltergeists aren't greatly respectful of what's polite and what's not, and charged forward. Instead of passing straight through, as he'd expected to do, his face collided with the door, and he staggered back, yowling.

"And because it's not a normal door. It's a ghost door to a haunted house," added Arthur, a bit belatedly. Tike whimpered, holding his nose.

"*Now* you tell me?" he said, tweaking his nose back into shape. It still looked a little bit crooked, but it was close enough.

"Are you going to tell us what this is all about?" asked Montague.

"We'll explain it all when we get inside," Tom replied, knocking again on the door. For a brief, sickly moment he worried that there was nobody inside, but as the familiar sound of locks being unlocked and bolts being unbolted rattled through the woodwork, he breathed a sigh of relief. Mrs. Scruffles stood in the doorway, smiling at all the ghosts waiting on her doorstep.

"Oh my, but what a pleasant surprise!" she said, clapping her hands together. The warm smile lapsed briefly, as she looked behind them, scanning the garden for anything out of place, and then she visibly relaxed when she saw the coast was clear. "I hadn't been expecting so many of you. I'll have to dig out the decent guest china! Come in, come in, and don't forget to wipe your feet. No point trailing the garden indoors if we can help it."

And so, one by one, the ghosts marched in. Grey Arthur, Montague, Tike, Mildred, the Harrowing Screamer, Woeful William, and last but by no means least the very real, very human, Tom Golden.

Mrs. Scruffles bustled about, preparing the kitchen table for tea, and Tom and the ghosts all grabbed a chair and sat at the table. Well, every ghost except the Harrowing Screamer, who preferred to stand. He stood by the kitchen counter, as all the cats milled around him, looking distinctly out of place in the homely setting. A small white kitten was brushing up against the Screamer, who didn't quite know how to respond. He stood there awkwardly as the kitten nuzzled up against him, purring loudly. In the end, he held out a clawed hand, and the baby cat ran up and down, dragging the claws through its fur, enjoying the scratching.

"Well, aren't you a fierce little ghost," Mrs. Scruffles said to the Harrowing Screamer, before passing him a cup of warm, steaming tea. The Screamer hissed gratefully at the compliment, but didn't drink any, as it's frightfully difficult to clutch a cup of tea when you have long, curling talons. Mrs. Scruffles sat down at the round table, which seemed to have grown to accommodate all the extra guests, and set a plate of freshly baked biscuits down in the middle. William took one, and chewed thoughtfully, sighing all the while. Tom was secretly a little impressed at how he managed to look like he was thoroughly miserable, and yet enjoying a biscuit, all at the same time.

"So," Mrs. Scruffles said, pouring everyone a cup of tea. "Let's get straight down to business. Tell me what Sorrow Jane said to you, Tom."

All eyes were fixed on Tom as he began to explain what had happened at the castle.

"She didn't actually tell me anything, so much as *show*," Tom said, through a mouthful of warm biscuit. He swallowed, taking a swish of tea to wash it down, and described to everyone that weird, watery vision that Sorrow Jane had given him: the scared Snorgle, the cobbled streets, taking refuge in a building, the Collector suddenly vanishing to somewhere far off, howling all the while. . . . "And that's it, pretty much. The Collector is real after all—well, as real as a ghost ever is."

Mrs. Scruffles nodded thoughtfully, taking it all in. "So," she said, topping up everyone's tea, "I wonder why she chose that particular moment to show you. If she just wanted to prove that the Collector exists, then there are simpler ways to do it. No, there has to be something else we're meant to be learning about how he does what he does, or how that poor little Snorgle managed to fend him off."

"It's all so hazy," complained Tom.

"Come on, Tom. Try," said Arthur. Tom sighed, and concentrated, trying to remember.

"He dropped something. When he vanished. The Collector dropped something. I think it might have been, no, I'm *sure*, it was a coin. But that doesn't make sense. Why would a ghost need money? It's not like you go shopping. Is it?"

"Well actually, I do," replied Mrs. Scruffles. "Only during the sales, but I do. But I can't imagine the Collector standing in line to buy groceries. No, it has to be something else."

"A Wish Coin," Montague said, looking seriously at Mrs. Scruffles. "Well, that's got to be it, surely. He uses Wish Coins."

"A Wish Coin?" asked Tom.

Mrs. Scruffles was nodding. "You know how you humans have this strange custom of making a wish on money . . . Not paper money, as that would go soggy, but coin money, and then you throw it into a well, or a fountain? Well, those coins, all heavy with wishes, that's how they get their name. Wish Coins."

"Like on the news, eh Tom?" said Tike. Tom looked at him, lost for a while, before he realized what Tike was talking about.

"Actually, he's right. It *was* on the news! Erm, something about coins vanishing all over the country from wishing wells and so on. The police think it might be antique-coin dealers or something like that." Tom looked at Mrs. Scruffles, hoping that this information would help.

"Well, the police are very much out of their depth.

Okay . . ." Mrs. Scruffles sipped her tea thoughtfully. "So it looks like he is using Wish Coins. So we have to assume that's how he does it."

"Does what?" asked Tom.

"Collects the ghosts," replied Mildred, following Mrs. Scruffles' train of thought. Tom began to feel that familiar headache feeling that built whenever the ghosts started talking about things that were far too weird for him to understand. He massaged his forehead.

"You're really going to have to spell this out for me. How can coins, Wish Coins, or whatever, collect ghosts?" The ghosts at the table looked at each other, waiting for someone else to respond. In the end, as usual, it was Mrs. Scruffles who took on the task.

"It's so hard to explain this to someone who's spent so long seeing the world from a strictly human perspective, but I will give it a go." She topped up Tom's tea again, for the umpteenth time in as many minutes, and continued. "The world is riddled with different types of magic, Tom. Just because most humans choose not to believe it, it doesn't change the fact that it's true. When humans take a coin, a strictly normal, could swap-it-for-penny-sweets or put-it-in-a-piggy-bank coin, and they make a wish on it, it changes. The wish clings to the coin, melds with it. It makes it special. It makes it *magic.*"

Tom's brain groaned. "But I thought that you said before that wishes don't come true. Remember, when

I asked you how I could see ghosts, when all this first happened?"

Mrs. Scruffles was shaking her head, smiling. "Oh, wishes come true all the time, Tom. See, it's ever so hard to explain this to you."

"Try?" he asked.

"Okay . . . It's not enough to just *make* a wish, and some wishes never come true, no matter how much you want them to. Say, if you make a wish to wake up tomorrow all full grown and adult, or if you wish that you could fly, or that your parents were royalty—wishes can only stretch so far, like an elastic band, before they snap."

"Right . . ." said Tom, following as best as he could.

"But," she continued, "some wishes can come true, if you add enough luck, or talent, or hard work, or best of all, a mix of the three. Say, if you wish to be a famous musician, it won't come true if you sit on your human bottom and wait for it to happen. You need to practice, and try, and nudge the wish into coming true. Are you following?"

"So far." Tom nodded.

"Okay then. So wishes, really, are just hopes under another name. And hope is a very potent thing. You humans have turned your back on magic for so long, that you just assume it has done the same to you. Why do you think ghosts hear human emotions? Why do you think Screamers revel in fear? Or Sadness Summoners feast on miserable moods? You humans positively drip with magic, every single day of your lives, and you don't realize that anger, or sadness, or fear, or hope, it's all every bit as magical as the ghosts you can now see. Do you understand now?"

"Ish . . . ," muttered Tom.

"Thomas, let me see if I can explain it better to you." Woeful William flapped his handkerchief at Tom to get his attention. "Normally, when humans are close by me, they feel sad. They'll sigh, and walk a little slower, and possibly pout. Now, if I've just been to the cinema, and watched a film where everyone in the audience is sobbing their hearts out, I come away positively radiantly blue. People all the way across the street will start thinking sad thoughts, and sighing deep sighs. Just drinking in all that emotion in the cinema, well, it makes you feel deliciously recharged, and wonderfully wretched."

"So, what you're saying is that humans' emotions can make a ghost stronger? Like a magical . . . rechargeable . . . *battery*?" asked Tom, slowly understanding, although his nose creased slightly at the absurdity of it all.

"Precisely!" Mrs. Scruffles nodded enthusiastically. "You're getting there. So he takes these coins, these coins that have all these wishes and hopes embedded in them, and he uses that magic for something it was never meant to be used for."

"He uses that magic to help him steal ghosts?" Tom asked.

"At a guess, yes. There's no way any normal ghost

would be strong enough, powerful enough, to steal other ghosts. He has to be using these Wish Coins to help him."

"Okay. So how does this help us stop him?" Tom waited for a response. There was an awkward silence around the table. William sighed, more deeply than usual. "What? Come on, how does this help us stop him?"

"It doesn't," Mrs. Scruffles said sadly.

"Well, that's just marvelous. What's the point in knowing it then? What's the point of that stupid vision if it doesn't help?" Tom fumed.

"It does help. It helps us understand how he's doing it. We just need to work out how to stop him." Mrs. Scruffles knocked back her tea in one go, and sat there, lost in thought.

"I could go steal all the coins myself?" volunteered Tike. "Get 'em before he can. It'll take blimin' ages, but . . ."

"You can't steal people's hopes, Tike," Montague said, ruffling the Poltergeist's hair.

"Well . . . I could . . ." Tike muttered.

"No, you can't. That would make us no better than him. Besides, it wouldn't help us get back the ghosts he's stolen," Mrs. Scruffles replied, smiling softly at Tike, who blushed slightly.

"You think we can? Get the ghosts back, I mean?" Arthur asked, looking hopefully at Mrs. Scruffles.

"I hope so. After all, what's life without hope? So, come on, enough of these sad faces, let's go through what else she showed you, Tom."

"Why?" asked Tom, looking miserable. "It's pointless."

"Nothing is ever pointless. Come on, Tom, pull yourself together. You're acting like a Sadness Summoner. No offense, William."

"Oh, none taken," William replied.

Tom took a deep breath. "The Collector came in, took a coin, sorry, a Wish Coin, from the bag, and then he just, I don't know, *vanished*."

"Just like that?" Mrs. Scruffles asked.

"Yes, just like that."

"And what was the Snorgle doing?"

Tom sighed, exasperated. "I don't know. Looking terrified."

"Anything else?"

Tom shrugged. "He was holding something up to protect himself. Just something he grabbed off the table."

Mrs. Scruffles leaned forward in the chair, her interest growing. "What was it?"

"I don't know. Everything was all wobbly and watery. It was hard to make out. I'm sorry."

"Well, it's a start. It's a *good* start, Tom. We need to know what it was that Snorgle was holding. It might be just the clue we're looking for." Mrs. Scruffles leaned back in her chair, mulling it over. "So I suppose, the obvious place to begin would be finding out who the Snorgle was."

"He wasn't exactly wearing a name badge." Tom

was beginning to feel more and more depressed the more they looked into this. It all felt a bit hopeless. Another awkward silence descended, while everyone pondered over what to do.

"You could always call in at the museum," suggested Mildred.

Mrs. Scruffles clapped her hands. "Of course! Why didn't I think of that? That's an excellent idea, Mildred. If they'd know about it anywhere, that'd be the place."

Tom was looking blank. "The museum? A Snorgle museum? Is that near here then?"

"Oh no, it's up in London."

Tom shook his head, looking apologetic. "There's no way that Mum and Dad will let me go up to London, and it's not like I can sneak there during my lunch break. My parents have been a bit wary ever since the Dr. Brown thing. So we're back to square one."

"Not necessarily . . ." Mrs. Scruffles grinned at Tom, and he knew that a plan was forming. He raised an eyebrow as a question, but Mrs. Scruffles simply smiled widely. "Just leave it to me, Tom. You guys had better head off home. Oh, except you, Mildred. You stay here with me." She caught Arthur's look, and pre-empted what he would say. "Don't worry, I'll walk her back home when we're done." Tom looked at Mrs. Scruffles suspiciously, but he knew that whatever she was planning, she wasn't going to say. "You did well, Tom. You really did. Now, come along everyone, get moving, you mustn't make Tom late."

So Mildred and Mrs. Scruffles stayed behind, plotting and planning, as Tom Golden, Grey Arthur, Montague Equador Scullion the Third, the Harrowing Screamer, Tike, and Woeful William wandered back to Aubergine Road, and waited to see what was going to happen next.

Mystery Guests

THE GHOSTS DARTED THROUGH THE CLOSED DOOR AND dashed upstairs, leaving Tom to unlock the front door and wander in alone. It was always easier to act like he wasn't surrounded by ghosts when they really weren't there, after all. Dad was home by the time he got in, and both his parents were chattering in the kitchen. Tom came in to join them. Mum glanced at the clock, and smiled at Tom.

"And with five minutes to spare, too," she said with a grin, before turning back to Dad to carry on the conversation where it had left off, interrupted by Tom's entrance. "So, you were saying?"

"Well, that's it, pretty much. Nothing's changed. Promotional leaflets, special offers, even a full-spread article in *Your Feet Weekly,* and nothing's changed, not a single pick up in sales. If anything, it's gotten worse. It looks like we may well have to consider moving in with your mother after all. . . ."

Tom's ears pricked up, and Mum glared at Dad, who looked suddenly flustered.

"We're moving in with Granny Green?" Tom asked, eyes wide. Mum sighed, and tried to explain.

"Not necessarily, sweetheart. It's just something we're having to consider. If we can't keep up with the payments on this house, then we're going to have to move out, and because we can't afford to get another place straight away, we have to look into other options. One of them, one of *many*, being moving in with Grandma. Nothing's certain yet, we're just weighing it all up."

Tom tried very hard not to look concerned, but it wasn't easy. Living with Grandma Green would be an absolute nightmare, for oh so many reasons. Firstly, she still spat on a tissue and cleaned him, even when he wasn't really dirty. Secondly, she would never let him forget the time he was sick on her, even though he had only been six months old at the time, and she wound him up about it endlessly every time she saw him. Thirdly, and perhaps most significantly, Grandma Green was catastrophically awful in the kitchen. She had an astonishing inability to know how long to cook anything for, which was rather awkwardly paired up with the fact that she loved cooking, and took to the kitchen at any given opportunity. For Sunday roast, she would cook the tiny, tiny little peas for the same amount of time as a chicken big enough to feed four. The result was, quite frankly, terrifying, and it was only a combination of politeness and years of training that prevented Tom from spitting the food back out onto the plate, and running away to wash his tongue. The peas would be a green, mushy horror, and the meat so tough that you would either need a diamond to cut it, or a small amount of dynamite to blow it into mouth-size pieces. And that was if you were lucky! The worst meals were the ones where the peas were cooked perfectly, and the chicken was still pink. Those were the times that Mum distracted Grandma Green, and Dad scooped everyone's food up in a napkin, and hid it in his pocket.

"So, anyway Tom, tell me about your day," said Dad, swiftly looking to change the subject.

Well, Mildred managed to be seen by humans for the first time in her life, and then I went to Thorblefort Castle to meet the world's strongest Sadness Summoner, and she showed me a vision of the past, and through that I managed to work out that the Collector is real, and that he's responsible for all the ghosts vanishing. Then I met Mum in the tea shop, and discovered that the woman she works with is actually a Faintly Real, and then I came home, before dashing over to Mrs. Scruffles' house with all the ghosts that are secretly living in our home, and our shed, and we had an emergency meeting to see how we could put everything right. . . .

"It was okay," said Tom, nonchalantly. "Bit dull, really. The castle was nice."

The doorbell rang. "Are you expecting anyone, Tom?" asked Dad. Tom shook his head. Mum and Dad shrugged at each other, and trotted down to see who was at the door, with Tom following not far behind them.

Can Tom Come Out?

"HELLO, MOTHER AND FATHER OF TOM."

An exceedingly strange-looking girl was peering up from the doorstep. Her jet black hair was cut at perfect right angles, framing unblinking eyes in shockingly different colors—one bright green, the other so dark a brown that it seemed to be black. It was all Tom's parents could do not to gasp. Her skin was deathly pale, and she wore a black school uniform, complete with black tie and black tights, the look finished with black dolly shoes. She smiled at them, and Dad was reminded of a cat trying to expel a hairball. Tom's parents smiled back nervously. Tom, who had been standing behind them, shocked silent by this latest turn of events, finally found his voice.

"Mum, Dad, this is one of my friends from school. This is Mildred."

Tom's parents muttered vague greetings, unable to peel their eyes away from that nauseous smile on Mildred's face.

"And I'm her mother. Mrs. Scruffles."

The parents had been so distracted by the odd little girl that they hadn't even noticed the woman standing behind her. They looked incredulously at this sweet, cuddly, grey-haired lady, and then at the odd-eyed, deathly serious-looking child all draped in black, and then they looked at each other.

"She takes after her father," explained Mrs. Scruffles.

"Must have been an interesting-looking man . . . ," muttered Dad, prompting Mum to elbow him in the ribs. "It's a pleasure to meet you, Mrs. . . . Scruffles." Dad held out his hand for her to shake, and Mrs. Scruffles looked around awkwardly, suddenly thrown by this attempt at touching. She glanced anxiously at Tom.

"Mrs. Scruffles can't shake hands, Dad. She's . . . erm . . ." Tom floundered, searching for a reason. "She's . . ."

"I'm allergic to hands," interrupted Mrs. Scruffles, smiling warmly. "They give me a terrible rash."

Dad retracted his outstretched hand, and he and Mum exchanged perplexed looks. Mildred had stopped smiling now, worn out from all the effort, and had fixed her stare on Dad. He tried his hardest to avoid eye contact with her, as he found it distinctly unsettling, and so instead he studied his tie, pretending to see something very interesting there. Mum spotted this, and it was all she could do not to laugh, watching

Dad squirm. That soon stopped though when Mildred decided to look at Mum instead, and she too became immediately transfixed, with the woodwork of the doorway.

"So, I take it Tom didn't remember to say we would be popping over?" Mrs. Scruffles asked.

"I must have forgotten . . . ," Tom said, playing along. What on earth were they up to?

"It's my darling Mildred's birthday this weekend, you see," Mrs. Scruffles said, draping her arm around Mildred's shoulders.

"Really? How old will you be?" asked Mum.

"Twenty-six," replied Mildred, improvising. Tom cringed.

"Such a joker, this one!" laughed Mrs. Scruffles, seeing Tom frantically shaking his head. Mum and Dad looked at the very serious Mildred, and nodded quietly. "No, really, she will be"—Mrs. Scruffles glanced at Tom, who was waving his fingers at her from behind his parents' backs—"*twelve*. She will be twelve." Tom sighed with relief. "And so we were wondering if it would be possible for Tom to stay over at our house for the weekend. We'll be having a very normal party. With cakes. And bouncy castles. And dancing monkeys."

Dancing monkeys? Tom laughed nervously.

"Tom's never mentioned you before . . . ," said Mum, looking at Tom suspiciously. Tom grinned, a picture of innocence.

"Yes, I have. I think you were vacuuming at the time though. You must not have heard me." Mum thought about it, and then nodded, seemingly satisfied by that explanation.

"We'd come and collect him on Friday night, for a sleepover, and then on Saturday we would have the party, with the cake, and the castle, and the monkeys, and on Saturday night we would watch films, before returning him to you on Sunday." Mrs. Scruffles smiled warmly at Tom's mum and dad. "We'd take very good care of him. I promise."

"We would have a lot of fun," said Mildred, sternly.

"I don't know . . . Tom's been through ever so much recently, and I'm not sure he's ready to stay out for a whole weekend yet," said Mum. Mum, the overprotective. Mum, the worrier. What she really meant was that she wasn't sure that *she* was ready to let him out of her sight for an entire weekend. Tom groaned.

"I'm fine, Mum. I want to stay out. And you said ages ago that you wanted me to make new friends at this school, didn't you?" Tom was doing puppy eyes now, his deep brown chocolate eyes all big. Mum frowned, and Tom pushed on. "It's a birthday party. What's the worst that can happen? And Mrs. Scruffles will be there the whole time, to keep an eye on me. And you could have her phone number, because she has a phone, and I'll stay in touch and let you know what's going on. Please? Pretty please?"

"It could give us a chance to visit Grandma Green, to sort out plans if we did have to move out there," Dad said thoughtfully.

"Well, she *would* like the company . . . ," Mum agreed.

"And I've been so busy with work recently, it would be nice for us both to get away, spend some time together."

Mum nodded, still unsure.

"I promise I won't let anything happen to him," said Mrs. Scruffles. Mum looked at her warm smile, her friendly, open face, and she trusted her. Mrs. Scruffles had that effect on people.

"So can I? Please, Mum? Please?" Tom asked, tugging on her sleeve. Mum sighed, giving in.

"Okay! Okay, you can. But next time, I'll need more warning." Tom yelped with joy, throwing his arms around Mum, who smiled, returning the hug. "So, you'll pick him up tomorrow?"

"Straight after school. Thank you very much. This means so much to my Mildred. Well, to all of us. It's been a pleasure meeting you both." Mrs. Scruffles grinned at Tom, and Tom grinned back. They'd done it! They'd actually done it! Tom heard clapping from behind, and he turned to see that all the other ghosts had gathered on the stairs to watch what was happening. Arthur was jumping up and down, looking delighted.

"Bravo!" called Montague. "Bravo! An outstanding performance!"

Mrs. Scruffles and Mildred waved good-bye, and Tom's Mum and Dad closed the door, and wandered back into the kitchen. Mildred, now invisible again to humans, darted through the closed door, and looked at Tom.

"How did I do?" she asked.

"You were fantastic," he whispered.

In the kitchen, Mum and Dad were talking in low voices, and a triumphant Tom raced upstairs, and left them to it.

"What an odd-looking girl . . . ," Mum said, and she couldn't help but laugh. "So serious!"

"I'm sure we had stranger friends when we were younger," Dad replied, and they both paused a while, thinking back. They looked at each other, shook their heads, and laughed. "Okay, maybe we didn't! But it's good that Tom is making friends. Even if they are a little . . . *different.*"

And that was how the daring plan was put into action. A weekend, free of parents, to visit Ghost museums, to follow clues, and to hopefully put an end to the Collector's collecting. The rest of the night passed quietly, with everyone praising Mildred's performance, and with planning, and plotting, and at last, high hopes.

If only things were going so well elsewhere.

You Don't Have to Be a Ghost to Work Here . . .

ESSAY DAVE, THE FAMOUS PAPERWORK POLTERGEIST, floated through the door to his office and glided to his desk, his shiny immaculate shoes hovering a good inch above the carpeted floor. The door obediently clicked shut behind him. His trademark paperwork suit rustled as he settled into his chair, and he loosened the tie that bore the legend TOP SECRET running down the length of it. It had been a long day. He opened his briefcase, unceremoniously tipping its contents all over his desk. Grabbing the nearest piece of paper that had spilled free, he smiled quietly to himself. He turned it over in his hands, tracing his fingertips across the words scrawled there, savoring each new gem of information he had "acquired." Sneaking into offices, gliding invisibly from desk to desk, place to place, ethereal hands quickly stealing away notes, letters, reports, memos; that was the bulk of Essay Dave's work. But it was this, the time he spent carefully sorting through everything he found, gleefully absorbing every new tidbit of knowledge, this was the part he relished the most. This was the part that made it all worthwhile.

With a flick of his wrist, Essay Dave sent the letter he had been reading across the room, where it obediently fell on top of a pile of papers. It had been written by some high up politician, someone always seen smiling insincerely on TV and in newspaper photos, and was addressed to someone else called "My darling muffin-cake." Essay Dave chuckled, picturing the look on his face when he found his letter gone. You shouldn't leave these things just lying around in locked drawers, hidden inside a book on modern politics, inside an office with a six-number combination lock on the door. Not when Essay Dave is about. Another flick of his wrist, and a hot mug of coffee appeared in his hand. On the side of the china mug was written, in bold letters, YOU DON'T HAVE TO BE A GHOST TO WORK HERE—BUT IT HELPS! He sipped slowly, savoring the taste, and leaned back to read the rest of his new material.

The phrase "organized chaos" could have been invented purely to describe Dave's office. All around where he sat, lost in the study of his latest findings, towers of paper stretched toward the ceiling, precariously balanced, leaning at impossible angles yet never quite falling. The fluorescent light overhead still hadn't been fixed (he had much better things to do with his time) and it flickered constantly, creating a strange strobe effect. A fan in the corner of the room whirred away, swirling Post-it notes and scraps of paper around the free floor space. The walls were plastered with posters and letters, some printed in ink and some in delicate handwriting, some in languages from far away and some in languages from times forgotten. Somewhere amongst all the clutter, nestled next to a handwritten note from Winston Churchill complaining about the stocking of the

Downing Street liquor cabinet, was pinned the front page of an old *Daily Tell-Tale,* with the headline INVISIBLE FRIENDS SAVE THE DAY.

Essay Dave sorted the remaining items from today into order: a report on Diminishing Haddock Stock Levels; someone's essay on "The life and times of Henry VIII," complete with numerous historical inaccuracies; a Classified Document detailing the movement of America's president during his visit to England, a scrap of paper that said "Lovely night, had a great time, call me–Marina," (lots of kisses and a phone number followed); and a request lifted from a milk bottle for "two more pints of full cream tomorrow please." Each was sent flying to its respective piles, each filed away for future reference, or just as a trophy to keep and relish.

He'd been to all his favorite haunts today, everywhere from Downing Street to Gatwick (how he loved those little boarding passes), all the way to tiny rural villages where people's accents were thick and lilting, and where the countryside crept all the way up to their back gardens. It had been the visit to the MI5 offices that really stuck in his memory though. He'd floated unseen past all the guards, through doors with so many security devices that they seemed as if they'd been plucked from the future, straight through to the main offices without so much as a moment's hesitation, when something unexpected happened. Someone had beaten Essay Dave there. A Poltergeist was already sitting at a desk, transparent fingers pawing away at an unmanned computer, grinning gleefully at the bounty she found within. She was a small, young ghost, with bright pink hair standing tall in a Mohawk, and wearing a dress embellished with CDs like oversize sequins. She'd waved cheerily at Dave, and introduced herself as "bYtE mE," making sure Dave knew to capitalize the alternate letters of her name, insisted on being referred to as a Cybergeist instead of a "plain old *boring* Poltergeist," and then quickly settled back to causing havoc on the computer system. It was all Dave could do to shake his head in disbelief, before grabbing the itinerary of the president's visit and making a hasty exit. The times were definitely changing.

It hadn't been so long ago that everything was scratched on parchment with an ink-dipped feather, and now . . . E-mails. Text messages. Whole correspondences across cyberspace. Essay Dave sighed, and shuffled a pile of papers left on his desk. Maybe in a century or so he should think about retiring. Settle down in a big library somewhere, whittle away his time messing around with the Dewey system, putting history books in the cooking section, sabotaging the alphabetical order in the fiction department . . . Leave the Poltergeisting, or even *cybergeisting,* to younger ghosts, and enjoy a mischievous retirement amongst thousands of beautiful books, full of millions of pages of words. He smiled, full of paper orientated thoughts.

The sound of his office door clicking shut pulled

him from his daydream. He hadn't even heard it open.

"Hello?" he called, sitting up straighter in his chair. He glanced around his office, but there was nobody to be seen. Raising his voice, he called out again. "Hello?" Nothing. "Look, this isn't a good time. I've got a lot of work to be getting on with. If you could call back later?"

The only sound was the constant hum of the electric fan, and the buzz of the ever-temperamental fluorescent light overhead. Essay Dave shrugged. Obviously, whoever it was had changed their mind, and wandered off again. It happens, occasionally. Ghosts come from miles around to seek out information, and then sometimes think the better of it. After all, you might not like what you find out.

A pile of paper in the corner of the room suddenly tumbled, sending pages cascading across the floor. Dave leapt to his feet, spilling coffee across his desk. It was greedily absorbed by the various papers strewn there, handwritten words bleeding out of shape as the paper became soggy. Dave growled, and began hastily mopping it up before more damage could be done.

"I really don't have the time for this." He glared around the room, searching for the unseen intruder. With so many towers of paper, it made it easy for someone to hide out of sight. "Either come out, or disappear, but I don't want you tiptoeing around my office. Do you have any idea how long it took to arrange that stack?"

Still no response. Whoever, *whatever,* was in his office didn't want to be seen. At least, not yet. Dave mopped up the last of the coffee, dropping the sopping wet tissue into his bin. "I don't know what kind of game you are playing," he muttered darkly, "but it's getting pretty old, pretty quickly."

Rustling over on the other side of the room grabbed his attention, and he turned quickly, but not quickly enough to catch sight of whomever, whatever, was in the office with him. Dave began feeling uneasy now, and stood up slowly from his desk. Movement caught his eye, this time on the exact opposite side of the room from which the rustling had come, but it was too brief to make out anything other than a vague blur of motion.

"Stop playing around now. I warn you, I'm not in the mood," Dave snapped. As if in response, another stack of paper crashed to the floor. He winced as decades of filing crumbled into chaos. Still no sight of his mysterious guest. An unfamiliar feeling nestled inside Dave, and when he realized what it was he almost laughed. He was afraid. A ghost, *afraid?* This was ridiculous.

"I'm going to give you to the count of three to show yourself," he called, trying to push the worry aside. He hoped it didn't show in his voice. In the most authoritative tone he could muster, he began to slowly count out loud.

"One . . ."

"Two . . ."

As Dave saw what stepped out in front of him, the number three lodged in his throat, unsaid. He shook his head in a mixture of disbelief and fear.

There were many things he wanted to say. He wanted to scream out in shock, he wanted to demand how this was possible, he wanted to refuse that this was happening, he wanted to shout, oh cliché of clichés, that the ghost in front of him was just a myth, a legend, a lie, a childhood ghost story, but instead Essay Dave trailed off into silence, unable to find the words he wanted. This wasn't happening. It couldn't be.

The Collector wasn't meant to exist.

The Collector simply smiled from beneath his cape, a smile colder than winter at its bleakest, and with a slight motion of the hand he flicked something toward Essay Dave. It happened quickly, too quickly, not even enough time to fall through the floor, or dart through the door, not enough time to do anything but watch in transfixed horror as an old coin flew through the air toward him, still shiny, glinting from the faltering fluorescent light that caught it as it spun. Essay Dave threw his hands up instinctively, and as the coin hit him he shimmered, a brief flash of despair registering on his face, and then he was gone.

The coin continued its path, landing on the desk, spinning to a halt amongst all the clutter. It tarnished, the sheen instantly fading to moldy greens and rusty grime, all the luster taken from it. The Collector reached over, picking up the coin with sinewy fingers, and dropped it into a bag, where it clanged against the other coins held inside. Many coins, each one a ghost stolen from existence.

He grinned triumphantly, and opened the door to Dave's room, slowly walking away. He left behind him an empty office, illuminated by the flickering glow of a dying light.

Just Biding Time

IT DIDN'T TAKE MUCH TO GET TOM OUT OF BED THE next day. Even if he'd wanted to sleep in, the ghosts were all far too hyperactive to ignore. Tike had been up at six, bouncing on Tom's bed, all ready and raring to start the day, and the others hadn't been much better. Mildred making notes; Montague pacing dramatically; William writing a poem that might even for once have a happy ending, entitled "When Ghosts Disappear from the World"; the Harrowing Screamer testing out his claws on Tom's wooden cupboard, and Grey Arthur perched patiently on the end of the bed by Tom's feet, Tom's schoolbag already packed and waiting for him. So it was no surprise then that Tom was already up and about when Mum burst in to wake him, and she looked at him, amazed that for once she wasn't needed.

"Excited about the party then?" she asked, pulling his curtains open.

"The what?" Tom asked.

"Mildred's birthday!" Arthur hissed at him.

"Oh, yes! That's why I'm up early," agreed Tom. Mum flustered around the room, and it made it very hard for Tom not to giggle, seeing all the ghosts diving out of her way to avoid her marching through them. If things continued this way, he was going to need a bigger room. She stopped, perhaps standing a little too close to Woeful William, and sighed.

"I'm sorry if I smother you a bit sometimes, Tom. I don't mean to. It's just . . . it's hard for me. I just want everything to go right for us, and we've been through so much since we moved here, and now, with your dad's job, and the thought of having to maybe move out . . ." She stumbled into silence, and then as William realized what was happening and sidestepped away, she began to compose herself. "I'm happy that you've got a new friend, and I'm glad that you've been invited over to stay for the weekend. I just . . . I worry. It's what mothers do."

"I know, Mum. I understand. But everything is going to work out. I have a good feeling about this." And he did. They'd visit the Snorgle Museum, find the Snorgle who'd seen the Collector, find out what he'd done to get rid of the Collector, and then Mrs. Scruffles would work it out, work out how to fix it all. Everything would end up fine. The ghosts would all come back, Dad's business would pick up, and everyone would be happy. Tom grinned at Mum, and she smiled back. The moment passed, and she changed the subject.

"Now, your dad and I are going straight to Grandma Green's from work, so I won't see you this evening. I've left Gran's phone number downstairs on a scrap of paper for you to take, in case of an emergency, and I dug out a card for you to give Mildred for her birthday, and I've sorted out your nice clothes for the party, and I've made you a big packed lunch because you're going to have a busy day, and, erm . . . Have I forgotten anything?"

Tom laughed. "No, I think that's everything. Don't worry, Mum! It'll be fine."

"Okay . . . Okay." She smiled, and gave him a hug, not for any particular reason, but just *because*. "I'll see you downstairs for breakfast." She left the room, and closed the door behind her.

And so Tom and the ghosts prepared for school, all full of energy, and high hopes, and dreams of putting everything right. Even William seemed almost upbeat.

"THOMAS GOLDEN!" a rather angry-sounding Mum shouted from downstairs. Tom stopped what he was doing, and listened. "Thomas Golden, you get down here this instant!" When your parents call you by your full name, you know that you're in trouble. Tom looked nervously at the ghosts, who appeared as confused as he was. He pulled on his shirt, and dashed down the stairs, Grey Arthur hot on his heels, and the rest of the ghosts in pursuit. Mum was standing in the kitchen, glaring at him, hands on her hips.

"What? What is it? What have I done wrong?" Tom asked.

"What. Did. I. Tell. You. About. Feeding. Stray. Cats?" she replied, breaking each word down into an individual statement, as only annoyed mothers can. Tom looked at her blankly, not understanding. Mum leaned over, and flung open the kitchen curtains, showing the garden outside.

Tom's mouth dropped open.

"I told you!" Mum shrieked. "I told you this would happen!"

The garden was full of cats, all of them meowing silently, the noise blocked out by double glazing. Cats were perched on the bird table, crowding the windowsill, covering the patio, lining the fence. Agatha Tibbles and Carrot Cake stood in the middle of the garden, meowing pitifully.

Tom knew. It hit him in the pit of his stomach, a sick fear, and behind him he heard Grey Arthur wail.

Mrs. Scruffles.

"This is the last thing I need, Tom. I've just had a phone call from the castle saying that Janet hasn't turned up for work, which is completely unlike her, and we're away for the weekend, and now we've got a hundred and one cats doing whatever it is cats do all over our garden, and who knows what the neighbors are going to think—Tom, are you listening to me?"

"I've got to go," Tom said quietly.

"What? You've not even had breakfast yet. Tom, what's going on?"

"I've got to go. I forgot I had to be in early today. Sorry." Tom was gathering his schoolbag, throwing his packed lunch and the birthday card in hastily. He ran up, and kissed Mum good-bye. "I'll see you after the weekend, Mum. I've got to go."

Mum growled, but Tom was already on the move.

He was rushing toward the door as Dad emerged from the bathroom, towel wrapped around his waist.

"You off already, Tom? Not even a good-bye for your old man?" Dad asked, as Tom tore past. Tom paused, and waved at his dad, before carrying on charging out the front door. "Have a nice weekend then!" shouted Dad after him. "And behave yourself!"

But Tom was already gone, racing toward Mrs. Scruffles' house. Deep down inside though, he already knew what he would find.

The Loneliness of Empty Homes

THE DOOR TO MRS. SCRUFFLES' HOUSE WAS WIDE open. They stumbled to a halt on the doorstep, almost afraid to step inside, afraid to know for sure what they all suspected. Tom was the first one through, the first one to snap free from the silent staring, and he broke into a run, dashing into the kitchen, and the ghosts weren't far behind him. What he saw though caused him to stop dead in his tracks.

The table had been turned over, and Mrs. Scruffles' prized tea pot lay on the floor, smashed into several thousand pieces. The tea that had been inside was spilled all over the carpet. A few cats remained, howling sadly amongst the chaos. The curtains had been torn from the rail, hanging in rags by the sink. Her beloved grandfather clock was lying on its side, its ticking silenced, the glass face smashed.

They were too late.

The Harrowing Screamer hissed angrily at the empty room, bristling. Mildred looked around dumbly, for once too shocked to write anything down. William held his handkerchief to his face, as if he could somehow block out what he was seeing. Tike's usual impish grin was gone, and he looked like a little boy lost.

"Oh, no . . ." Montague looked at the damage around him, and he placed a hand on Arthur's shoulder. "I'm so sorry."

Grey Arthur crumpled to the floor, heavy sobs racking his tiny, see-through body.

"Can you . . ." Tom found his voice was choking, and he cleared his throat. "Can you just give us a second?" he asked the ghosts. They nodded quietly, and retreated to the doorstep, leaving Tom and Grey Arthur alone. Tom crouched down at Arthur's side. Huge tears rolled down his pale, ghostly face, and he looked around the room, shaking his head.

"We shouldn't have let her walk home on her own last night, Tom! This is my fault. We were so excited that the plan had worked that we . . . I didn't think . . . I can't believe she's gone. . . ." He buried his face in his hands, crying.

"It'll be okay, Arthur," whispered Tom. "We'll find a way to fix this."

"How? How will we?" Arthur howled, looking up at Tom, his eyes framed red in a face that was now pasty blue. "We can't do this without her, Tom. She is . . . *was* . . . she was clever. Cleverer than all of us put together. How are we supposed to work this out without her?"

"We'll find a way," said Tom sternly. Arthur looked away, shaking his head.

"It's just scary, Tom," he said quietly. "I don't want to disappear. I've only just found out what I am. I've only just made friends with you."

"Stop it!" snapped Tom. "You can't do this, Arthur. You can't give up. I won't allow it. We'll go, and we'll figure this out ourselves. We'll fix this ourselves. We've got Monty, and Tike, and Mildred, and William, and we've got the Harrowing Screamer, and together we will work out how to make this right." Arthur sniffed, wiping his face with the back of his hand, the shock of the normally mild-mannered Tom shouting jolting him out of his tears. "So, come on, stand up. We've got to go to school now, and once that's finished we've got a lot to get done. There's not enough time to be sad. *Stand up.*"

Arthur shakily got to his feet, and looked at Tom. Tom had never seen Arthur look so small, so sad, so frayed, so scared. It made Tom angry; angry that someone could hurt so many people, angry that his friend was afraid, angry for his parents worrying they would lose the house, angry for all the other people affected too, angry for all the ghosts that had vanished. He felt his nails digging into the palms of his hands, and he realized that his fists were clenched. He was going to fix this.

Now all he needed to do was work out how.

"Come on, Arthur. We've got to get going." Tom gestured toward the door.

Arthur nodded, and took one last look at the broken room, at the damage strewn amongst the usually warm, safe home of Mrs. Scruffles. It felt so quiet, so lonely without her there, without all the cats meowing, without the ticking of the clock, without the constant sound of a kettle boiling in the background.

"I'm ready," he said. Tom nodded, a determined look on his face.

"Good. Then let's go to school."

Counting the Hours

THE SCHOOL DAY PASSED IN A MISERABLE BLUR. TOM tried to concentrate, tried to pay attention, but his mind constantly wandered to what they were going to do, and his eyes constantly wandered to his watch, counting the seconds, the minutes, the hours. Big Ben wisely kept his distance, possibly deterred by the stronger air of misery that William radiated, and the fiercer sense of menace that surrounded the Harrowing Screamer. Tom didn't even notice their effects. He was worried enough, and sad enough, that he didn't need to be influenced by the ghosts around him. Peter sensed that something was up, and kept pressing Tom to tell him what was going on, but what could Tom say? Hi, I know we've only just made friends, but I have to tell you I can see ghosts, and two of my ghost friends have vanished without a trace? So Tom would just shrug, and say it was nothing, and although Peter didn't believe him, he didn't push the matter. He just decided to give Tom some space.

Grey Arthur didn't say, or do much all day, lost in bleak thoughts, with Invisible Friend duties being the last thing on his mind. Tom even wandered around for the best part of an hour with a sign on his back reading FREAK BOY LOVES PICK-NOSE PETER before Mildred noticed and quickly ripped it away. When he lost a pen, it was Montague who replaced it from the stash in his shirt pocket. When Tom daydreamed, it was Tike who shouted in his ear to drag him back to reality. The final straw came at lunchtime when Kate deliberately barged into Tom as she walked past, sending him face first into a locker, and Arthur didn't even notice it had happened. While Tom held his nose, checking for signs of bleeding, his eyes watering with pain, Woeful William took Grey Arthur by the shoulders, and led him out onto the playground.

"Why are we out here?" Arthur had asked, as William pushed him through the unopened doors. The noise of the playground washed over them, and Woeful William had to raise his voice to be heard.

"Because," William said with a sigh (every sentence he uttered tended to contain a sigh at some stage), "I wanted to have a word in your dear little lopsided ear. It's a frightfully awful thing that has happened to Ballpoint Bill, and Mrs. Scruffles, and if I vanished I'd like nothing more than for you to mope around in a delicate shade of blue, perhaps a few tears, maybe a poem about how much you'll miss me—"

"I'm terrible at poetry," Arthur interrupted.

"Wouldn't matter a bit—it's the thought that counts. Anyway, what I'm trying to say, in a round-about way, is that if I vanish, then it would be a fitting tribute for you to act this way."

"But?" added Arthur, sensing that one was coming.

"But," continued William, "it's the last thing in the world that Ballpoint Bill or Mrs. Scruffles would want.

You're so busy being so spectacularly sad that you're missing what's important."

"And what's that then?" Arthur was kicking at the ground, scuffing his already scuffed grey ghostly shoes.

"Look around. What do you see?"

Grey Arthur sighed, not particularly in the mood for a pep talk. He glanced at the playground, and shrugged. "Children . . . grass . . . a soccer ball . . . a teacher . . ."

William flapped his handkerchief in front of Arthur's face, admonishing him. "I don't believe for one miserable second that you've been hanging around with these humans for so long that you've forgotten everything I taught you. Now, have another look, and look properly this time."

Grey Arthur rolled his eyes, but did what William asked. The playground stretched out before him, a slew of grey concrete that slammed into grass and mud. Children milled all over the place, gathered in groups, sitting in pairs, some perched on walls eating their lunches, some lounging on the grass, talking and laughing. Lunchboxes, schoolbags, notes being passed, giggling, graffiti, a boy sitting beneath a tree, some kids playing tag . . . Grey Arthur halted, backtracking. Frank Longfield was sitting on his own, back resting against the trunk, knees tugged in toward his chest, and even from this distance it was ragingly obvious that he was upset. His sweater sleeve was ripped, falling open at the seam to reveal the white shirt below. There was just something in the way he held himself, something in the way his arms wrapped tightly around him, that made Arthur believe it wasn't just the sweater that had been mauled. Arthur looked at William, suddenly understanding what this was all about. When he looked back at the playground, it was as if someone had thrown on the light switch in a gloomy room, and he could finally see what was going on. The noise, and the playing, and the apparent happiness of the playground were swept away, and Grey Arthur saw everything that was wrong simmering beneath it. On the other side of the field, far away from teachers' sight, two boys were fighting while a crowd watched, egging them on excitedly. Just as Grey Arthur had started to look at them, Holly Mayer fled past, red-eyed, teeth biting her lip, and spiteful shouting followed her from a group of girls who were watching her run, and laughing. Elsewhere, some older kids deliberately kicked a soccer ball into a huddle of younger boys, and cheered when it connected with someone's face.

"This place is riddled with sadness, Arthur. Sometimes it's hard to spot, especially if you aren't looking for it, when it's hidden beneath all the shouting and playing and horrible giggling, but if you look hard enough, it's there, plain as day. Of course, I think it's fantastic, but that's why I'm a Sadness Summoner, and not an Invisible Friend."

Arthur nodded, feeling more than marginally

guilty. The trouble with being sad is that sometimes it's hard to see any farther than the tip of your transparent blue nose.

"Well, if we're quite finished here, I think your human is in need of a friend right about now, and your ghosts are in need of a teacher. Goodness knows this school could do with a few more Invisible Friends scattered around the place." William nearly added, *"Even if it will put me out of a job,"* but didn't. Instead, he gestured toward the door, and Arthur was already dashing back inside, detouring via the boys' toilets to get some cold wet toilet tissue for Tom's nose. William followed behind, at a much slower pace (Sadness Summoners simply don't go any faster than a depressed amble). When Arthur arrived, Montague was trying to cheer Tom up with a scarily accurate impersonation of Kate Getty, even down to the missing eyebrows, and in between twinges of pain as he held the soggy toilet tissues to his face, Tom managed to grin at Arthur, who grinned back.

William might have smiled as well, if Sadness Summoners did that kind of thing, but they don't, so instead he flapped his handkerchief, and sighed, and moped, but inside he felt something (not that he'd EVER admit it) that nudged toward happiness, or at the very least, a lighter shade of gloom.

Back on Track

IT WAS STRANGE, WALKING HOME PAST THE EMPTINESS that was Mrs. Scruffles' house, and it didn't exactly serve to boost the mood. The Spitting Kids had been standing around outside it, looking more than a little suspicious, eyes wandering to the broken, open door, but they soon dispersed when the Harrowing Screamer charged toward them in full howl, shadows streaking behind him like exhaust fumes. A wave of terror had bowled into them, and they ran away in different directions, suddenly feeling too terrified to stay put. Later on, they'd put it down to thinking that someone was watching them, or say that they were convinced the police were on the way, or something equally macho, but the truth was simply that they were scared out of their wits by the unseen ghost in their midst.

The Harrowing Screamer was handy like that.

They stopped off at Mrs. Scruffles' empty house just long enough to put straight, where possible, the damage the Collector had done—picking up the broken shards of the tea pot, standing the now silent grandfather clock back up again, rehanging the shredded curtains. The place still looked like a supernatural bomb had hit it, but it was a start. Tike had somehow managed to "borrow" enough leftovers from the school dining hall to feed all Mrs. Scruffles' cats (Tom dreaded to think what his pockets smelled like, watching him drag handful after handful of fish and meat scraps from his tatty trousers). This was greeted by much appreciative meowing, and Tom and the ghosts paused at the house to give every cat that wanted it a little fuss, before dashing back to Number 11 Aubergine Road.

"So, here's the plan," Tom said, as he paced around the lounge. It felt strange, having the home to himself, without Mum and Dad flustering around. It felt quiet. The ghosts had settled on the settee, apart from the Harrowing Screamer, who was standing in the most shaded corner of the room. All eyes were on Tom, and for once, it didn't bother him that they were expecting him to know what to do. "Me and Arthur are going to go to the museum. We *will* find this Snorgle, and we *will* work out exactly what he did to stop the Collector. If Mrs. Scruffles was here, that's what she'd be telling us to do, and so that's what we will do. The rest of you, you need to go out there and warn the other ghosts. Warn them that it's not safe out there on their own."

"So where do we tell 'em to go?" asked Tike. He was curled up in Dad's armchair, knees tucked to his chest. Tom remembered Tike's meaty, fishy pockets, and hoped quietly that the smell wouldn't seep through. He pushed that thought aside.

"Tell them to come here, if they have nowhere else to go. Mum and Dad will be gone for the whole weekend, so it will be okay for the time being. They can stay wherever they like, just not in Mum and Dad's room. That's out of bounds. But there's plenty of room in the attic, in the shed, in the kitchen, the lounge. In my room, if they have to. But just make sure they are safe. That's the main thing. Someone also needs to contact the *Daily Tell-Tale,* let them know what's going on, tell them what we're actually up against. They can help get the word out too." Tom was pacing as he spoke, his hands twitching, his thoughts whirring.

"We'll get straight on it, Tom," replied Montague. Mildred nodded.

Tom glanced at his watch. It was just gone three o'clock. "We need to work out how to get to London, Arthur."

"It's okay. I've already got an idea." Arthur had managed to pull himself together slightly since this morning—whatever William had said to him in their private aside had obviously worked—but he was still more blurred, more see-through, more ghostlike than normal. He stood up, and gestured for Tom to follow him. "We'll be gone for a few hours, but we'll try not to be too late," he said to William and the trainee Invisible Friends. "Just . . ." He struggled for a suitable good-bye, but couldn't find one that fit the circum-stances. "Just look out for one another, and get the warning out."

The ghosts nodded, faces serious, and they watched Tom and Arthur wander out the front door.

"Well then, my little ghostly friends," said Montague, smoothing down his mustache. "Let's get this show on the road."

A Twist on Public Transport

"So, can you see it?" asked Grey Arthur, looking hopefully at Tom. Tom frowned.

"See what?"

"It? Can you see *it*?"

Tom scratched his head. Whatever *it* was, Tom was pretty sure he couldn't see it. Arthur had hurried him through the streets, a left turn here, a right turn there, a brief dash down an alleyway overgrown with stinging nettles and laced with dog mess, and then he had stopped at a very specific spot, and looked at Tom expectantly. Tom scratched his head. He could see pavement, he could see a wall where people had written their names in spray paint, he could see a discarded crisp packet, he could see where someone had obviously ignored the sign saying PLEASE DO NOT LET YOUR DOG FOUL THE FOOT PATH, but nothing ghostly or weird sprung to view.

"Is it definitely here?" Tom asked. "What exactly am I looking for?"

"It's . . . It's hard to describe. You'll know it when you see it. You just need to concentrate."

Tom shook his head. "This isn't going to work."

"It will, it will," Arthur insisted. "You're just look-ing at this with human eyes."

"They're the only eyes I've got!"

Grey Arthur ignored that point, and continued regardless.

"If you can see me, and other ghosts, then you must be able to see this. It's right here. Concentrate."

Tom growled under his breath, but Grey Arthur just looked hopefully at him. Taking a deep breath, Tom stared at the area Arthur had shown, teeth gritted, brow furrowed, eyebrows scrunched. *Concentrate . . . Concentrate . . .*

Suddenly, the air by Arthur flickered, then shimmered, and there *it* was.

Grey Arthur hadn't been lying when he said it was hard to describe. There was a hole in the air that resembled an upright puddle. Colors danced around inside as if someone had shaken all the different hues from a rainbow within a giant snow globe. They drifted, slowly falling within the hole, before a faint shudder would send them all up in the air again. Trailing behind the hole were shiny strands of silver and gold, stretching out far into the distance. Tom's mouth dropped open.

"So you can see it?" Grey Arthur asked excitedly. He took Tom's amazed expression as a yes. "I told you that you could do it!"

"What is it?" Tom murmured. It was beautiful, it was mesmerizing, it was—

"A ley-line," said Arthur, clapping his hands. "You're looking at the entrance to a ley-line!"

Tom had seen a program about ley-lines ages ago. The TV presenter had said that they were lines of psychic and supernatural power that crisscrossed over the land, connecting important areas. His dad had said it was a "bunch of hippy nonsense."

It would seem Tom's dad was wrong.

Tom edged toward it slowly, holding out his hand. He gingerly touched the surface, tracing his fingers across it. The colors gravitated toward him, pooling around his fingertips. He'd been expecting it to feel wet, but instead it felt tingly, like when you place your hand on a television screen. He withdrew his hand, shaking his fingers.

"This is so weird. . . ." With his hand gone, the colors continued their gradual fall, before shimmering back up into the air and starting all over again. "So now what?" he asked Arthur.

"Now, we travel on it. It's only a short trip, we change at Stonehenge, and then we're—"

"We *what*?" Tom interrupted.

"We travel on it. What did you think it was for?"

"I . . . I don't know. I just didn't think about it, to be honest." Tom looked at the ley-line. "Is it safe?"

Grey Arthur paused, which really wasn't the most reassuring response.

"Oh, don't look so worried, Tom. It's not that it *isn't* safe—well, it's not that I *know* it's not safe—"

"Not helping," Tom said quickly.

"I've never been on one before," admitted Arthur.

"Great." Tom leaned against the graffitied wall, and stared at the shimmering ley-line in front of him. "That's just marvelous."

"I just tend to run everywhere," Arthur said apologetically.

"This is a nightmare," muttered Tom.

"I'm sure it will be fine. Ghosts have been using the ley-lines for thousands of years."

"But I'm not a ghost!"

"But you're hardly a normal, run-of-the-mill human either," Grey Arthur said, smiling hopefully.

"Come on, Tom, what's the worst that could happen?"

Tom could think of quite a few worst things that could happen, most of them involving exploding, disappearing, or ending up in Timbuktu and having to try to explain to his parents how he got there when he was meant to be at a very normal birthday party.

"Okay, okay, I just need to wrap my head around this. . . . How exactly does this all work?" asked Tom, biting his lip nervously.

"Erm . . . Exactly? I'm not sure. Nobody is. They've just always been there, as far as I know. I suppose the nearest human equivalent would be train tracks, without the train, or motorways, without the cars. You just step into them, and"—Arthur made a *whooshing* noise, waving his hands for emphasis—"and you're at the other end. Does that help?"

"Not greatly," Tom said truthfully. He stared at the shimmering colors before him, lost in thought. "Come on then, before I change my mind," he said suddenly, surprising even himself.

"Really?"

"Really," Tom said, hoping he sounded convinced. He didn't feel it. *Deep breaths, Tom Golden, deep breaths* . . . He straightened up from where he had been leaning on the wall, and strode toward the ley-line, stammering to a halt just out of its reach. It seemed to crackle with anticipation, as if it knew that Tom was ready. "I just step into it?"

"As simple as that. So I've heard." Arthur gestured toward the entrance. "I'll be right behind you."

"Well . . . here goes." Tom grimaced, heart pounding, teeth gritted. He edged forward, tiny steps, hands held in front of him as if he was playing Murder in the Dark. At the last second, he hesitated, trying to pull back, changing his mind, but it was too late. The ley-line surged forward, and gathered Tom up, plunging him through the opening.

Keep Your Hands Within the Ride at All Times

IF TOM WAS EVER TO BE EATEN ALIVE BY A RAINBOW, he imagined this is how it would feel.

Colors swarmed and whirred around him, and he hurtled forward, lost in a sea of lights. Gravity loosened its grip, and Tom realized with a faint pang of worry that his feet weren't touching the ground. Beyond the radiant walls of the ley-line, Tom could just about make out the Real World, rushing past at an unearthly speed. Noises would flit past—the sound of a busy road, of a police siren, a blaring stereo—and be gone as soon as Tom had even begun to hear them. It was as if the world had become liquid, and it flowed past in a torrent of blurred images. In front of him, Tom saw a building approaching at a terrifying speed, and no sooner had he begun to scream and pull his hands up to cover his face then he had passed through the wall, past someone sitting on the settee watching telly, and he was back outside again. He was mildly relieved at not being splatted all over the wall, but at the same time a little bit concerned about the fact that he could pass straight through, unharmed. Hopefully, this was just a temporary thing. He'd have a lot of explaining to do if the effects lasted. . . .

He tried to look behind, to make sure Arthur was there, but turning his head made him so giddy that he had to give up.

Onward, onward, faster and faster, floating feet and flashing colors, flowing scenes and fleeting noises, hurtling on and on and on and on . . .

Tom crashed back into the world, knees hitting grassy earth, hands slamming to the ground, and for a while he couldn't move, couldn't even look up. His head spun, and nausea chewed at him, making his mouth taste of salt and sweat. He was aware of Arthur tumbling out alongside him, but couldn't bring himself to move his head to see how he was, or even where they were. He just wanted to stay stock-still, and wait for the sickness to pass.

"That . . . was . . . *awesome!*" shouted Arthur, bending down to Tom's ear. "Wasn't that awesome?"

Tom spat, frothy flecks of white landing on the grass. He was glad that Arthur seemed to have perked up, but at the moment the last thing he wanted was someone being chirpy in his vicinity. He was sure he looked every bit as pale as Grey Arthur right now. Still, the ground felt reassuringly solid beneath him, and it was lovely not to be moving anymore. The sickness began to fade, slowly, and Tom took deep breaths, trying to push it farther away. *In through the nose . . . Out through the mouth . . . In through the nose . . .*

"Are you okay, Tom? Are you all right? What's going on? Didn't you enjoy that? Are you all right? Tom? Tom? To—"

"I'm fine! I just . . . need . . . a second, Arthur," Tom gasped, still staring at the ground. "I just need to be still for a while."

Arthur paced around Tom, which didn't help much, but thankfully he stopped talking. Tom rubbed his face with his hands, trying to chase away the last of his travel sickness, and finally forced himself to sit up and look around.

As Tom took in the grand stone blocks, towering high above him, carefully arranged amongst the rolling greenery, he instantly knew where he was.

Stonehenge.

In history class, Mr. Hammond had said that nobody really knows what Stonehenge was built for.

Perhaps it had been a calendar for keeping track of the seasons, or a way of mapping the stars. Perhaps it had been thought of as holy, a place to pray, or dream, a place to remember the dead or to hope for better tomorrows. Perhaps we'll never know, Mr. Hammond had said, smiling wistfully, because there is nobody left who can tell us.

Tom looked around, and he knew. He understood. Lying stark before him was the answer.

In between the gaping mouths of stone, the carefully constructed heavy stone frames, were entrances to ley-lines. Each one housed perfectly its own pool of light, its own shimmering gateway to ghostly travel. Beautiful strands of metallic light stretched out across the horizon in every direction, streams of golden and silver magic unfurling against a backdrop of green.

Doors.

Stonehenge was a set of *doors.*

"So this is what it's for," Tom whispered, eyes wide. Arthur chuckled.

"Of course," he said, matter-of-factly. "What else?"

"So . . ." Tom looked around, feeling a little awestruck. "Who made it?"

"The Druids did, to repay a favor to the Ghost World. The ley-lines were already there, they just made them all fancy with stone. History is not my strong point, and Mrs. Scruffles could probably have explained it better, but it had to do with helping them scare away villagers, or pillagers, or something. At least, that's what I was told."

Tom grinned, picturing the look on Mr. Hammond's face if he told him the real reason behind Stonehenge. Of course, he couldn't, and naturally, he wouldn't, but it made a nice thought; Tom Golden, the pupil, setting his history teacher straight.

As Tom got to his feet, he began to take in everything else around him. There were ghosts here, multitudes of ghosts, appearing and disappearing at a steady pace through the doorways. Some stood around, milling aimlessly, some grouped together and talked, some decided to wander off across the grass toward the gift shop and car park, and some looked worried, urgent, racing through the entrances, hurrying other ghosts along with them. . . . Nobody seemed to take much notice of Tom, which suited him just fine, as they all appeared to have something to do or somewhere to go.

Stonehenge had always looked fairly dull to Tom in photos. Seeing it with new eyes though, seeing it in person, made everything different. Each doorway was made of two huge pillars of stone, carrying the weight of a third one that rested across the top. The main doorways formed a large circle, although in places the stones had fallen, or been destroyed, leaving gaps. In the not-so-far distance, Tom could see the wire-mesh fence that kept Stonehenge tidied away from the rest of the world, and beyond that was a busy road. It seemed odd, to have such an ancient place tainted with wire, and pavement, and all things modern. That was something the postcards never showed.

Tom trailed his hands against the stonework of the door he had fallen through, feeling the coldness of the rock, the roughness against his skin, tracing with his fingertips the patches where moss grew, a distant smile on his lips. There was something so perfect, so right, about the clash of the heavy stonework with the delicate lights and colors of the ley-lines. As Tom was lost in his thoughts, a ghost dived out through the ley-line, a faint shimmer across the surface the only warning that someone was approaching. She looked briefly at Tom, smiled a smile that boasted too many teeth, and quickly darted across to an opposite point, vanishing as she plunged back into the waiting doorway.

"Incredible," Tom muttered. "Just . . . incredible. So this place is like a station?"

"Of sorts," Arthur agreed. "It's a place where lots of ley-lines converge, so you can change route here. That one there," he pointed at door in the distance, "will lead you straight to London, and that one goes all the way to John O'Groats. Some of them have broken over the years—the usual things, weather, wars, thieves—but the main doors still stand."

"And what about these ones?" Tom wandered toward some stones that stood apart from the rest, in the middle of the circle. In each case, the two main pillars were placed so closely together that the gap was too narrow to form a doorway. Light seeped out from between them, like when you leave a bedroom door ajar with the landing light on. The ley-line behind it still pulsed, as if desperate to escape its confines, but the heavy stones shut it away.

"Those doors are closed. Have been for a very long time . . . ," said Arthur, stepping warily away.

"Closed?" Tom asked, running his hands across the rough stones. Arthur made a yelping noise, and tugged Tom's sleeve, pulling his hand away.

"Closed, or sleeping, or waiting . . . There are some places that even ghosts are afraid to travel to. Or are afraid what will travel from them . . ." Arthur looked at the stones, and he couldn't help but shiver. "For now, they are closed. That's the way they are, and that's the way we are happy for them to stay. So no touching. Or loud noises. You have to behave yourself here, Tom."

Tom shrugged, hands safely tucked away in pockets, and stared hard at the thin band of shimmering colors that meshed the sealed entrance. Something stirred distantly, a faint outline amongst the chaos of lights, and Tom's breath caught.

"What? What is it? What did you do?" Arthur demanded, a touch of panic in his voice.

"Nothing! Nothing. I just . . . I thought I saw . . ." he stammered. He looked again at the closed ley-line, and everything was still. "It was nothing. Honestly." He turned quickly, walking away, all the while carrying an unnerving feeling that he was being watched. When he glanced back, there was still nothing there, just a slice of light wedged between rocks, but it was a long while until his pulse returned to normal. Arthur frowned, but said nothing more. He wandered across the center of the circle, weaving in and about the throng of ghosts, and Tom followed him.

Arthur stood in front of a ley-line that looked very much like every other, and nodded to Tom.

"This is the one we want. Are you ready to go?"

"Do I have a choice?" Tom asked. Grey Arthur grinned in response. "I didn't think so . . ."

And through the ley-line they plunged.

There's No Such Thing . . .

FACE PRESSED AGAINST THE CHICKEN WIRE FENCE THAT enclosed Stonehenge, young Nikki Ferguson from Tennessee in the United States of America stared hard at the distant stones, lost in thought, one hand clasping a cheap disposable camera. Her parents, distinctly less interested, stood by her side, Dad reloading his far fancier camera with a new film, and Mom regretting that she didn't pack warmer clothes for this sightseeing trip. It really wasn't that cold, for an English day, which is admittedly positively gloomy for a day anywhere else.

"I always imagined it to be bigger," Dad uttered, as he tried for the fifth time to get the new film to load up.

"Well, we are quite far away," replied Mom, blowing onto her hands, trying to force some heat back in.

"Honey, you didn't want to pay to go in. You said you can see it just as well from the side of the road, which is where we are. If you wanted to go in, you should have said."

"No, it's fine. We can see it okay from here. You can see it okay from here, can't you, Nikki?"

Nikki didn't respond. She simply stared, fingers from her free hand curled round the metal mesh.

"I just imagined it to be more . . . mystical. It just looks like a pile of stones," Dad whispered.

"Old stones."

"A pile of old, English stones." He laughed. "Well, it's another thing done from the list of Things to See When You Are in England, at least. Next is to visit a castle, and eat some jellied eels."

"I am *not* eating jellied eels," objected Nikki's mother.

"It's traditional," her dad replied.

"I don't give two hoots about traditional, there is no way on earth that *eels,* let alone *eels in jelly,* are going anywhere near my taste buds."

"But we're on vacation, you're supposed to be open to new ideas, to new experiences, to new . . ."

Nikki had mastered the art of tuning out her parents' conversations a long time ago. It was a talent she prided herself on. While they argued the nutritional and cultural merits of jellied eels, she was busy watching a boy in the middle of Stonehenge. He was sitting on the ground, head down, as if he was sick. After a while, he stood, and began wandering around, touching the stones, and seemingly talking to himself. Nikki watched with interest, taking photos all the while.

"Besides, I seem to recall you refusing to eat haggis when we were in Scotland."

"But that's different. That's *intestines*. I'm not asking you to eat *intestines*. I'm just suggesting that while we are here we take the opportunity . . ."

The boy approached a gap in the stones, took a deep breath, and leaped forward, disappearing in midair. Nikki's breath caught.

"Mom! Dad!" she gasped, eyes wide. The parents' conversation stopped, all attention turned to their daughter. "I think I just saw a ghost!"

Her parents shared an amused glance, each wearing quiet smiles.

"There's no such thing as ghosts, sweetie," they said, at the same time.

Nikki Ferguson looked back at the now empty Stonehenge, and she wasn't quite so sure.

Follow Your Nose

THE LEY-LINE SPAT TOM AND ARTHUR OUT AT THE OTHER side, and this time Tom managed to keep his balance, though he still felt giddy. Arthur twitched excitedly at his side.

"Ta da!" cried Grey Arthur, gesturing dramatically toward the Snorgle Museum.

Tom couldn't have looked less impressed if he tried.

"This is it?" he asked.

"You were expecting something a little grander?" Grey Arthur asked innocently.

"Maybe. Possibly. I didn't really know what to expect." Tom shook his head, staring at the museum before him. "If I'd thought it would be like this, though, I'd have brought some rubber gloves to wear."

Tom had been to several museums in his lifetime, some monstrously dull, such as the one that his mum had dragged him to that was dedicated to old shoes (Dad had quite wisely talked his way out of that trip), and some just indescribably amazing, like the one that boasted towering rooms filled with gigantic skeletons of dinosaurs—but this museum, this was something else all together. There were no grand roman pillars framing the entrance, no Ye Olde-style signs pointing the way, nothing about it that looked even vaguely museumlike. The building was dumped, unceremoniously, anonymously, at the end of a dank alleyway. Ugly, graffitied, vacant tower blocks enclosed it on every side, blocking out any hope it had of ever seeing daylight. In the distance, unseen, a busy road roared with relentless traffic, but here everything was still and abandoned.

A yellowing poster, its corners curling away from the wall, warned that the building was condemned. Tom wasn't even faintly surprised. He found it difficult to imagine this place, even in its heyday, as looking anything other than ugly and run-down, and that must have been the longest time ago. Small windows, some smashed, stared out glumly from the crumbling walls, films of grime rendering them almost black. A rotten door hung in place, held by one solitary, remaining hinge. Discarded rubbish piled steeply up against the walls—split bin liners, spewing waste out of their sides; fast food wrappers; cigarette packets; and even, rather bizarrely, an old sofa, propped against the wall, its material streaked with dirt, stuffing and springs jutting out from threadbare cushions. A plaque on the wall contained the words PUBLIC TOILETS, although this helpfully had a line marked through it, like a child scrawling out a mistake in their homework.

"It's an abandoned toilet," Tom said, as if Grey Arthur didn't already know. "You're absolutely sure this is the place?"

"Oh, definitely. Can't you smell it?"

Tom frowned, shaking his head. He inhaled deeply, frowned again, and took another pace forward, led by his nose. Smell it? Smell what? A few paces more . . .

And then it hit him. The rankest aroma, a mixture of damp dog, rotten eggs, boiled cabbage, neglected toilet, and a few other smells Tom had never encountered before and hoped to never encounter again, bowled into him. Instinctively he leaped two paces back, waving his hands in front of his face as if he could somehow fend off the haunting stench. This was definitely the right place.

"And you want me to go in there?" He gasped at Arthur, his eyes watering.

"Oh, come on, Tom. It's not that bad."

"It's every inch that bad, Arthur." Tom replied, pinching his nose. "This will never work."

"Don't say that, Tom," said Arthur with a sigh. "It's not like we have much choice."

An idea struck Tom, and he grinned suddenly.

Tom rummaged in his pockets as a bemused Grey Arthur watched on. Finding what he was after, he pulled out a strip of chewing gum, waving it at Arthur with a pleased smile. Grey Arthur just looked at him blankly, and Tom held up a finger to motion for him to watch. He crammed the chewing gum in his mouth, and chewed noisily. Then, with all the finesse of a magician showing off his finest trick, Tom pulled the chewing gum from his mouth, stretching it into a thick, minty strand. Arthur looked at him as if he was mad. Satisfied that his creation was ready, Tom turned his back to Arthur, and then spun round to face him again, a self-satisfied grin on his face. A peppermint chewing gum mustache clung to his top lip, hovering just below his nostrils.

Grey Arthur burst out laughing.

"You look *ridiculous!*"

"But it fills my nose with minty freshness, so I don't care," replied Tom with a grin.

Grey Arthur cringed but said nothing more. Humans can be so terribly stubborn when they put their minds to it. Instead, he smiled indulgently at his mint-mustache-wearing friend, and gestured toward the rickety door. Tom saluted (it felt appropriate with his new facial "hair") and marched into the Snorgle Museum. Grey Arthur paused just long enough to roll his eyes, and then took after Tom.

A Sculpture Emits a Thousand Smells

THEY FOUND A SNORGLE IN THE ENTRANCEWAY, snoring heavily, asleep in an old wooden chair. With the best will in the world, he was an ugly ghost, even by Snorgle standards. He was short, no more than three feet tall, with a little potbelly that spilled generously over the confines of ill-fitting boxer shorts. His toes (stubby, hairy toes) boasted thick, discolored toenails. His skin was the color of algae, and his long gangly arms twitched with each snore that shook his unevenly proportioned body. A large nose dominated his face, and his wide mouth gaped open in sleep, revealing small, blunt little teeth unevenly distributed inside. Tom and Grey Arthur stood for a while, unsure of the politest way to wake him. Tom decided in the end for a short, sharp, coughing noise, and the Snorgle woke up with a start. Bulbous fingers rubbed small eyes, trying to chase away the remnants of sleep. Tom and Arthur waved at him.

"Blimey, talk about giving a ghost a fright." The Snorgle sat up, straightening out the creases in his boxer shorts. "Welcome to the Snorgle Museum, and all that. You just caught me catching up on my beauty sleep." Tom nearly burst out laughing, but Arthur gave him a look, and Tom managed to hold it in. "If you've come for the guided tour, though, you're in for a disappointment. Museum's closed at the moment."

"Why is it closed?" Tom asked. The Snorgle peered up at Tom, studying him.

"Do you know you've got something stuck to your face?" he asked. Tom reddened slightly.

"He knows," Arthur replied.

"And he stinks of soap," said the Snorgle, not even attempting to hide his disgust. It was Arthur's turn to suppress a laugh.

"Yes, well, sorry about that. His mum makes him shower quite regularly." Tom turned bright crimson and glared at Arthur, who shrugged. "Well, it's true."

"But you didn't have to say it!" an embarrassed Tom muttered.

Arthur smiled apologetically at his blushing friend, and tried to steer the conversation back on track. "So you say the museum is closed?"

"Yeah, not enough ghosts visiting, something along those lines. Real shame, it is. No idea where they've all gone, but you know ghosts these days."

Tom and Arthur shared a knowing look. It was no wonder attendance was down, with so many ghosts vanishing. The Snorgle seemed oblivious to it all, though. He reclined back in his chair, picking something dubious out from his teeth. He studied it, shrugged, and popped it back in his mouth. Tom grimaced.

"I don't suppose there's any chance you could help us out, is there?" Arthur asked hopefully. "We've come here hoping to track down an old Snorgle. Thought here was a good a place as any to start."

"Well, I can give it a go, but can't see how I'd be able to help much. I'm only the caretaker." For the second time in as many minutes, Tom fought against laughing. For a caretaker, it seemed like this Snorgle couldn't care less. Cheese-and-onion crisp packets and assorted debris gathered in the corners, and more spiderwebs than Tom had ever seen in his life clung to the ceilings. But then, perhaps, this was how a Snorgle museum was meant to look. "So, who you looking for then?"

"Ahh. See, that's the problem. We don't know the name," answered Grey Arthur honestly.

"That's a cracking start." The Caretaker chuckled. "Got any more to go on?" Grey Arthur looked at Tom hopefully.

"He was short . . ." Tom said. The Caretaker rolled his eyes. "And it was a long time ago . . ." The Caretaker audibly sighed. "And he somehow managed to scare away the Collector."

"Now we're getting somewhere!" The Caretaker

leaped down from the chair, and grinned impishly at Tom and Grey Arthur. "You mean Stinklebert? Nice to see someone with an interest in the old Snorgle legends. I suppose I can open up for you, as long as you promise to behave?" Tom and Arthur nodded enthusiastically, and the Snorgle grunted as he rummaged for his key. "Come on then, you two. Got something in here that might interest you . . ."

He waddled forward, his fat, flat feet scuffing their way through the dirt. He led them to a large set of old doors, which he carefully unlocked (though he did have to stand on tiptoe to reach). With a terrific effort the Caretaker pushed the heavy doors wide open.

"After you," he said, gesturing inside. Tom wandered through, and then stopped, dead in his tracks, amazed at what he saw.

The hall was deceptively large, and filled with glass casings buried under dust, framed pictures held behind cracked glass, and strange shapes draped with discolored, mud-splattered sheets. Toilets were still plumbed into the walls, and signs above them listed the many Snorgles that had haunted each one—Grelch Gruntington, Pobble the Wiffy, and Blech just some of the visible names. For reasons of historical accuracy, or laziness, or maybe deliberate intent, the toilets remained every bit as filthy as the day they were last in use. And the smell! Tom pressed his minty mustache against his face, and was grateful for its presence. The room smelled genuinely appalling. It was almost enough to make Tom flee, even with the aid of his gum, but curiosity and necessity forced him to venture inside.

Tom strolled from spot to spot, hands smearing windows in the grime to see the contents of display cabinets. One contained nothing but cheeses in various stages of decomposition. A rusty plaque beneath labeled it SMELLY CHEESES OF THE WORLD. A painting on the wall, seemingly done by smearing mud on canvas, was said to carry a likeness to "King Aromaticus." Tom wandered around, lost in a cross between admiration and horror.

"I hope you appreciate this. It's bad enough you bring a human here, but a freshly washed one?" whispered the Caretaker to Grey Arthur as they watched Tom traveling the room. Arthur grinned. "Don't know how you put up with it. It's going to take me ages to shift the smell."

"So where am I meant to be looking?" called Tom.

The Caretaker strolled purposely across the room, and halted in front of one of the weird shapes smothered with a sheet. He grasped a corner, and gave it a firm tug. The sheet fell away, revealing a statue beneath it. A statue that seemed to be carved entirely from mold. Tom had no idea what the mold was growing on—cheese, perhaps?—but maybe some things are best left unknown. It was a small Snorgle, and, given the unorthodox material it was carved from, not a bad likeness. The little ghost was standing triumphantly, one scrawny arm raised in a victory salute. Tom gasped, immediately recognizing him from Sorrow Jane's vision.

"That's him, Arthur! That's the one!"

"Stinklebert the Malodorous. Legend has it that he was one of the few ghosts known to have seen the Collector, and survived to tell the tale," the Caretaker said proudly. "It's a nice little statue, eh? You know what they say, about a picture painting a thousand words and all? Well, it's kind of a Snorgle tradition, to make a statue that, you know, embodies the essence of the ghost. You smell that, and that's exactly what the little blighter would have smelled like. Allegedly. Never met him myself, he stopped existing a good few years before I came to be, but I have it on good authority that it's a very good smellness. You're inhaling a bit of history there."

Tom dearly wished he wasn't, but was too polite to say otherwise. He studied the statue, and saw that the figure of Stinklebert was clutching something. His fat Snorgle fingers were firmly gripping a mirror, also modeled from mold (with silver foil to make the reflective face). Tom grinned at Arthur, eyes wide.

"So now we know," Arthur said, understanding. "It was a mirror."

"Still doesn't help us find *him,* though." Tom stopped short of saying *the Collector,* but Grey Arthur knew what Tom meant. Arthur bit his lip, thinking furiously. Tom was right. They'd found out what the Collector's weakness was, but they were still no closer to finding the Collector himself. With ghost disappearing at a rate of knots, and Tom's parents only away for the weekend, they couldn't afford to just sit around and wait for him to find them. "So now what?"

A polite coughing—well, as polite a sound as a Snorgle can possibly make—interrupted Tom and Arthur. The Caretaker smiled at them. "Now, I couldn't help but overhear your conversation, being as you were right in front of me when you said it. Now, I'm not making any promises, and I really don't even want to know what you two are up to—any business of a ghost that chooses a human as a companion is business I'm well clear of—BUT . . . I know a ghost that might be able to help you. She comes in here a fair bit, when it's open. She's, ahh, well, she's *different,* put it that way."

The Caretaker leaned in and said to Arthur in an aside, "She's one of those Contrary types." Grey Arthur nodded, and Tom just looked confused.

"Anyway, she lives not far from here. I can give you directions if you like, but there's one condition." The Caretaker paused dramatically, making sure he had Tom and Arthur's full attention. "Don't be too . . . horrified . . . by her. She can be a real shock when you first see her, but deep down, she's not a bad sort."

Tom glanced anxiously at Arthur, and Arthur shrugged.

"We promise," said Arthur. The Caretaker looked at the worried expression on Tom's face, and then looked back at Arthur. "He promises too." The Snorgle

Caretaker nodded, satisfied, and began reeling off a list of directions. Arthur concentrated on remembering them all, while Tom stared off into the distance, his face creased with fretting. If a ghost looks so horrific that a Snorgle has to warn you about it, then it has to be very bad indeed.

"Well, this should be interesting . . . ," Tom muttered to himself.

Almost Too Much to Bear

THE CARETAKER, ON ARTHUR'S INSISTENCE, HAD locked the door behind them (not that they were sure it would do any good), and they left him to the delicate business of dehumanizing the museum. He'd been opening packets of cheese-and-onion crisps when they'd departed, and putting them around the place like grandmothers do with potpourri. Arthur led the way, and Tom distracted himself by peeling away his mint mustache. Down the alleyway, a left at the ley-line, cross the road by the burned-out building, a turn, another . . .

It didn't take long to find the ghost they were looking for. She was, by all accounts, rather hard to miss.

She was sitting on the only patch of grass for miles around, humming to herself, making a daisy chain. Tall, grey, bland blocks of flats that jutted up all around where she was sitting only served to accentuate the defiant little refuge of greenery. There was no litter, no dog mess, no cigarette butts. . . . It was like someone had cut out a little patch of the countryside, and planted it in the last possible place you'd expect to find it, and there, in the middle, like the cherry on the cake, she was.

She looked like a Snorgle, with the same little potbelly, the same knobbly knees, but she was the most delicate shade of lilac. Her nose, while as broad as a conventional Snorgle's, ended in a sweet little snub. She wore a frilly dress, instead of crisp packets or shopping bags, and it was decorated with tiny little embroidered flowers. Around her neck hung a necklace of petals. Shiny pink patent shoes with just a hint of a heel hid away the ugliness of Snorgle toes. As they approached, Tom realized that she smelled most distinctly un-Snorgley. A gentle breeze carried to them the undeniable scent of roses, and freshly washed clothes, and the type of perfume that mums wear on special nights out.

Tom and Arthur walked up behind her, and she didn't even notice, lost in girly thoughts as she plucked flowers out of the grass, counting the petals on each.

"Hello?" called Tom, and the little ghost jumped, the flowers tumbling free from her hands. She turned to look at them, a cute little frown on her face.

"You shouldn't go creeping up on ghosts. You made me jump. Now I'll have to start all over again." She sniffed, gathering the flowers back up. Up close, there was something almost unbearably adorable about her, and Tom struggled to think what it reminded him of. And then it suddenly occurred to him what it was.

Tom remembered a time when his parents had taken him out for a birthday meal at a pizza restaurant. The dessert had been self-service, and Tom had stacked his bowl-sky high with ice cream, sprinkles, chocolate chips, glacier cherries, sticky sauces, jelly sweets, fudge pieces, toffee crumble, and anything else he could lay his hands on. The result, far from being his dream dessert, had left him nearly paralyzed with nausea, and his dad had had to actually carry him out to the car while he moaned and clutched his stomach.

Looking at this little Snorgle felt like a very similar experience.

She was almost too sweet, too cute, too over-whelmingly *nice*. And yet, somehow, you couldn't stop looking. Tom's mouth ached from grinning at her. The little Snorgle noticed the way Tom was smiling goofily at her, and she looked quizzically at Grey Arthur.

"I'm sorry about him. He's a human, so you have to forgive him," said Arthur. He glared at Tom, but Tom was oblivious. "The Caretaker from the Snorgle Museum said we could find you here. We need your help."

The lilac ghost got to her feet and gave a little curtsy.

"Well, in that case, let's start again. Miss Lilly. Pleased to meet you." She sat back down again, cross-legged, and Tom and Arthur followed suit. The grass was surprisingly spongy and soft. "I don't know what it is I can help you with, though. Unless you want a daisy chain?"

Grey Arthur looked over at Tom, hoping he would explain why they were there, but Tom was just grinning, and sniffing Miss Lilly when he thought she wasn't looking. Arthur sighed. "He seemed to think you might know some ghosts that could help us. We've lost our friends. We know what's going on, we know what's taken them, but now we need to work out how to get them back. And to do that, we need to find the Collector."

"How horribly serious." Her nose creased up with disgust. Tom and Arthur were expecting a stronger response than that, but Miss Lilly seemed far more pre-occupied with playing with her bunch of flowers. "I think I know what the Caretaker meant, though. He's talking about the other Contraries." Lilly gave a flower to Arthur, who dutifully put it in his buttonhole. "Freddie there should be able to help you—if anyone can find anything, it's Lost and Found Freddie."

Tom finally discovered his voice, which was a welcome relief from his moronic grinning. "What's a Contrary then?"

"I'm a Contrary. Freddie's a Contrary. It's like a social group for ghosts that don't do what other ghosts expect us to do. Ghosts can be so cruel sometimes. If you're a Snorgle that smells, well, lovely, if I do say so myself." Tom nodded in silent agreement. "Or a Sadness Summoner that would much prefer to make people happy, then you're seen as a Contrary. It can be lonely sometimes, when you're different. So we stick together. They hold meetings every week. Should be one tomorrow."

"And where is this meeting?" Arthur asked. Miss Lilly shrugged.

"It changes every week. It has to. Some ghosts can be very . . . intolerant . . . of us. They see us as freaks, or an embarrassment to their ghostly type. Silly really. There's enough space for all of us in the world, don't you think?"

Arthur nodded, understanding. He knew what it was like to not fit in. Before he'd found Tom, before he'd realized he could be an Invisible Friend, he'd felt so very alone, and there was no loneliness deeper than being surrounded by ghosts when you just don't belong. Tom understood as well. Sometimes ghosts and humans weren't as different as they seemed.

"So how do we find out where it is?" Tom asked. Miss Lilly smiled.

"Lost and Found Freddie is the chairman of the Contraries. He puts out cards all over the country, telling you where to go. You just have to find one."

"And so where do we look?" Arthur asked. Lilly giggled.

"Where do you look when you need to find any-thing?" Lilly asked. Tom and Arthur looked at each other blankly. Lilly rolled her eyes. "Down the back of the settee, of course."

Of course. How could they not have guessed?

They escorted Miss Lilly back to the museum (she had a horribly cute habit of skipping, instead of walking, and singing to herself while she did so), and the Caretaker let her inside for safekeeping. Tom was quite happy to see her go, as it meant he could finally stop smiling. He felt like he needed to watch a game of rugby, or play a fighting game on the computer, just to purge all the cuteness from him.

"Ready to head home?" Arthur asked, nudging his head toward the waiting ley-line.

"Ready as I'll ever be," Tom replied.

Standing Room Only

"OH . . . GOOD . . . GRIEF!" TOM GASPED AS HE STARED at his home, slack jawed, eyes wide.

Madness bubbled within the confines of the Golden home, spilling out the front door and into the garden. Shadows seemed to seep from the brickwork, a testament to the number of Screamers that had taken up residence inside. The pretty garden, with its patch of grass and its mundane shrubbery, was crowded with all manner of supernatural creatures. The lace curtains twitched as eyes, sometimes far too many eyes, peered out from inside. Even from where Tom was standing, the sound of chains being rattled, of low, melancholic wailing, of ear-piercing screams, seemed deafening.

"Well, you did say to bring the ghosts here if they had no where else to go . . . ," Arthur said, although even he was surprised by just how many ghosts had taken up the offer. There were ghosts sitting on the roof, hanging out the windows, milling in the doorway. A group of Thespers was arguing in the front garden over which one of them was the most dramatic. The sun was setting, and in the long shadows that stretched from the house Screamers lurked, looking mildly out of place amongst Mum's prized begonias.

"Welcome to England's most haunted home . . . ," Tom said, more to himself than anyone else. Arthur laughed. Tom didn't. He just kept shutting his eyes, and shaking his head, hoping that when he looked again, everything would be normal. It wasn't. It was so far from normal that you couldn't even see normal through the Hubble telescope. A Headless leaped in front of Tom, threw his head in through the top window, and then dashed inside to reclaim it. A Sadness Summoner kept on touching Mum's flowers while crying, and each one she touched would wither and wilt. Tom had to shout at her to stop, and she looked most put out. Tom half expected all the neighbors to be outside, lining the street, demanding to know what was going on, but luckily everyone who lived on Aubergine Road seemed to be oblivious to its new ghostly residents. Tom half wished he was in the same position. It was quite positively the weirdest thing, to see such a mass haunt-ing in his own little home. He'd suspected a few ghosts might have taken him up on his offer, but not this many. . . .

Tom took a deep breath, and made his way through the garden, and nobody even seemed to pay much attention to him.

"Excuse me . . . Coming through . . . Mind the way . . . ," he muttered, weaving a path through the throng of ghosts, with Arthur at his side, who was busy waving cheerfully at familiar faces. The front door was open, and Tom and Arthur edged their way through the lounge. The TV was blaring, the volume cranked all the way up to maximum, and ghosts were piled on the settee, and taking up every inch of floor space. There were Thespers, Sadness Summoners, Poltergeists, every ghost under the sun and a few that Tom didn't even recognize, perched in the distinctly unghostly setting of magnolia wallpaper, school photos, and Dad's collection of *Your Feet Weekly* magazines. All of the ghosts were staring, transfixed, at the television.

"EXCEEDINGLY HAUNTED HOMES OF ENGLAND," flashed the opening sequence, and a big cheer went up from the ghostly crowd. The scene opened to a nerv-ous-looking presenter, standing in the great hall of a mansion. It was dark, and she held a candle, the light flickering on her face. Next to her stood a stocky, wire-haired man, who was sniffing the air and grimacing.

Subtitles flashed up beneath—MAXWELL MABBUTT—
WORLD-FAMOUS PSYCHIC. The ghosts burst out laughing, pointing at the screen. Maxwell Mabbutt, *alleged*
world-famous psychic, took in a deep breath, and
began humming. The ghosts laughed louder.

"Can you . . . *sense* . . . anything?" the presenter
asked, looking around fearfully. Maxwell held up a finger, signaling for her to be quiet.

"There is . . . a dark presence here. Foul, it is. Evil!
It's evil!" He wailed dramatically. The presenter gasped,
and visibly paled. The ghosts were near screaming with
laughter now. "Why are you here, oh spirit? Begone!"
he intoned. "BEGONE!"

The camera panned out to where Maxwell was signaling the ghost was, and there was nothing there.
Suddenly, from out of nowhere, a small Poltergeist ran
on screen, mooned the camera, and darted away again.
That was it. That was all it took. All the ghosts in the
lounge fell to absolute pieces, one laughing so much
that he actually retched, a splodge of ectoplasm falling
out onto Tom's carpet, which caused all the other
ghosts to laugh even harder.

Tom switched the television off, and a universal
noise of displeasure came from all the ghosts.

"Come on, shift off the settee. We need to look
down the back of it." Tom was standing in front of the
telly, hands on his hips, with Arthur grinning apologetically at his side. "If you really have to watch it, there's
a TV up in my room as well." As soon as he said that,

the ghosts were up and moving, floating through the ceiling to resume their viewing.

"Nicely done," Arthur said. Tom nodded, dreading to imagine what state he'd find his bedroom in. He was going to have a whole lot of tidying up to do before Mum and Dad got home.

"Okay then," he said, staring at the settee before him. "Let's get looking."

The Secrets That Lurk Down the Back of Settees

"FOUND ANYTHING?" ASKED GREY ARTHUR HOPEFULLY, as Tom groped around down the back of the settee, his entire arm swallowed up behind the cushions.

"Not yet, give me a tic," muttered Tom, his face furrowed in concentration. He pulled out his arm, revealing a fistful of fluff, a hairband, a five-pence coin, and a solitary, old-looking peanut. He grimaced. "This is disgusting. Can't you do it? You know, go all ghosty arm and have a look for this card?"

"I could do," agreed Arthur, nodding with a smile. "But it's much more fun to watch you do it."

Tom sighed, and thrust his arm back down the side of the settee. "Yuck, yuck, yuck . . . ," he muttered, as he rummaged about. His fingers found something sticky, and he quickly decided to search a different area. Crumbs . . . crumbs . . . toffee? Pen . . . coin . . . "Wait, wait, here we go. . . ." Tom pulled his arm back out, and clamped between his fingers was a business card. He blew the fluff and crumbs off it, and showed it to Arthur.

L. F. Freddie—
official secretary of the
Contrary Ghosts Association (CGA).
Meetings held every Saturday at twelve noon.
This week's meeting at Pebblebeach
Village Hall, Biddeltown.
If you wish to contact me, simply leave your
correspondence down the back of the settee,
and I will find it.
CGA—
Embracing ghosts of every Contrary disposition!

"They meet in a Village Hall?" asked Tom. "That's not very ghostly."

"The Contraries are . . . different," said Arthur diplomatically. "What's the time now?"

Tom glanced at his watch. "Wow. It's late. I'd best give Mum and Dad a ring."

Tom grabbed the phone away from a Thesper, who was in the process of dialing an exceedingly long number, and after holing himself away back in the lounge, he dialed Grandma Green.

Tom hated lying to his Mum and Dad, and he would have loved more than anything to tell them the truth about what he'd been up to, and maybe one day he'd be able to, but today was not that day. Even if Dad was beginning to come round to the idea that Tom could see ghosts, Tom was sure he wasn't quite ready to hear every weird detail of it, and Mum, well, Mum was a long way from ready to hear about Snorgle museums, Contrary ghosts, and the secrets that lurk down the back of settees. So Tom lied, and he hated every second of it.

"Yes, Mum, I'm having a lovely time . . . Mildred loved the card, thank you. . . . No, we won't stay up too late—in fact, I'm going to bed soon. . . . Yes, it has been a long day. . . . Of course I am behaving myself. . . . Yes, I'll call you again tomorrow. . . . Okay . . . Okay . . . Okay . . . Good night, Mum." He hung up the phone, and rubbed his eyes tiredly.

"What do you think the chances of getting a good night's sleep before tomorrow are?" he asked Arthur. Arthur tilted his head, listening to the sound of ghostly laughter and screaming coming through the ceiling. He shrugged, and Tom sighed.

"Okay, you go clear the bedroom of as many ghosts as you can, and tell the other Invisible Friends everything we've found out today. I'm going to get myself a glass of milk, and get ready to go to bed." Arthur nodded, and dashed up the stairs. As Tom wandered into the kitchen, he found the Red Rascal, sitting on the counter, telling an enthralled group of Poltergeists about the time he stole a hut from under Dr. Brown's nose, and by doing so whisked Tom to safety. He waved cheerily at Tom, and continued his tale.

"So there I was, crawling out of the smallest laundry basket, into this hut in the middle of Duskridge Woods." His familiar voice boomed. "And I see Tom Golden, He-Who-Can-See-Ghosts, hands tied with rope, in the middle of the room. Well, what's a Poltergeist to do? So, naturally, I . . ."

Tom poured himself a glass of milk, and slowly sipped it, the deep, dramatic voice of the Red Rascal roaring in the background. This was going to be one *long* night.

Where the Opposite Is the Norm

IT TOOK FOREVER TO GET TO SLEEP. IF IT WASN'T A Poltergeist trying to sift through Tom's laundry when he thought Tom was snoozing, then it was the Screamers trying to out-howl each other, or Thespers trying to upstage each other on the landing. The trainee Invisible Friends were very good, ushering the ghosts out of the room, telling them to be quiet, and it made Tom feel quite proud—well, in between feeling grumpy and tired. Eventually, despite all the noise, and the commotion, Tom managed to fall asleep.

He dreamed he was hurtling through a ley-line, the world screaming past, indistinct and blurry, and at the end of it waited Ballpoint Bill, and Mrs. Scruffles, and all the other ghosts who had vanished, each of them full of smiles and happy endings.

It was a good dream to have.

Morning came far too soon. Tom got woken up by a very young Faintly Real, who was peering at Tom's face, watching him sleep, and then trying to imitate the way Tom snored. He heard Grey Arthur from beneath the bed, telling the ghost to leave Tom alone, but by then Tom was already awake. He rubbed his eyes sleepily, and the Faintly Real copied him.

"That could get annoying," muttered Tom, sitting up.

"That could get annoying," repeated the Faintly Real, imitating the exact way Tom had said it.

"Arthur!" moaned Tom.

"Arthur!" said the Faintly Real.

"It's okay, Tom. I'm on it." Grey Arthur crawled out from beneath the bed, and grabbed the Faintly Real by the elbow, leading him away. The little ghost kept looking back over his shoulder, his transparent face mirroring the bleary frown on Tom's, and Arthur put him out onto the landing, and shut the door behind him. Not that shutting a door would keep most ghosts out, but at least it prevented Tom from seeing the Headless bowling competition taking place on the landing.

"What's the time?" asked Tom, rubbing the sleep from his eyes. Arthur glanced up at the clock on the wall.

"Eleven o'clock," he replied.

Eleven? Tom hadn't realized he'd slept in so late. He must have been exhausted. He leaped out of bed, forcing himself to wake up, slapping his cheeks to drive away the sleep.

"I'd best get ready then. Big day today," he said.

"The biggest," agreed Arthur.

If you should ever need to get dressed in a hurry, it's probably best to not live in a haunted house. There were three Screamers crowded into the shower, taking advantage of the acoustics to practice their haunting shrieks. The kitchen was so crowded that Tom could barely see the other side (and that's even taking into account the see-through nature of ghosts), let alone reach the fridge without having to walk through far more spooks than he would have liked. Woeful William was reciting poetry in the under-stairs cupboard to a group of very depressed-looking blue ghosts, and Montague was talking in a very loud voice in the lounge about the great new role that he had undertaken as an Invisible Friend, in between signing autographs. Tike was hanging out with a group of young-looking ghosts, and telling them some rather colorful jokes. Mildred trotted up to Tom, having carefully and lovingly prepared him breakfast. Two slices of burnt toast (Tike had obviously been fiddling with the toaster settings again) floated absurdly in a mixing bowl full of milk, with little lumps of Mr. Space Pirate Hoops bobbing around the edges.

"I know you like cereal, and I know you like toast, so it occurred to me that what you would like most is the two together," she said, odd-colored eyes fixed on him, pushing the bowl toward his face. Tom had smiled gratefully, taking the bizarre concoction away, and when Mildred's back was turned, he quickly poured it all away into the kitchen bin, nearly drowning the Snorgle who was sleeping in there. All this madness, especially first thing in the morning, was a little hard to bear. In the end, Tom had sneaked out into the shed to get changed, turfing the Harrowing Screamer out into the back garden. Finally dressed, and running more than a little bit late, Arthur and Tom slipped out the door, grateful to leave all the chaos behind, and wandered back to the local ley-line. A turn this way, a turn that way, another jog down dog-mess alley, and there they were.

Tom saw the ley-line immediately this time, bristling with energy, bursting with shimmering colors, waiting for its next passengers. It even seemed to glow brighter as it saw them approach. No time to hesitate, no time to slowly edge your way forward, this time Tom just closed his eyes, and ran straight toward the entrance.

Tom was convinced he'd never get used to riding the ley-lines. It didn't seem to phase Grey Arthur at all, who appeared to actually quite enjoy the sensation, but Tom got the distinct impression that humans simply weren't designed for this kind of travel. Colors hurtled through, fragments of noises, snippets of rushed-past conversations, smells tumbling in and then out of reach, and all the while the ground flowed underneath Tom's feet like a fast river. If Tom looked down he always felt instantly sick, so he either looked straight ahead, or closed his eyes and hummed to block out the sounds. Ley-line travel is fast, but it still felt like an eternity to Tom before the ground stopped moving, and the ley-line spat him out at their destination. The weirdest thing was that they didn't go as far as Stonehenge this time—the ley-line had thrown Tom and Arthur off early. It was almost as if it knew where they needed to go, and acted accordingly.

"That was fun." Arthur laughed as they tumbled out of the ley-line to the ground. Tom didn't respond. He was waiting for his head to stop spinning. "Come on Tom, no time to stand around. We've got some Contraries to meet."

Tom grumbled, but begrudgingly started following Arthur, who was already halfway down the street. At first his feet refused to go in a straight line, still all tangled up with dizziness, and he staggered from side to side as he tried to keep up, but soon he managed to shake it off. They'd arrived in a sweet little rural village, bursting with tiny thatched cottages, all boasting gardens laden with rosebushes, and lavender, and creeping ivy. The roads were quiet, not a car in sight, and the only sound to be heard were birds singing, and bees buzzing. An old English phone box stood proudly on the corner of the street, wearing its rich red paint with dignity and without a sign of a smashed window anywhere. Phone boxes from Tom's area looked very different indeed, and probably smelled it for that matter.

"Come on, slow-poke!" yelled Arthur, and Tom picked up the pace. They trotted round the corner with the red phone box on it, and came to face the Village Hall. It sat on the edge of a large field, and people were playing cricket on the grass, throwing Frisbees, walking dogs, doing whatever it is people do on big patches of rolling green. A children's playground nestled in the corner of the scene, and Tom noted with surprise (and a pang of envy) that all the slides, and rides, and round-abouts were still in working order. No, it was better than that, still in *pristine condition*. Brightly colored paint, laughing children, parents pushing their kids on the swing; it felt like the ley-line had spat them out not just far away, but into an entirely different world. The park near Tom had rusty swings that could throw you loose over a ground of gravel, cigarette butts and bro-ken glass. The bins overflowed with beer cans, and bottles. Someone had ripped the basketball hoops off the walls, and everyone knew there was no point in replacing them. Scorched patches of ground bore testament to where stolen vehicles had been set alight. Something inside Tom felt spiky and hot, seeing this Through-the-Looking-Glass version of what a park could be. Arthur noticed Tom's expression, and tugged at his sleeve, dragging his attention away from the park, and back to the Village Hall.

It was all neatly painted, with baskets of hanging flowers outside, and posters advertising an upcoming church fair carefully pinned to the doors. Tom smiled, imagining the building alive with rummage sales, and knitting circles, and old people dancing to old music. It just had that look. The entrance was left slightly open. Tom, still feeling a little out of breath, gestured to Arthur.

"After you."

And in they went.

C.G.A.

"And that about sums it up for this week's meeting of the . . ." The speaker stopped short as Tom and Grey Arthur wandered into the Village Hall. Everybody stared at the two visitors and, to be fair, Tom and Arthur stared back. It was certainly a strange sight, nestled in amongst the children's portrait that adorned the walls, a gilded framed portrait of the Queen, and pictures of boy scouts on their latest camping trip . . .

A circle of wooden chairs stood at the center of the room, and while many of the seats were empty, the ones that were filled held some of the more outlandish creatures Tom had ever seen (and by now, he was considering himself quite an expert on all things odd). The speaker, who was standing in the center of the chairs, had to be L. F. Freddie. He was a short ghost with ruffled, greying hair, and a friendly smile. Around his neck was a length of string, and hanging from that string were multitudes of keys: different sizes and shapes, some modern, some shiny, some old, some intricate, rusted-iron creations, each one subtly or strikingly different from the key next to it. Beneath that length of string hung another, this one holding rings: engagement rings, wedding rings, plastic rings from Christmas crackers, big fat bands of gold, thin delicate strips of silver, jewels of every different color. It looked as if the weight from these keys and rings alone would be enough to cause a normal person to buckle under it all, or at the very least, get a crick in the neck, but L. F. Freddie carried them with ease. He wore a large, baggy coat, the kind detectives do in old movies, and his shoes were scuffed. He looked at the two newcomers, raising a greying eyebrow quizzically. "And who do we have here?"

"Grey Arthur, at your service," said Arthur, bobbing his head in greeting. "And this is my friend, Tom Golden."

"*The* Tom Golden?" asked Freddie.

"The Tom Golden," replied Tom, a little embarrassed. Being a celebrity, even if it was only in the Ghost World, felt really odd. There was a murmur of noise from the other ghosts gathered, who all started to straighten their heads, and rearrange their limbs where appropriate. "But I prefer just to be called Tom. If that's all right with you."

Freddie nodded warmly.

"Tom it is then. Come in, come in, close the door, you're letting in a draft." Tom and Arthur shuffled farther inside the hall, pulling the door shut behind them. Tom waved nervously at all the eyes that were fixed on him. "Well, I suppose fair's fair, we know your names, so it's only right that you're introduced to everybody here. I'm L. F. Freddie, reverse Poltergeist, finder of all things lost, restorer of all things missing, and also secretary of the CGA. This is our chairman, the Calming Whisperer, but most people just call him Carl."

The Calming Whisperer was a Screamer, but instead of having the usual shadow-dark skin, his was lighter, dusty grey, like bonfire smoke, or grandma's hair. Tinted glasses hid the foggy eyes, and his claws looked distinctly pedicured. Hippy beads gathered at his scrawny wrists, and his taloned feet had been crammed inside some sandals. He waved amiably across the room.

"This is Henry, he's relatively new. Just been with us a couple weeks."

L. F. Freddie gestured to a very normal-looking ghost sitting in a chair—well, normal by ghost standards— slightly see-through, rather pale, but a distinctly person-shaped and person-sized ghost.

"And you are a Contrary . . . ?" asked Tom, waiting for Henry to fill in the description. Henry huffed.

"Headless. See. Look. I have a head." He tugged on it for effect. It didn't detach. "How can I be a Headless if I have a head?"

"Maybe you're just a normal ghost?" mused Arthur, and L. F. Freddie shot him a look that said, "Best not go down that route." It would appear that conversation had been had many times, and so far Henry was insisting he was Henry With-Head, and that was that.

"This is Silence Sally, the world's only Feather-Boa Rattler (apparently she went off chains in the 1920s, and hasn't looked back). There's Introverted Ian hiding in the corner over there (used to be a Thesper until a terrible incident during the Hundred Years War—won't talk about it at all, but now he positively hates the lime-light). I'm afraid we've got quite a few people missing tonight—the numbers just keep on dwindling away. This is Miss Lilly . . ."

"We've met," she said, waving cheerily at Tom and Arthur. Her little lilac feet didn't reach the ground from the chair she was sitting on, and her pink, shiny shoes swung back and forth. Tom and Arthur grinned at her. "Managed to find it okay then?" she asked. Tom nodded, and Freddie continued.

"And last, but not least, this is Vincent Dali, our very own Faintly Surreal."

A bundle of noses and eyes in the corner chair winked at Tom, and a detached hand from somewhere near the bottom of the pile waved. This creature had quite a few hands, scattered around the place, more ears than were strictly necessary, and no discernible mouth, although there were several chins in a row where a mouth maybe could have gone. Possibly. It really was hard to tell.

"We've always got space in our ranks for a new Contrary, and I suppose a human who can see ghosts definitely fits the bill. I assume that's why you're here?"

"Lilly didn't tell you?" Arthur asked. Lilly smiled sweetly, shaking her head.

"All far too serious for me. I thought I'd leave that to you." She leaned over, and began tying a daisy chain around one of Vincent Dali's many wrists. A couple mouths smiled appreciatively. Tom sighed. It felt like they had been over this so many times now, and he hated having to repeat himself.

"It's a long story, but basically, we need you to find something for us," Tom said, scrimping on the details. Freddie nodded thoughtfully.

"Say no more. I know exactly what you're after. We're just about done here, and so if you follow me to my place, I'll sort it out for you." Freddie turned and faced the rest of the ghosts. "So, that's it for today. Meeting the same time next week. Don't forget to look out for the card to find out where we will be. And . . . take care of yourselves. There's something funny going on in the Ghost World at the moment, and so we don't want you taking any unnecessary chances." He busied himself about, shaking hands, saying good-bye to everyone, while Tom and Arthur just stood by, waiting. Shaking all of the Faintly Surreal's hands took a rather long time.

"So where is Freddie taking us now? To his house?" asked Tom in a low voice. Arthur shrugged.

"Not my house . . . no." Freddie had overheard, and wandered back over to where Tom and Arthur were. "You'll see. But it's a long old trek from here. I'm not quite sure how we're going to go about it."

"Oh, that's okay. Tom can ley-line," replied Arthur proudly. L. F. Freddie looked at Tom in surprise.

"He can? Well, that's perfect then. There's a line just around the corner that will drop us pretty much right on the door."

Another ley-line. Tom's heart sank, but he put on a brave face. "What are we waiting for?" he said cheerily.

"That's the spirit!" said Freddie, leading the way. His keys jangled noisily as he walked, and his baggy grey coat, which was just that little bit too long for him, trailed behind him on the ground. Tom and Arthur, after waving good-bye to all the other Contraries, and Miss Lilly in particular, followed him out the door.

Mind the Gap

To say Tom was surprised at where the latest ley-line had dropped them off would be an understatement. . . . They staggered to a halt in a large stone archway, and immediately the sounds of central London roared into place. A woman dragging a large suitcase stared at Tom in shock as he appeared in front of her, and she shook her head, as if trying to make sense of it, and then simply steered around him, muttering about him creeping up on her. Tom apologized, every bit as shocked as she was.

"Here we are," said Freddie, waiting for Tom and Arthur to catch their bearings. They looked around, open mouthed, taking it all in.

London's Victoria Station was buzzing with life. Businessmen, businesswomen, tramps, families, teenagers with wild hair and wilder clothes, people from all different walks of life gathered and milled, wandered or stood, lost in thoughts of the day gone by or the complex art of working out when their train would be arriving. The air was cluttered with noise and smells: mobile phones ringing, chatter, newspaper vendors shouting headlines, the aroma of warm pretzels mingling with that of cooking burgers, the delicate hint of flowers from the flower stall occasionally overwhelmed by trails of cigarette smoke. It reminded Tom of a human version of Stonehenge, only with more people drinking coffee from cardboard cups.

"Stay close," informed Freddie, authoritatively. "It's very easy to get lost or separated here. Ready?"

Grey Arthur nodded, eyes wide, a look of wonder on his face. He'd never been to Victoria Station before. "This place is *busy*," he breathed.

"Always is," L. F. Freddie said, toying absentmindedly with his necklace of keys. "You should be glad it's not rush hour. Makes this look tame. Come on, it's over this way, between platforms seven and eight."

Freddie began working his way through the station with the practiced ease of someone used to navigating through crowds. Grey Arthur and Tom didn't find it quite so easy, Tom especially being at a disadvantage due to the fact that he couldn't simply walk *through* people who got in his way.

"Sorry . . . Sorry . . . Excuse me . . . Coming through . . . Excuse me . . . Sorry . . ."

Determinedly, the three pushed forward, ducking between gaps, avoiding elbows, narrowly missing the widespread newspapers held aloft by people trying to kill time.

"Not far now!" called L. F. Freddie, surging forward, his collection of keys and rings jangling like the bell on a cat's collar. Both Arthur and Tom picked up the pace, as best they could, but going anywhere fast in Victoria Station is about as easy as going anywhere slowly on a roller coaster.

A hand grabbed Tom's shoulder, making him jump, and it forced him to stop. He spun round, and came face to face with a train guard. Tom smiled nervously. She leaned forward, looking concerned. She was large woman with rosy cheeks, and she frowned as she talked.

"Are you lost?" she asked, glancing around Tom. "Where are your parents?"

"No, I'm not lost, I'm here with—" Tom caught himself, and ground to a halt. I'm here with two ghosts? Not the best answer to give, by all accounts. Arthur and Freddie had realized by now that Tom had stopped, and they watched nervously from a distance, willing Tom to say something sensible. Tom fumbled. "I'm here with . . ." The train guard's frown deepened. Grey Arthur and L. F. Freddie were frantically gesturing, which was more than a little distracting, encouraging him to say something, *anything*.

"Him!" Tom pointed at a man in a suit who was struggling to drink his coffee, eat a pretzel, answer his phone and keep hold on his newspaper and briefcase at the same time. "I'm here, Dad!" he hollered at the man, smiling winningly. The businessman, who currently had the pretzel lodged in his mouth for safe keeping, could only look around confused as Tom bounded over to his side. The guard smiled, satisfied that Tom wasn't lost after all, and wandered off back into the crowd.

"Do I know you?" the businessman asked, hastily withdrawing the pretzel from his mouth, and balancing it on top of his coffee cup.

"No, I don't think so," said Tom. "I'm Tom Golden."

The businessman frowned, looking perplexed.

"You just told that woman I was your dad."

"Did I? I must have been confused. Sorry about that." Tom glanced behind to make sure the guard had definitely gone, grinned a good-bye to his surrogate "Dad," and then quickly ran back over to join Grey Arthur and L. F. Freddie.

"That was close," breathed Arthur, relieved.

"Don't I know it!" replied Tom, his heart still racing. At least he was getting better at thinking on his toes.

The businessman stared over at the odd boy—who was currently talking to thin air—and looked puzzled briefly, before shrugging and returning to eating his pretzel. Stranger things happen at Victoria Station all the time. . . .

"Come on, this way. This is no place to dawdle, and we can't have that guard spot you on your own again. Stay close," commanded Freddie. They pushed forward with renewed energy, navigating their way across the station.

There were a few ghosts scattered around, but they were very much in the minority here. A fragile looking Sadness Summoner, all dressed in rags, sat at the feet of a street musician playing violin, seemingly lost in the beautiful music. A couple Poltergeists were climbing the display board, fiddling with the numbers, and laughing raucously at the accumulative sighs of disbelief that arose from the crowd when they succeeded in getting a train time to disappear. Several Faintly Reals milled about, trying to strike up conversation about the train delays, or simply copying everyone else and staring up at the ever-changing train times. There was a group of Thespers doing some street performance, but nobody seemed to be paying much attention, much to the annoyance of the lead Thesper. By and large though, this was distinctly human territory.

It was slow work moving through this many people, and a trip of just a few short meters was taking an unearthly amount of time. On they pushed, through the crowds, past the group of people who were arguing heatedly about an article in the *Financial Times,* past the old lady who was dancing to a song that only she could hear, past a couple tearfully saying good-bye to each other between noisy kisses and noisier sobs, until finally . . .

"Welcome to my humble abode," declared Freddie. They were standing outside a rather bland-looking door. "Someone stole the sign," he mumbled, apologetically, "but I'm working on finding it again."

He fumbled through his chain of keys until he found what he was looking for, and unlocked the door. One by one, they stepped through, and the door shut behind them. Immediately all the hustle and bustle, noise and clamor of the train station disappeared, and they were left in quiet darkness.

"Hold on . . . just got to find the light switch . . .

Where are you ... Oh, this is embarrassing ... It's around here somewhere ... A-hah!"

The room sprung into light.

And what a room it was.

There were boxes everywhere, piled ceiling-high. Some were closed, with labels on the side giving a hint as to what lay within—

BOOKS AND MAGAZINES

BIRTHDAY CARDS

JEWELRY

MOBILE PHONES

KEY RINGS

GLASSES

GLASS EYES

"Glass eyes?" asked Tom, incredulously.

"You'd be surprised what people lose," replied Freddie.

WALLETS/PURSES

PHOTOGRAPHS

Some boxes held items too large for the lids to close, and curious objects jutted out from inside. One box contained a collection of false legs, in various shades and sizes. Another contained a fake skull, an African tribal head-garb, a jar full of tadpoles, and a tambourine. It was like a very bizarre version of Aladdin's Cave, holding everything you could imagine, and a few things you couldn't imagine even if you tried really hard. Lamp shades, wigs, a complete train set, a soldier's uniform from the Napoleonic war, a fourteen-foot miniature boat that really wasn't all that miniature . . . Tom reached out curiously to touch a box that was hissing faintly.

"Careful. That's the box I keep all the lost snakes in," L. F. Freddie explained, and Tom quickly retracted his hand. "I used to keep it over there, next to the box of lost mice. Well, long story short, I don't do that anymore. So now I store them next to the box of novelty ties. It's better that way."

Grey Arthur was trying on the African tribal headgarb, and grinning excitedly.

"What do you think?" he asked, posing.

"Different . . . ," replied Tom, tactfully. Arthur looked a little crestfallen, and put it back where he found it.

L. F. Freddie had managed to find a ladder from somewhere, and was scaling the wall of boxes.

"So, you said wanted to find something, Tom . . . ," he called down, wrapping his arms around a rather cumbersome-looking box.

"Yes, that's right. I'm sorry I didn't go into more detail, it's just—"

"No need to explain," interrupted Freddie, making his way back down the ladder with the box. "I know exactly what you're looking for."

"You do?" asked Arthur, sounding pleased. Freddie placed the box on the floor, and began rummaging inside, brow furrowed with concentration. "It's in here somewhere . . . Typical. It's right at the bottom. Still, you know what they say, it's always the last place you look . . . Here we go!" Freddie grinned victoriously, and pulled the object out of the box.

"Ta da!" he cried, thrusting a mess of fur, limbs, and seaweed smells toward Tom's face. "Reunited at last!"

"Madame Twinkle Bear?" gasped Tom.

Grey Arthur began to chuckle. One of the teddy bear's eyes was missing, a tangle of thread the only indication that it had ever been there in the first place. The bear had obviously been much loved in its time, with as many threadbare patches as furry ones, and the smell of the sea still clung to its pretty, yet faded, patchwork dress. The words "I Love Tom" were embroidered on a pocket. Tom began turning bright red. Freddie held up a little tag that was around Madame Twinkle Bear's neck.

"Lost on Bognor Beach, Sunday, third June... I can't quite make out the year here, the tag must have gotten damp, but look, clear as day: 'OWNER: Thomas N. Golden.' Tell me I'm good!"

"You're fantastic." Arthur laughed. Tom snatched the teddy bear from Freddie, blushing heavily.

"It was from my aunt. She always buys me girl presents. And I haven't had a teddy bear for years," he muttered.

"I'm sure it wasn't *that* many years. If I squint, I can just about make out the date here, hang on . . ."

"Besides," said Tom, hastily interrupting him (much to Arthur's dismay), "that isn't what we are looking for."

240

"Really?" Freddie looked disappointed. "My mistake. If you don't want it, I can always take it back?" He reached out to take back the very tatty bear.

"No, no, I'll keep it," replied Tom, quickly moving Madame Twinkle Bear out of reach. Grey Arthur grinned knowingly. "I mean, just because you need all the space you can get in here, don't you? So really, by taking it, I'd be doing you a favor. Not because I want it, you understand. But to help you out."

"Of course. Very kind of you."

Tom nodded brusquely, trying his very hardest to look cool while cramming a teddy bear in a dress into his pocket. She didn't quite fit, and a sad-looking face and a solitary paw protruded out of Tom's bulging jacket.

"So, back down to business then," said Freddie. "If it isn't Madame Twinkle Bear that you've lost, then what is it?"

"We've lost two friends," said Grey Arthur, solemnly. The amusement of Tom's long lost bear was instantly gone, as they were reminded of why they had come. "Ballpoint Bill, a Poltergeist, and Mrs. Scruffles, a Faintly Real."

"Vanishing ghosts," replied Freddie, his voice heavy.

"Vanishing ghosts." Nodded Tom.

Freddie went quiet, and he sat down on the box in which Madame Twinkle Bear had been stored. He played with the keys and rings around his neck absently, toying with them as if they were worry beads.

For a while all that could be heard was the sound of jingling. Arthur and Tom exchanged worried glances. They'd been hoping for an altogether more positive response.

"So you already know about the ghosts disappearing?" asked Arthur, trying to break the silence.

"I know," he said finally. "Sadly, it seems as if there are some things that even I can't find. You're not the first people to have lost ghosts recently, and I'm afraid you won't be the last either. I've looked, and I've searched, but it's as if . . ." He hesitated, carefully weighing up the words he was to use. He suddenly looked tired. "It's as if they no longer exist. I'm sorry. Ghosts come and ghosts go, that's the nature of haunting, but recently, so many ghosts have disappeared—too many, too many for coincidence, too many for chance—and there's nothing I can do to find them. Nothing at all." He looked down at the ground. "I'm sorry you have lost your friends, I really am, but I'm afraid I don't think I can help you. *Lost and Found Freddie* . . ." He laughed, and it was a sound without humor. "Maybe I don't deserve the name after all."

"We know what's happening," said Tom. Freddie looked up, his face still lined with worry.

"You do? Well, don't just stand there. Tell me! What's going on?"

"Have you heard of the Collector?" asked Arthur.

Freddie's expression darkened.

"Now, there's a name that's been lost in history for

the longest time. I thought he was just a myth. You know, a story told to scare young ghosts. *'Behave, or the Collector will get you.'* You're saying he's real?"

"As real as ghosts get," replied Tom.

"And he's responsible for this?"

"Sorrow Jane seemed to think so."

"You *spoke* to Sorrow Jane?"

"Not spoke, as such," Tom explained. "She just did this weird visiony thing on me, and I—"

"Cried," said Arthur.

"Thanks," said Tom, dryly. Arthur smiled helpfully.

"But Sorrow Jane communicated with you? You're just full of surprises, Tom Golden. And you shouldn't feel embarrassed about crying. I just *think* about that ghost and I feel miserable." He stood up, smoothing out the creases in his baggy overcoat. "So how can I help you?"

Tom and Arthur looked at each other, each hoping his friend would break the news to Freddie. It was a stand off of seconds, which felt like minutes. In the end, Tom buckled first.

"We need you to find him. *It*. The Collector. We need to know where we can find him, and soon, before any other ghosts can go missing," he said. Tom waited for an outright refusal, that telltale look that said "Are you crazy?", but none came. Instead, Freddie was quiet for a while, mulling it over.

"And if I find him, what will you do then?"

"We have a plan," declared Tom proudly.

"Well, more of an idea," clarified Arthur.

"Well, okay, more of an idea, that might work."

"Or might not," added Arthur.

"Will you stop doing that!" cried Tom.

"Sorry. I'm just being honest, that's all," muttered Arthur.

"So, you want me to find the Collector because you have an idea that might, or might not, work?"

"Yes," agreed Tom. Said out loud like that, it did sound a little bit ludicrous.

"Rather you than me . . ." Freddie shook his head, and the long overdue "Are you crazy?" look appeared. Tom and Arthur smiled back at him. Freddie sighed then, as if he couldn't believe what he was about to say. "Listen, I'll do my best, but you'll need to give me a little time. I've never looked for anything before that doesn't want to be found. It's not going to be easy. And it's probably going to be dangerous. I find missing wedding rings, children's lost comfort blankets, the scrap of paper that you wrote a phone number down on, that kind of thing, not ancient evil ghosts. I can't promise you that I'll be able to do it."

"But you'll try?" Arthur asked hopefully.

"Of course I will. Whatever he's done with the ghosts he's stolen, he's collected them in such a way that I can't find them at all. But now I know what I'm looking for . . ." He looked into the distance, nodding to himself, before turning his attention back to Tom and Arthur. "I'll meet up with you again later, say five?

At yours? To discuss what I have discovered, if anything at all. That's if I even make it back . . ." L. F. Freddie looked worried, his ghostly fingers wrapped tight around his necklaces. Grey Arthur stirred guiltily, seeing the fear on Freddie's face.

"You don't have to do this. I know it's a lot to ask," said Arthur. Freddie shook his head.

"Of course I have to do this. I've been waiting my whole life to find something so important. And you wouldn't be here if you didn't need my help, would you?" Tom and Arthur shook their heads. "Well then, there you go. That doesn't mean that I can't be scared though. I'd be silly not to be."

"We can always let you in on our plan? So that, if he did catch you, you'd at least have a chance of . . ." Arthur trailed off into silence, seeing Freddie shaking his head.

"That's not what I do, or who I am, Arthur. I find things. It's not my place to make a stand, or fight. Different ghosts have different roles. You know that."

"Then we can send some ghosts with you? To make sure that you aren't alone?" Tom volunteered. "There's plenty at my house to go round."

"That would be lovely." Freddie sighed. "But I'm afraid that's not how it works. It takes a lot of concentration to find things, which is why I always work alone. Less distractions that way." He took a deep breath, and rubbed his hands together. "No, this is how it has to be. I'll try not to let you down." They shared a silent moment then, each one of them aware of just how much rested on this. L. F. Freddie was the first to speak again, his tone deliberately chirpy. He rubbed his hands together. "So then, assuming everything goes to plan, I'll be seeing you both at five."

"Five it is," replied Tom, nodding, as he and Arthur headed toward the door. "Oh, wait, Freddie, do you know where I live?"

"I'm sure I'll be able to find it." He grinned.

The Waiting Game

TOM HATED WAITING. IT WAS THREE THIRTY BY THE TIME they finally got back home, and it took another ten minutes for Grey Arthur and the trainee Invisible Friends to reclaim the lounge. It transpired that Woeful William had led an expedition of Poltergeists over to Max's Videos, and they'd "borrowed" (in the loosest possible sense of the word) a collection of exceedingly sad films. The lounge had been full of sobbing Poltergeists when Tom entered, and it had been all he could do not to flee the room in floods of tears himself.

Still, ten minutes and five persuasive ghosts later, they had the lounge to themselves, and together they sat. And waited. Time seemed to slow down, the minutes defiantly dragging. Tom was glancing at his watch every five seconds, then sighing, pausing, and looking again. There was a heavy tension in the room, everyone feeling so very helpless, having to simply sit, and wait, and hope that Freddie managed to succeed. Tom flicked through the channels on the television, never settling on any one program long enough to get into it before changing the station again. Montague sat in Mum's chair, his eyes closed, running through in his mind the possible scenarios they might face. Four o'clock came and went. Mildred was desperately reading through her notes, trying to find something, anything in there that might help. She would start to write, and then, with a frustrated sigh, scrawl it all out and start again. Four thirty . . . Tike was being distinctly un-Tike-like, and was sat quietly in Dad's big armchair, staring into the distance. Four forty-five . . . the Harrowing Screamer was standing, stock-still, in the corner of the room, slowly breathing in light, and breathing out shadows. His ancient claws creaked as he flexed them. Tom pulled back the curtains and opened the window, to let in more light. Four fifty-five . . . Grey Arthur was pacing, his ghostly shoes hovering an inch above the floor, so as not to wear a hole in the carpet.

Five o'clock came.

And went.

"Where is he?" demanded Tom, tapping his watch to make sure it was still working properly. "He should have been here by now!"

Grey Arthur didn't respond. He just paced, a sick feeling of worry growing and growing in his stomach.

Five ten.

Five fifteen.

Five thirty.

Six o'clock.

Arthur ground to a halt, staring down at the carpet.

"He's not coming." He sighed, and sunk down into the arm chair next to Tom.

"No, he has to be. Just give him a little more time," said Tom, refusing to believe it.

"Tom . . . ," said Montague gently. Tom knew what he was going to say, and he shook his head.

"No," he said simply. "He's coming."

And so time drudged on, each tick or tock of the hands of the clock another second that Freddie was late. Six thirty, seven, eight o'clock came . . .

Freddie flew through the walls of the lounge, staggering to a halt in front of where everyone was waiting. His grey coat was torn, his cheeks flushed, and he looked around desperately, his breathing heavy.

"I don't have much time." He gasped, nearly doubled over, his hands holding his side. "I couldn't lose him. He's close. I can't afford to bring him here, when there are so many ghosts around."

It was as if time had started up again, running twice as fast as before. Everyone leaped to their feet.

"You found him!" yelped Arthur.

"I found him. But listen. It's not going to be easy

for you. He doesn't just collect ghosts. He *uses* them. The place is flooded with them. It's horrible. Like little blank-eyed puppets. I only just managed to get away from the guards, and even then—"Freddie stopped suddenly, lifting his head, and he looked around in alarm. "He's coming. I have to go. It's me he's after. He doesn't know about this place. He *mustn't* know about this place."

"I'm sorry," muttered Arthur, his voice sad.

"Don't be." Freddie smiled, feverish energy forcing his mouth into a wild-looking grin. "A ghost lives for moments like these. And, if I vanish for them too, well . . . that's the way it has to be." He rummaged urgently in his large coat pockets, and pulled out an old map. He handed it to Mildred, and flashed that smile at Arthur and Tom, a smile that managed somehow to be both scared and brave, exhilarated and tired, all at once. "I've done my bit. Now it's up to you. Good luck!"

"You too," said Tom gently, but they both knew luck wasn't going to be enough to keep Freddie safe.

It was his time to be found.

L. F. Freddie winked at Tom, and then he turned and ran straight through the wall, his torn coat flapping behind him, his keys clattering together. "Come on!" He could be heard yelling outside, "Hide and Seek is a game for children! Surely you can do better than this? I could keep going all day! Catch me if you can . . ."

His voice trailed off into the distance, and Tom and

the ghosts stared quietly at what Mildred held in her pale white hands.

"This is it then . . . ," said Tom. Mildred unfolded the map, its yellow brittle pages held carefully open, and they looked at where exactly they needed to go. Despite the circumstances, Tom couldn't help a wry smile as he looked at what was drawn there. "Just like the films," he said, looking up at Arthur. "*X* marks the spot."

All Systems Go

TOM LED EVERYONE UPSTAIRS, RELOCATING THE Sadness Summoners once again (amidst obscene amounts of sighing), and together with Arthur and the trainee Invisible Friends, he began getting ready for the adventure that lay ahead. Woeful William, sensing that something was about to happen, stayed with them too, forsaking watching the end of *Orphans in a Storm*. Nervous energy bristled in the air, and even the other ghosts who had moved in could sense it. The sheer insanity that had roared freely through Tom's house reduced itself to a light simmer, and everyone gave Tom and the Invisible Friends space to think. Before they even started, Tom phoned his parents again, and after assuring them that the birthday party was going wonderfully, and yes, he was making lots of new friends, and no, he *still* wasn't misbehaving, and after several good-byes, he began the very serious business of plotting the big attack.

"So," said Tom, pointing at the map with a pen he had found, "this is where the Collector is based. This is where he goes when he's not out stealing ghosts, and so this is where we are going to face him." He swallowed, his throat feeling dry. "We know that his weakness is seeing his own reflection, and so we will be prepared." Tom showed everyone the hand mirror he had borrowed from Mum's room. Its handle was covered in little blue flowers. It seemed somehow right that something so dainty would be the thing that would defeat the Collector. Tom put it in his back pocket, the handle jutting out above his trousers. "We don't know for sure that this will work, but it's the best shot we've got. Now, me and Arthur, we have to go, we have to do this, but the rest of you don't. You can stay here, if you want. Look after the other ghosts while we're gone."

"And let you steal the limelight?" asked Montague, leaning against the wall. "Preposterous. You'll need our help, especially as Freddie said there were guards there, and goodness knows what else. No, you can count me in. I'm coming."

"And me," Tike piped up. "You never know when an ex-Poltergeist can come in handy."

"And I'll also be joining you." Mildred looked at Tom, her mismatched eyes locked on his. "You can't teach us to be Invisible Friends and then expect us to stay behind while you go and do something like this. I'm sure you will need all the friends you can get. Isn't that correct, Arthur?"

Grey Arthur nodded, a little teary, but very proud.

The Harrowing Screamer howled loudly in agreement, head tilted back, showing off his razor-sharp teeth. William sighed. "Well, I suppose that means I should come along too. I always knew I'd meet a tragic end, anyway. I know I'm not an Invisible Friend, and frankly, I have no desire to be. You're so horribly optimistic to be around. But, if I can help in any way, I would like to."

Tom nodded, a determined look on his face.

"Okay then. So we follow this map, somehow get past the guards, confront the Collector, show him his reflection, and then we're done."

"*That's* the big plan? Bit dodgy, isn't it?" came a tiny voice from Tom's desk. "I mean, what if it all goes pear shaped? What then?" A little Bug fluttered out from his hiding place beneath a stack of Cold Fish CDs, and flew ungracefully through the air, landing on the Harrowing Screamer's shoulder. The Screamer hissed at it. Tom knew who the Bug was straight away, before he'd even set eyes on it, just by the way he spoke.

Ladybug.

Ladybug adjusted his little costume, smoothing down his black-spotted red wings, and got out a notebook and a pencil. He sat down, his tiny feet hanging off the Harrowing Screamer's shoulder. The Screamer didn't quite know how to react, and he glared at the ghost with the shock of red hair, neck craning. Ladybug ignored his irate seat, and looked at Tom, pencil poised, waiting for a response.

The last time Tom and Grey Arthur had seen Ladybug, he'd been flying out of Tom's bedroom window, muttering darkly. Bugs were the ghost equivalent of journalists, and Ladybug's role had been to listen out for when humans tell white lies, and report them in the *Daily Tell-Tale,* where Poltergeists can pick them up as freelance mischief jobs. Ever lied and said you couldn't make it to work because of a flat tire? If you were unfortunate enough to have a Bug overhear then it would go straight into the paper, and the next day Poltergeists would come and let down your tire for real, knowing that you can't use the same excuse twice. Said you couldn't hand in your homework because your printer was broken? Poltergeists would sneak in while you slept, and make sure that the next time you needed it, it really wouldn't work. Ladybug had caught Tom out in a white lie, and Grey Arthur had trapped him until he promised not to report it. He had been as good as his word, and hadn't mentioned it all. No, instead he ran with the scoop of the year—Tom Golden, the boy who can see ghosts. It was Ladybug's fault that Tom's school trip had ended up a disaster, after every ghost under the sun made their way to Thorblefort Castle to meet him. Tom glared at Ladybug.

"What?" asked Ladybug. "Why are you looking at me like that? Oh, don't tell me you're still sulking about that front-page scoop. I made you famous. You should be happy." Tom's look assured Ladybug that he wasn't happy at all. "Fine. How can I make it up to you?"

Tom shook his head. "It doesn't matter. We've got other things to worry about right now."

"I know what I could do . . . ," said Ladybug, pretending that he hadn't heard Tom. "I could come with you, and record everything that happens, and get the exclusive story. How's that sound?"

"That doesn't sound much like you'd be doing that for me," replied Tom suspiciously. Ladybug threw his hands up in the air, in a "You've got me!" way.

"Right. You've caught me out. Boss sent me down. Reckoned, since me and you go way back, that I was the Bug for the job."

"We don't go way back," Tom said.

"We do, you just never realized," Ladybug said with a grin. He saw Tom was still frowning, and changed tack. "Look, truth be told, I'm more of a gossip ghost than a frontline-reporter ghost, so I'm not exactly tap dancing at the thought of heading into a dangerous ghost's lair. However, since you guys thought it wise to let the paper know what was happening with the Collector, my editor thought it wise to throw me at the story. So, like it or lump it, I'm tagging along."

Tom groaned, too distracted to put up a fight.

"Fine. Just don't get in the way."

"Look at the size of me! I'm diddy. How could I possibly get in the way?" He flew off the Screamer's shoulder, and landed behind Tom's ear. It tickled. "Pretend I'm not even here," he whispered.

Tom rubbed his eyes tiredly, and carried on where he left off. "The one thing I don't get," he said, trying to ignore the itch behind his ear, "is this whole thing that Freddie said, about the guards, about using the ghosts like puppets." Tike shot his hand up in the air, as if he was answering a question in the classroom. Tom looked at him, and Tike grinned, pleased to be useful.

"I think I know. It's a bit like stealing, isn't it?" When Tom looked blank, he carried on. "I mean, when I steal socks, they're mine to do with as I want. I can wear 'em, use 'em to store marbles in, make sock puppets . . . When I steal someone's homework, I can read it, use it to make paper airplanes, tear it up and make confetti . . . When I steal—" He caught Arthur's look, and decided to stop his list, and skip straight to the point. "Anyway, when I steal, it's mine, and I can do what I like with 'em. Not that I steal anymore, well, much, because, you know, Invisible Friend now, but what I'm saying is that maybe stealing ghosts, it's the same kind of thing?" He looked at Tom, eyebrows raised, waiting for a response. Tom didn't know what worried him more;

the long list of Tike's stealing habits, or the fact that what Tike was saying made vague sense. He'd definitely been spending too much time in the company of ghosts.

"If that's true . . . ," mused Montague, "then judging by the amount of ghosts that have gone missing, we could have one almighty greeting party waiting for us."

Nobody much fancied responding to that statement, so instead Tom just clapped his hands, Mrs. Scruffles style, and looked at the ghosts in his room. Arthur, Tike, Montague, Mildred, the Harrowing Screamer, and Woeful William stared back.

"So, are we all set?" he asked. The Invisible Friends and Woeful William nodded quietly. "Arthur, you know where we're going?" Arthur looked at the map in Mildred's hand, and bobbed his head as a yes. Tom's hand patted his back pocket, just checking that the mirror was still there. "Well then. I guess it's time."

Tom suddenly remembered Madame Twinkle Bear, and with a bit of effort, pulled her free of his pocket. He placed her on the shelf, tapping her on the head for good luck. In a gesture of solidarity, Mildred placed her sinister monkey next to it, and nodded quietly up at Tom. It was a small act, but it meant a lot. Tom smiled at her, touched.

They walked slowly out through the house, and ghosts lined the stairs and the hallway, clapping, or shouting words of encouragement, or, in the case of the Screamers, just hissing loudly and spitting shadows out on the floor before them. There were so many ghosts now that they spilled out into the street, and took up every inch of space within the home. Tom's skin bristled as he walked, as it was impossible to navigate through without brushing against ghost after ghost. A Sadness Summoner threw flowers at him (Mum's begonias, in actual fact). A Thesper yelled a battle march that had been plucked straight out of the Middle Ages. A Screamer howled to the Harrowing Screamer, and the Harrowing Screamer threw his head back, and howled in reply. It was all a little overwhelming. Tom spotted the Red Rascal by the door, and after pushing his way past and through many ghosts, he beckoned the famous Poltergeist to one side.

In a quiet voice, hoping that the other ghosts didn't hear him, Tom whispered to the Red Rascal, standing on tiptoe to even get close to his ear. "I need you to stay here, and look after the ghosts. If anything should happen, if we should fail, you need to get them to safety. If anyone can do that, it's you. Don't move the whole house though. My parents will have a fit if they come back and it's gone." The Red Rascal nodded, understanding. From the Red Rascal's neck still hung a red tie, stolen from Dr. Brown's hut, a reminder of what they had all been through. Tom nodded back at the giant ghost, and raised a finger to his lips to tell him to keep it secret.

He needn't have bothered. All the ghosts in the house had heard, as well as the ones in the garden, because the urgency in Tom's voice amplified it a hundred times to ghost ears, but they pretended, for Tom, that they hadn't. It made them a little quieter though. None of the ghosts wanted to imagine what would happen if this didn't work.

They marched out of the house, and weeping Sadness Summoners, and cheering Thespers, headless Headlesses, and Chain Rattlers solemnly rattling their chains, stretched the length of the garden path, bidding them good-bye. A row of Screamers lined up against the wall, screaming in what was almost harmony. Tom and his ghostly companions walked in silence, each one full of heavy thoughts, marching forward like a small, strange-looking, mismatched army into battle. The crowds thinned the farther they walked in the fading light, one turn, another, a trip down dog-mess alley, and before they knew it, they were there, standing alone. Even the ley-line seemed to glow brighter for them, its entrance sparking with energy, colors fizzing faster than usual. With one final look good-bye at Thorbleton, Tom stepped into the ley-line, and everyone else followed behind.

The End of the Road

THE LIGHTS OF THE LEY-LINE SWALLOWED TOM, AND he felt that familiar tug as gravity loosened slightly. The ground flowed beneath his feet, a torrent of colors, and sparks of magic flickered around him. Faster, and faster, and faster it went, hurtling forward, the world blurring so much that it all seemed to merge into one long streak of indistinct shapes. Fragments of noise, snippets of smell, flashes of scenery, all rushed through the ley-line and were gone as soon as they arrived. The walls of the portal shimmered and pulsed. Faster, and faster, and faster still. They passed straight through Stonehenge, and out the other side, the circle of stones gone in an instant, the ley-line carrying them along without pause. Across grass, across roads, across gravel, across fields . . . The ground beneath Tom fell away, and the ocean took its place, at first shallow enough to see pebbles and sand beneath, but soon changing to darker shades of blue, with no bottom in sight. Tom gulped the air, his heart racing. The colors in the ley-line began to warp and fade, dark greys and rotting greens seeping in where rainbow sheens had been. Shadows started to crawl the walls, twisting, grappling with the little sparks of light, and smothering them. Tom gasped in alarm, calling out to Arthur, but the ley-line swept his words away as soon as he said them. Decay crept around Tom, the silvery walls seeming to weaken and fade, and beneath him the dark, deep sea waited. He began to feel cold salty water seeping into his shoes, the magical floor becoming flimsy. The ley-line surged on, dragging Tom forward, and tears of fear pricked his eyes. Cracks appeared, darkness etching across the tunnel of light.

Suddenly, the ley-line tore apart, and Tom felt himself falling into water, arms flailing. Panic surged through him, the cold water dragging him under, his clothes becoming heavy . . .

His feet hit the ground, and Tom stopped flapping his arms. They were on the shore! He giggled, a little deliriously, splashing the water with his hands. The ghosts, hovering above the water, looked at Tom in confusion.

"I thought I was going to drown!" laughed Tom, wading toward the shore.

"In two feet of water?" asked Tike.

"Well, I didn't know that, did I?" He stood on the pebbly beach, wringing the water out of his clothes. "It's all right for you lot. You can float."

"That shouldn't have happened though," said Montague thoughtfully, looking at where the ley-line had crumbled to an end. Dark tendrils, like smoke, crawled across where the ley-line had broken. "He must really not want any guests."

"Well, that's his tough luck," Tom said in an act of

bravado. He looked around, trying to get his bearings. The beach they were standing on was deserted. Huge pebbles, dusky greys and mellow browns, felt uneven under his wet feet. The sea looked almost sickly in the light, a pale mimicry of the sky, with white-crested waves crashing into the shore. A tired sun hung low on the horizon. "So where are we?"

"We're in Ireland," said Grey Arthur, studying the map.

"Really?" Tom said. He'd always wanted to visit Ireland. He'd imagined going on a holiday though, or a school trip, not being dumped in the sea with ghosts for company, after traveling there on a ley-line. He took off his shoes, and tipped out the water. His socks were soaked. "So where do we go from here?"

"It's not far. Maybe half a mile down the beach." Arthur was holding the map in front of him, and already walking in the right direction. Tom hastily put his soggy shoes back on, and followed. His feet squelched as he walked, and without even thinking his hand shot to his back pocket, to make sure the mirror was still there, and hadn't been stolen by the sea. It was, and he smiled, relieved. They walked, in silence, along a bleak beach in Ireland, darkening sky and grey cliffs above them, and all that could be heard was the squelch of Tom's shoes, the crunch of stones beneath his feet, and the roar of the Irish sea.

Dark Cave, Darker Secrets

"WE'RE HERE," ARTHUR SAID, POINTING AHEAD. Tom, Arthur, Mildred, Montague, Tike, William, and the Harrowing Screamer were crouched behind some conveniently placed clumps of shrubs on the beach, hiding out of sight. Before them, like an angry wound in the face of the cliffs, opened up a dark cave mouth. Screamers milled in the shadows of the entrance, sniffing the air, hissing to each other. Even at this distance, Tom could feel the menace radiating from them, and he paled.

"Tom, you know the ghosts can't harm you, don't you?" Montague asked. Tom nodded, mouth dry, eyes fixed on the cave. "But they will throw every trick in the book at you. They will try to scare you, to make you cry, to make you turn and run. You need to be strong in there. We'll try to help as much as we can, but we don't know what's going to happen when we get inside. You have to be brave, Tom—you're the only one out of all of us that he can't steal."

"I'll be fine," Tom muttered, trying to make himself mean it.

"I can't believe he has done this. Those poor ghosts." Arthur was peering over the leaves at the Screamers standing guard. The Harrowing Screamer growled at seeing his fellow spirits used in such a way. "It's so wrong."

"It won't be for long, Arthur. When we're done, we'll let them all go." Tom hoped he sounded convincing. Ghosts have a very good ear for emotions, and he was trying to keep all his worry bottled up inside, out of sight. When you have as much worry though as Tom had right then, it made it difficult. His palms felt clammy.

"So, what's the plan?" asked Tike. He'd smeared the dirt on his face into streaks, like camouflage, and his usually spiky hairdo looked even more defiant than normal. The white in his hair was the only part of him that stood out, a bright trail of color amongst all the grime.

"I was thinking that we just charge in," said Tom. From behind his ear, he heard a little sigh. He'd almost forgotten about Ladybug. He tutted, annoyed. "Fine then, you have a better idea?"

"No. But that doesn't mean I can't think yours is rubbish," came the reply.

"Well, we can't just sit here, there's no way we can sneak past them unseen, and—" Tom started to argue back, when he noticed the Harrowing Screamer leap to his feet, and charge across the beach. He raised his sharp-taloned hands, old bones creaking, shadows trailing behind him as he ran. Tom and the other ghosts watched in shocked silence. "What's he doing?" breathed Tom, scarcely believing his eyes. The Harrowing Screamer ran toward the guards, his taloned feet making short work of the pebbly shore, and stopped just meters before them. There was a brief, uneasy second when they watched him, not knowing what he was going to do.

And then he howled.

The Harrowing Screamer threw his head back, and let loose the most astounding noise. It sounded like a million cats fighting, like an angry wind trying to tear down whole cities, like molten lava screeching free from a volcano. The scream tore across the beach, bouncing defiantly from the cliffs, racing out to sea, and long after it was gone, its echo vibrated along the waves. The Harrowing Screamer flexed his claws, his smoky eyes watching the other Screamers, his sharp teeth displayed in a wicked grin, and he waited.

The guards twitched their claws, a low murmur rising from them, and then they charged, moving eerily fast, their sinewy limbs hurtling them forward on a collision course with the Harrowing Screamer. Tom could barely bring himself to watch.

Just as they were about to reach him, the Harrowing Screamer turned and ran, his speed easily a match for theirs, and he fled down the beach, leading them away from the entrance.

A distraction.

"Now!" yelled Grey Arthur, and they leaped from behind the shrub and charged down the beach toward the waiting cave. Stones crunched noisily under Tom's feet, but the sound of howling and screaming drowned it out. They dashed across, Tom's heart racing, and it felt like the ground stretched for miles before them, like it took an eternity to reach the entrance. Each step was painful, the pebbles bruising his feet through his soaking wet shoes, but he forced himself forward, head down, not daring to look up. The entrance loomed imposingly before him. With the Screamer guards gone though, it was the easiest thing to dart inside. Tom fell heavily against the walls of the cave, back pressed tightly to keep out of sight, as he struggled to get his breathing back under control.

"I can't believe he did that . . . ," said Tom, bending over slightly to ease the pain of a cramp. The ghosts didn't seem out of breath, but they were shaken by what they had just seen. Tike was staring around in wide-eyed shock, and Mildred looked almost tearful. Monty put a reassuring hand on her shoulder. William was just shaking his head, as if he couldn't believe he'd volunteered for this. Arthur simply nodded, trembling hands folding away the map. They didn't need it anymore. Not now that they were inside.

"He was very brave," Arthur agreed, his voice strained. The screaming was fading now, growing ever distant. "We don't have time to stop. We've got to press on."

It took a while for Tom's eyes to adjust to the gloom inside the cave. It stretched out before them, burrowing deep into the cliff face, curving away out of sight. A sickly pale green light radiated unnaturally from the walls, and the air was clammy. Tom shivered, his cold wet clothes sticking to his skin. Every inch of him screamed that this wasn't a place for humans to be. There was just something that felt wrong about it, something about the light, the air, the cave itself, something that shouted inside Tom, demanding he turn round, leave now. He bit back on it, refusing to give that feeling any ground. He was here, and that was that. No turning back. Arthur gestured for everyone to follow, and they walked on into the cave, Arthur leading, Tom close by, with Mildred, Tike, Montague, and Woeful William at the back. They walked in silence, creeping forward, and Tom was horribly aware of how much noise he made compared to the ghosts. His breathing sounded ragingly loud to him, and his clothes and shoes squelched. With every step he took, he grimaced.

The cave twisted from side to side, growing tighter in places, wider in places, the ceiling lowering until Tom had to stoop, then stretching out way above, stalactites clinging to the cave roof. There was a constant sound of dripping. It felt as if they were burrowing into the depths of the earth, and Tom felt more and more anxious the farther he got from the exit, the farther he got from the sky. Claustrophobia began to creep into his thoughts, and he swallowed dryly, having to force each step farther in. Grey Arthur turned and looked at him, his ghostly figure illuminated by the sickly light from the walls, and he did that thing that only good friends can do, whole conversations carried by the slightest gesture, a raised eyebrow, a miniscule tilt of the head. *Are you all right? Do you want to stop?* Tom bit his lip and shook his head, and Arthur nodded before pressing on. The walls crept in tighter, forcing them to walk in single file, with Arthur taking the lead. Tom felt that if they didn't reach somewhere soon, he just might start to scream.

They turned a corner, and the cave suddenly fell open into a gigantic room, with ceilings so tall that you could barely focus on them. The room was almost perfectly round in shape, with angry stalagmites jutting out from the floor, and sharp stalactites clinging to the roof, like stone teeth in an open mouth. The space was simply huge. Tom might have been grateful for that, grateful to finally be someplace where it didn't feel like the walls were closing in on him, if it wasn't for everything else he saw. Arthur stopped, his breath catching in his throat. Tike swore quietly under his breath.

This was going to be more difficult than they thought.

Hundreds of ghosts filled the room, dead-eyed, empty, ghosts the Collector had stolen and then conjured up again to keep him safe. A supernatural shield. Freddie hadn't lied when he had called them puppets. They stood, waiting, ghosts of every type, ghosts of every shape, some so old that time had made them crooked, some young, like Mildred or Tike, some so very different that Tom could hardly bear to look at them, as they unsettled him so. Each ghost stood there, blankly, their personalities stripped away, hollow husks, gently rocking back and forth as if some breeze was stirring them. The air was stale and still though. Tom looked at Arthur, alarmed, but Grey Arthur could only stare at what lay before them, a silent horror on his face.

"This is never going to work," Arthur said. There was no emotion in his voice, just an unnatural calm. "We'll never get through." He slumped to the floor where he was standing, his eyes still locked on all the ghosts that stood in their way.

"Then I guess you'll have to leave that to us." Montague cracked his knuckles, and with a gesture of his hand his clothes changed back into the costume he had worn when he had first arrived at Tom's house. Gone was the sweater with reinforced elbows. Gone, the tweed trousers. A large cloak hung from his shoulders, and a top hat perched on his head. His mustache had regrown into twiddley points. Grey Arthur looked up at him in silent admiration, not knowing what to say. Montague ruffled Arthur's hair affectionately, and then turned his attention to the other ghosts "Mildred, Tike, William . . . Are you ready for the performance of your lives?"

Tike grinned mischievously, hands twitching, feet jiggling on the spot. Mildred stood stock-still, a look of quiet contemplation on her face, and Woeful William flapped his handkerchief as if his life depended on it.

"I had a terrible feeling you'd say something like that, Monty." He sighed, his voice echoing faintly in the dank corridor. He tucked his handkerchief into his sleeve, for safe keeping. "Woeful William, tragic hero. I suppose it does have a certain ring about it."

Monty looked at Grey Arthur and Tom, and bowed deeply, doffing his hat. "It has been the greatest pleasure, working alongside you two. But this is our grand finale, right here, and so this is where we must part ways. We'll hopefully buy you enough time to make it through, so no time to stop and watch the show." He grinned at Mildred, Tike, and William, and they nodded back at him, ready.

"Break a leg," whispered Tom.

"Several, if I'm lucky," laughed Montague. Mildred looked at Tom, a quiet respect passing between the two. Tike flicked a thumbs up toward Grey Arthur. William was muttering to himself, and shaking his head at the absurdity of what he was about to do. Montague cleared his throat theatrically. "One last time, for old time's sake . . . Enter stage right," he intoned, "Montague Equador Scullion the Third!" The sound of trumpets filled the air, and a bright flash of light made Tom shield his eyes. When he looked again, Monty, Mildred, Tike, and William were already running into the room, a gentle slope pitching them forward toward the waiting masses. The puppet ghosts stared at first, slow, clunky thoughts forming, so shocked by the sights and sounds that they didn't know how to react, and then chaos broke loose as they realized what was happening. The crowd surged forward toward the four charging ghosts, and for a brief second, seemed to swallow them whole, before the scene broke off into fragmented sections of scrapping.

William was shouting out lines from his favorite poem, and several ghosts crumbled to the floor, turning a deep shade of blue, and sobbing. Mildred had thrown herself onto the back of a Screamer, and was hitting him over the head with her notebook, while he flailed around howling. Tike was tripping ghosts up, laughing naughtily, and darting through their legs when they tried to grab him. Montague was dashing around, bursts of light following him, plumes of colored smoke obscuring him and allowing him to appear in a different location, leading the ghosts in a merry dance.

Tom was so transfixed by the mayhem they were causing that it took a while for him to notice that Arthur was already on the move, and with a start he followed, edging around the outskirts of the madness, trying to be as inconspicuous as possible. As soon as Tom stepped foot into the room though, a tide of emotion crashed into him, and after a few hesitant steps he buckled, legs shaking. So many Sadness Summoners in one place, so many Screamers, it was more than any human could be expected to withstand. A group of ghosts began closing in on Tom, their pale blue faces streaked with tears, and it was all Tom could do to hold his ground, to force his legs to hold him up. Arthur stopped, seeing Tom in trouble, and with a shout ran back to his side, urging Tom on, but Tom could only shake his head, pinned in place. He clung to the wall, biting back tears and screams, teeth gritted, and as much as Arthur tugged at his sleeve, or begged him to move, he couldn't. In desperation, Grey Arthur called out for William, his voice carrying above the sound of clashing ghosts, and in a flash William was there, standing between Tom and the other specters, battling sadness with sadness, misery with misery. The stalemate caused the ghosts to turn their attention away from Tom, and it was just the chance he needed to break free and push on. Another ghost spotted Arthur, and charged toward him, howling, and just before it reached Arthur Tike appeared, rugby tackling the ghost, and throwing him to the floor.

"Get a move on!" Tike yelled, and Tom and Arthur hurried on, leaving the two ghosts scrapping on the ground. Tike was trying to give his opponent a Chinese burn, and yelping with glee as he did so. It was out and out chaos, and thankfully, amidst all that, nobody else seemed to notice the small ghost and the human creeping around the edge of the room.

"Bravo, Mildred! Bravo, Tike! Bravo, William!" cheered Montague, as he let loose another plume of smoke. A Chain Rattler grabbed him from behind, throwing his chains around Monty's neck, but one flash of light later and the Rattler was bound from head to foot in his own chains, and looking thoroughly confused by it all. Montague grinned, adrenalin surging.

This was far more exciting than anything on the stage. He saw Mildred across the room, trying to jab a Faintly Real, who had hold of Tike, in the shins with a well-sharpened pencil, and he quickly dashed to their aid. William was holding his own in the center of the room, a trail of sobbing ghosts showing where he'd been.

Montague just hoped that what they were doing would be enough.

Tom and Arthur slipped, unseen, through the small exit at the back of the cave, and stumbled straight into the Collector's room.

Face to Face with a Nightmare

"And then there were two." The Collector sat on a throne carved roughly from stone, his eyes, only just visible through the shadows of his hooded cape, fixed on Tom and Arthur. If he was alarmed that they had gotten this far, he didn't show it. He reclined non-chalantly in his chair, simply watching them. The room was far smaller than the room before it, the ceiling lower, and Tom desperately looked around for another way out, should they need it. There wasn't one. This was the end of the line.

The Collector was shrouded from head to toe in a

heavy cape, thick, coarse, black material that hid away his shape. The only thing you could really see were his hands, pale, thin, resting easily on the arms of the throne. In front of his seat, so close that the hems of his cape trailed in the water, was a stagnant pool. It stank of mold, and damp, and decay, and made the air in the room thick, and humid. Green algae sprawled across the water's surface, and just barely visible beneath, lining the floor of the pool, thousands of Wish Coins lay. Each coin a stolen ghost. Arthur's nose creased in disgust. "Oh, don't look so put out, little ghost." The Collector's voice sounded like ice breaking. "That's where you'll be living, soon enough. You can join all your friends. Now wouldn't that be nice?"

Arthur growled, and anger flared inside Tom.

"Why are you doing this?" he demanded. He'd expected to be more afraid, but now he was here, face to face, the only thing he felt was overwhelming rage. The Collector laughed, a cold noise, and with a bemused smile he leaned forward in his chair. He pulled the cape away from his face, and for the first time Tom and Arthur saw what they were up against.

He looked almost disturbingly normal. Tom had expected red eyes, or sharp teeth, perhaps even horns, but the ghost that sat before them looked just like any other ghost. His skin was mottled, and his head was bald, but his eyes were almost a gentle grey. Somehow, though, that made it worse; it made him seem so much darker, to have such a terrible ghost housed in such a mundane appearance. Tom's skin crawled, and Arthur actually gasped.

"Why am I doing this? I would have thought that was obvious." He tilted his head, studying the two boys standing before him. One hand clung protectively to the velvet bag that hung at his side. "Because I want to." He grinned, enjoying the repulsion on Tom and Arthur's faces.

"I don't understand," muttered Tom. "That's not a good enough reason."

"What other reason should there be? What, you want to know the whole, dull tale? I have the time, though I'm not sure you two do." He smiled wickedly, thin grey lips tight over discolored teeth, and continued. "I used to be a Poltergeist, once. Many, many centuries ago. Stealing odd little bits here and there, but it wasn't enough. Trinkets, notes, socks . . . games for child ghosts to play. So I decided to collect ghosts. It really was as simple as that. Everyone has to have a hobby."

"You're disgusting," snarled Arthur. The Collector grinned.

"Why, thank you!" He reached into his bag, and took out a coin, twisting it between his fingers. "The problem with ghosts today is, they've gone soft. Can you believe that they're content to let humans ignore them, to live in the shadows, or in stories, and leave those fleshy, dumb creatures, those humans who see the world not in shades of magic, but in jobs, and money, and food, to think *they* own the world? It really is pathetic." He snarled disapprovingly. "You young ghosts have no idea how it used to be. Humans were terrified of us. Some even worshipped us. And now? They prance around on Halloween, dressed as us, thinking it's all very funny. Yes, I might have been resting these last few hundred years, getting my strength back, but I haven't been deaf. These ghosts need someone to take charge, to gather them all up, and it just so happens I'm the ghost for the job. Force the world to believe again. Make all humans afraid of the dark, just as they *should* be." He smiled slowly. "I'd have thought they'd have sent someone a little more impressive than you two. I'm almost offended. Still, it was very nice of you to come all the way out here to me. It saves me the trouble of having to hunt you down."

It happened in slow motion. The Collector threw the Wish Coin toward Grey Arthur, and it was all Arthur could do to stare in cold fear at the coin spinning through the air. Tom heard himself scream out, and Arthur's hands instinctively flew up to protect his face. But Tom had already dived, leaping through the air, urgency and panic forcing his body into action before his mind had even begun to grasp what was going on, and he snatched the coin before it could touch his friend. Tom landed awkwardly, crashing heavily to the ground, and he felt a sharp pain in his bottom, but he didn't have time to think of that. He staggered to his feet, the coin clutched in his hand. The Collector looked at him quizzically.

"Not a ghost," Tom said simply. He pocketed the coin. Arthur was lowering shaky hands from his face, checking himself, shocked to still be there.

"Thomas Golden . . . ," said the Collector thoughtfully. "I'd heard mutterings, but I'd thought it was just the Thespers telling silly stories. You know how Thespers can be. So you *do* exist. How interesting." He paused, his smoky grey eyes studying Tom, and Tom had to look away first. The Collector nodded. "Still, we can make this work to our advantage." He stood up, brushing out the creases in his cape.

"*Our* advantage?" replied an incredulous Tom.

"Now, Thomas, don't tell me that with your special gift, you've never thought about how you could make it work for you? How very human." Tom was glaring with open loathing at the Collector, who simply chuckled. "You could be my emissary, someone to negotiate with the humans, to explain to them the changes that will take place. Think of the power, Thomas. If humans were cruel to you, we could send Screamers after them, until people learned to fear you. We could make Sadness Summoners follow people, only leaving them alone when they were in your presence, so humans would think they felt miserable when you weren't nearby. Poltergeists, stealing anything you wanted. Don't tell me it's never crossed your mind."

"I just want my friends back," Tom said, his voice thick.

"Of course you do. And I'd give them back to you. In return for certain favors, of course."

"The mirror!" hissed Arthur, while the Collector was talking. Tom had almost forgotten. He discreetly reached behind him, into his back pocket, fingers edging toward it, when a sickening realization hit him.

The mirror was broken.

The sharp pain he had felt when he hit the ground had been the mirror shattering, breaking into hundreds of little pieces. Tom's hand came back red, sticky with blood. He hadn't even realized he was bleeding.

This couldn't be happening. To come so far, only to fail. The Harrowing Screamer, Monty, Mildred, William, Tike, they'd all been so brave for nothing. Tom felt like crying. He looked over at Arthur, who was subtly nodding his head toward the Collector, gesturing for Tom to act, and Tom shook his head sadly. He showed Arthur his hand, the blood on it, and in that terrible moment, Arthur knew what had happened. He didn't cry, or panic, or turn and run. He just looked tired, and that was the worst thing of all, because that was when Tom knew that Grey Arthur had given up.

"What's the matter?" asked the Collector mockingly, seeing their downcast faces. "Did your little plan fail?" He laughed, and Tom thought it was the worst sound he'd ever heard. "Oh, come on, Thomas. Don't be so glum. There's a whole world out there, just ripe for the haunting. You'll be famous. Respected. *Feared*."

"I'm sorry, Arthur," whispered Tom, looking over at his friend.

"It's okay, Tom. At least we tried," replied Arthur, trying very hard to be brave. He closed his eyes, bracing himself.

"Oh, for crying out loud!" came a tiny Cockney voice in Tom's ear. "Do I have to do everything myself?"

The Last Stand

LADYBUG FLAPPED OUT FROM WHERE HE HAD BEEN hiding, behind Tom's ear, his tiny wings sending him on an ungainly path, staggering through the air toward the Collector. Tom gawked in surprise, having forgotten all about his tiny passenger. Grey Arthur opened one eye gingerly, and saw Ladybug tumbling forward, his wings flapping manically. Arthur glanced at Tom, who seemed every bit as shocked as he was, and quickly looked back to the heroic charge of Ladybug.

The Collector sighed, reaching into his bag of coins, a dark smile spreading across his lips. "Far too easy," he said cruelly. Ladybug was close now, and the Collector toyed with the coin, feeling its weight, searching for the right moment . . .

"Say FLEAS!" yelled Ladybug, a flash of light springing from his tiny Bug hand.

The Collector faltered, and the light flashed again, and again, and again, its strobe effect in the dimly glowing room catching isolated moments of movement. Ghostly photos fluttered through the air, falling from Ladybug's outstretched hand, pooling at the Collector's feet. Tom and Arthur looked at each other in astonishment, realizing what Ladybug was doing.

Mirrors weren't the only way to capture someone's image.

The last time the Collector had ventured out, people had painted, and people had drawn, but this was a whole new world he was trying to conquer, and a whole new set of rules was in place. As humans had changed, so had the ghosts around them. *Far be it from Bugs to let humans be the only ones who knew how to take a photograph.*

The Collector stared in confused horror at the photos at his feet, and in that moment he saw his own face staring back at him. His inner ugliness, his rotten self, the withered core of what had once been Poltergeist but had now warped into something disgusting and hateful, stared back at him, accusingly. He screamed, throwing his hands up in front of his face, the Wish Coin tumbling harmlessly to the ground, but it was too late.

The damage was done.

There was a tearing sound, and an awful howl filled the air as the Collector folded in on himself. His limbs withered and vanished within the cape, his face shrinking, caving in, as if something deep inside him was collapsing. He stared accusingly at Tom, his pale grey eyes dimming, and Tom couldn't look away. A terrible gasp escaped the Collector, and then he was gone. The empty cape fell to the floor, and the bag of coins spilled open on the ground, surrounded by Ladybug's photos.

"You did it!" screamed Tom, as Ladybug came to a landing on the Collector's stone chair. "He's gone! The Collector is gone!"

Ladybug grinned proudly, his tiny wings bristling. "All in a day's work," he said with a wink. "What can I say? The camera never lies."

"Thank you!" cried Arthur, running up to Ladybug, and picking him up, holding him in his hand. He'd have kissed him, if he didn't think that Ladybug would protest bitterly. "Thank you! Thank you! Thank you!"

"And you nearly didn't let me come, eh?" Ladybug said to Tom. "Good job it worked though. We'd have been stuffed if it hadn't. I didn't have a backup plan." Tom laughed, so relieved, so happy that it was all over. They'd won! The Collector was gone, and . . . He stopped laughing, a sudden thought hitting him. "Where are all the ghosts?"

Arthur stopped, his grin frozen in place, and stared at Tom, the smile dropping, and a ghastly look of worry replacing it. Tom was right. Nothing had changed. "I thought they'd come back when he vanished," Tom said quietly. "But they're still not here."

A rather disheveled yet triumphant-looking

Mildred dashed into the room, followed by Tike, Montague, and William. Montague's hat was broken, the rim dropping low on his forehead, but his smile beamed. William still clutched his handkerchief, but it was little more than a rag now. Tike, well, Tike always looked a bit like he'd been dragged through a hedge backward, but at least now he had good reason. Following behind them, looking a little worse for wear, was the Harrowing Screamer.

"So, we're fighting, right?" Tike said excitedly, doing little boxing motions with his hands. "And I've got this Headless's head, and I'm running away with it, and then, suddenly, poof! They've all gone. I look around, and every single one of the ghosts has vanished, just like that. So that's how we knew you'd done it! You've actually done it!" Tike grinned at them, but when he saw the expression on Tom and Arthur's faces, his grin vanished. "You *haven't* done it?"

"We have," Arthur said, glumly. "It's just . . . they're still gone. Mrs. Scruffles. Bill. Freddie. All of them. Still gone."

"We knew there was a chance it wouldn't work, Arthur." Montague sat down in the abandoned throne, taking off his hat, letting it rest on his knee. He looked tired. "Mrs. Scruffles wasn't sure it was even possible to get the stolen ghosts back. We did what we could. Nobody could ask anymore."

Tom sank to the floor, suddenly feeling very worn out, and very, very sad. Montague was right. When

Tom had asked her if it would be possible to get the stolen ghosts back, all she'd said was, "I hope so. After all, what's life without hope?" Perhaps she'd known all along that there was no way to do it. Tom was soaking wet, freezing cold, with a cut bottom, and now it looked like they had lost after all. *Life isn't fair*, he thought, staring at the stagnant pool of coins before him.

Something was digging into his hip as he sat, and as he fished it out of his pocket, he realized it was the Wish Coin that had been intended for Arthur. He held it up, feeling the weight, surprised at how cold it was. It looked like it might be made of gold, and on one side a king's face was carved, although Tom had no idea which king it was. It glinted faintly, reflecting the unnatural light of the room. There was something about the coin that was different, something that struck Tom, though he couldn't place what. He picked up another coin that lay by the side of the pool. This one was grimy, tarnished. A film of green muck obscured the face of the coin, and it felt slimy in Tom's hand. One coin shiny, one coin filthy. This was important, he knew it was, but the significance of it all skirted just out of reach. He stared at the two coins, willing it all to make sense. Nothing came to him. He was so tired, so cold, that each thought was labored, slow, and heavy, and his mind was foggy. Frustrated, desperate, exhausted, sore, freezing, and defeated, Tom shook his head.

"I just wish I knew what to do," he said, and in a fit of annoyance he threw the slimy coin back into the pool, where it quickly sank.

"Tom . . . ," Arthur said, his voice rising in excitement. *"Tom!"*

Tom opened his eyes, and saw what Arthur was trying to show him. Standing in the middle of the water was a rather dusty Chain Rattler ghost. He was dripping with metal, dusted with cobwebs, and looking more than a little confused.

"What am I doing here?" he asked, staring at Tom. Tom leaped to his feet, with a roar of happiness.

"That's it, Arthur! *That's it!"* Tom cried. The Chain Rattler, who had been confused before, was now positively bewildered. Arthur was jumping up and down on the spot, clapping his hands with glee.

"What did you do?" Mildred asked, her mismatched eyes wide. Ladybug was watching Tom curiously.

Tom reached down, and picked up another coin from the pile. He held it tight in his hand, closed his eyes, and made a wish, then threw the coin into the water. The pool hissed and fizzed, and another ghost appeared next to the Chain Rattler. The two newly reappeared ghosts stared at each other.

"You genius!" screamed Arthur. "You absolute genius! You've just got to turn the coins back into what they were meant to be!" There was a yelp of delight from Tike and Montague, who were dancing around together, and even Mildred, serious, black-clothed

Mildred, was grinning widely. The Harrowing Screamer threw his head back and screamed, but this scream didn't sound scary—it was, undeniably, a scream of joy. William was flapping his handkerchief excitedly.

"Well, don't just stand there, Thomas!" he cried. "Get wishing!"

Tom smiled, elated but exhausted, staring at the huge pool full of coins before him. There had to be hundreds, if not thousands of coins there in the murky water.

It was going to be a long night . . .

And so Tom sat by the pool, and made wish after wish. Some were silly, and bound not to come true, because wishes can only stretch so far after all, but some had potential, and some came true that night. Tom wished for his friends to be safe, he wished for the ghosts to be returned, he wished for Dad's business to pick up . . . He wished for a Ferrari on his seventeenth birthday, and his own personal concert from Cold Fish to be played in his lounge, and he wished to be at least six feet tall when he stopped growing. So many wishes, and each one took away the taint that the Collector had made, and each wish set a ghost free. Some wishes he made twice, or three times, some wishes he made for the ghosts around him, who were putting in requests since only humans can make Wish Coins, and some wishes were as simple as hoping for a good night's sleep tonight, or more realistically, as time went on, tomorrow morning.

The sun was beginning to chase away the stars by the time Tom finished, and finally he staggered out from the cave, eyes wincing as they adjusted to daylight. Behind him stood more than a thousand ghosts, finally set free. Some had been trapped for centuries, and they rushed into the ley-line, or ran across the ocean, excited to see what the world had turned into while they had been away. Some had only been collected in the past few days or hours, and L. F. Freddie emerged, ruffled but unharmed, grinning broadly at Tom. And lastly, and most wonderfully, some were familiar faces, and Arthur and Tom yelled with joy as they found Mrs. Scruffles, Ballpoint Bill, Miranda, Janet from the castle, and Essay Dave amongst the ghosts Tom freed. The other Invisible Friends joined them on the shoreline, no longer trainee Invisible Friends but full-fledged members of the Ghost World's newest occupation. They had more than proved themselves in the past few days.

So, not only had all the ghosts that had vanished in the past few weeks been returned, but several hundred more that had vanished in centuries past were unleashed upon the world to haunt, and steal socks; to read miserable poetry, to rattle chains, to hiss in the shadows, to pretend to be real, to act out famous events, all the many things that ghosts do on a daily basis, things that humans don't ever see. Well, most humans, anyway, Tom Golden being the famous exception.

"So, as Invisible Friends . . . ," asked Montague, standing next to Tom and Arthur, "how did we do?"

Mildred, Tike, Monty, and the Harrowing Screamer looked at Tom and Arthur, who grinned widely back at them.

"You did brilliantly," Tom said, and Arthur nodded, bursting with pride. "Any human would be lucky to have you."

Tying Up Loose Ends

SO, YOU'RE PROBABLY WONDERING WHAT HAPPENED TO the Collector. After all, he came back once, he could do it again.

L. F. Freddie took the cape, and the now empty bag that had once held Wish Coins, and he hurried them back with him to his office in London's Victoria Station. There, he carefully put them inside a cardboard box, and he lined the inside with all the photos that Ladybug had taken, so that even if the Collector did ever start to come back, he'd only have to take one peep at his surroundings before he'd vanish all over again. Then Freddie taped it shut, and put it inside another box, and then another, and another, and marked, in big red letters on the outside, FOUND: ONE COLLECTOR. BOX NEVER TO BE OPENED. BY ORDER OF

L.F. FREDDIE. It went up on the highest shelf, far out of reach, and there it was left to gather dust and spider webs. A most fitting end for the Collector, after all, to join Freddie's collection of all things lost.

Freddie also returned every single one of the Wish Coins to its rightful place, which confused the British police no end. They decided, finally, to put it down to an act of conscience by the thieves who had taken them in the first place, and the case was closed.

The ghosts that had moved into Tom's house for safety were sent back to their homes, or their sewers, or castles, or wherever it is they used to haunt. Some took more persuading than others, having gotten a little too used to watching television, and the comforts of settees, but the Invisible Friends turned out to be very convincing. After a bit of a spring cleaning, orchestrated by Mrs. Scruffles, you'd never know that hundreds of ghosts had been staying there all weekend.

All the newly liberated Poltergeists decided to make up for lost time, and on Sunday night there was a Laundry Run the likes of which had never been seen before. There wasn't a household in the whole of England that didn't wake up Monday morning with a collection of odd socks, and a burning need to go out sock shopping. Dad saw his business turn around from nearly having to close down factories, to experiencing a massive sales boom, just over the space of one weekend. Nobody at Svelte Socks, or any of the other companies affected, could understand it, but they didn't complain. Socks were flying off the shelves, and the crisis was over. Dad's latest design, his Anti-Static-Shock-Sock, even broke trade records for the number of sales achieved! And if Dad suspected that his son had anything to do with the mystery of why sock sales increased, he didn't say anything. He just smiled quietly to himself.

Thorblefort Castle bustled once more with ghosts, and the tourists came back in droves, shivering in the dungeons, smiling wistfully on the battlements, or feeling a little sad inside when they wandered too close to Sorrow Jane. The human world went back to normal, and Tom was the only one who really knew what had happened.

It wasn't long until Mildred Rattledust, Montague Equador Scullion the Third, and Tike were settled down with humans of their own, and although none of the humans were aware that they had picked up a supernatural companion, it still made a big impact in their lives. They smiled more, and laughed more, and were just generally happier people now that they had an Invisible Friend to look out for them—to remember their lunch box when they forgot, to peel notes off their backs, and just generally to sit with them when they thought they were all alone. Frank Longfield was the first in line for an Invisible Friend, and Tike decided that he was the ghost for the job. Mildred adopted Holly Mayer, and after a couple false starts, she actually managed to become visible to her chosen human without scaring her away. It took a while for Holly to get used to her new friend, who tended to disappear quite often, only wore black, and was sometimes a little socially awkward, but then it took a while for Mildred get used to a girl who liked pink and giggled, so that made it all fair. Holly had no idea her new friend was a ghost, and was with her even when Holly couldn't see her, but Mildred was quite happy that it stayed that way. Montague took to his new career with all the dramatic flair that you'd expect from an ex-Thesper, and, in his spare time, the time when the Real World slept, he began writing a play based on his experiences. The last time Arthur checked, it was 947 pages long and showed no signs of stopping. The Harrowing Screamer wasn't quite ready to be unleashed on a human child yet, but Tom let him stay with them while Arthur tried to iron out the creases. It made Tom and Arthur ever so proud to see what became of the new generation of Invisible Friends, even if 11 Aubergine Road felt a little lonelier now, without so many ghosts haunting it.

And so life went back to normal. Mum and Dad returned from Grandma Green's house, a little hungry from avoiding her cooking, but otherwise none the worse for wear. Tom was waiting for them, a picture of innocence in a tidy house, and they hugged, and chatted, as parents and children do, before Mum began the very normal practice of sorting out what was for dinner. They'd never know the adventures their son had been on that weekend. Not unless they read a copy of the *Daily Tell-Tale*. Mum was a little confused by the re-emergence of Madame Twinkle Bear, and the disappearance of her mirror, but she just put it down to "one of those things."

The human papers were, as ever, pretty oblivious to the news around them. The story of increased sock sales snuck into the back of the business pages, next to a rather dull article about the value of the American dollar. The news of all the coins being returned to the wishing wells made the second page, nudged off the front by a story of an earthquake hitting Stonehenge, causing some of the ancient stones to shift position, or fall out of place. Tom was a little disappointed at being usurped from front-page position, but only a little. Second page was good enough.

Unbeknownst to Tom, he actually also made it into a small paper called *Mysteries of This World* where a couple of grainy, out of focus photos of him at Stonehenge, taken by young Nikki Ferguson, were printed with the headline IS THIS THE PROOF THAT GHOSTS EXIST? It was accompanied by an interview with Nikki that described a "mysterious boy figure appearing among the stones, and then vanishing again." If Tom had known, he would most definitely have cut the article out, and pinned it to his wall of memories, although it might have been a bit hard explaining to his parents what he had been doing at Stonehenge, when he was meant to be at a party in Thorbleton.

Of course, it was the *Daily Tell-Tale* that really got

the best story. Ladybug had the full, exclusive scoop of how they defeated the Collector, and how all the ghosts were set free. Since he wrote the article, he got to choose the headline too, and being a shy, retiring, modest type of ghost, this is the one he picked:

LADYBUG SAVES THE DAY!